## DEADLY CHALLENGE

Smoke Jensen slipped out of the house onto the stone-and-wood porch. He knew the chance of his being seen by the outlaws up on the ridges several hundred yards away was practically nonexistent, but he stayed low from force of habit.

Smoke darted off the porch to a tree in the yard, then over a fence and a footrace to the corral. Just one more stretch of open space before the safety of the bunkhouse, but as he got set for the run, a cold voice spoke behind him.

"I'll be known as the man who kilt Smoke Jensen. Die, you meddlin' bastard!"

# FICTION BY WILLIAM W. JOHNSTONE

BREAKDOWN                              (0-7860-0367-7, $5.99)

HUNTED                                 (0-7860-0194-1, $5.99)

THE LAST OF THE DOG TEAM  (0-7860-0427-4, $4.99)

PREY                                   (0-7860-0312-X, $5.99)

TALONS OF EAGLES                       (0-7860-0249-2, $5.99)

DREAMS OF EAGLES                       (0-8217-4619-7, $4.99)

EYES OF EAGLES                         (0-8217-4285-X, $4.99)

# WILLIAM W. JOHNSTONE

# JOURNEY OF THE MOUNTAIN MAN

## Zebra Books
## Kensington Publishing Corp.

http://www.zebrabooks.com

This novel is a work of fiction. Names, characters, places, and incidents are either the product of the author's imagination or are used fictitiously, and any resemblance to actual persons, living or dead, or events is entirely coincidental.

ZEBRA BOOKS

are published by

Kensington Publishing Corp.
850 Third Avenue
New York, NY 10022

Copyright © 1989 by William W. Johnstone

First printing: March, 1989

Printed in the United States of America

10

*It is only the dead who do not return.*
                    —Bertrand De Vieuzac


*Dedicated to: James Albert Martin*

# One

"I didn't think you had any living relatives, except for your sister?"

"I didn't either. But then I forgot about Pa's brother. He was supposed to have gotten killed at Chancellorsville, back in '63. I guess this letter came from his kids. It would have to be; it's signed Fae Jensen."

"I wonder how they knew where to write?" Sally asked. "Big Rock is not exactly the hub of commerce, culture, and industry."

The man laughed at that. The schoolteacher in his wife kept coming out in the way she could put words together.

It was 1882, in the high-up country of Colorado. The cabin had recently been remodeled: two new rooms added for Louis Arthur and Denise Nicole Jensen. The twins were approaching their first birthday.

And the man called Smoke was torn between going to the aid of a family member he had never seen and staying at home for the birthday party.

"You have to go, Smoke," Sally spoke the words softly.

"Gibson, in the Montana Territory." The tall, wide-shouldered and lean-hipped man shook his head. "A long way from home. On what might be a wild goose hunt. Probably is. I don't even know where Gibson is."

Sally once more opened the letter and read it aloud. The handwriting was definitely that of a woman, and a woman who had earned high marks in penmanship.

Dear Cousin Kirby,
    I read about you in the local paper last year, after that

7

dreadful fight at Dead River. I wanted to write you then, but thought my brother and I could handle the situation ourselves. Time has proven me incorrect. We are in the middle of a war here, and our small ranch lies directly between the warring factions. I did not believe when this range war was started that either Mr. Dooley Hanks or Mr. Cord McCorkle would deliberately harm us, but conditions have worsened to the point where I fear for our lives. Any help you could give us would be greatly appreciated.

Respectfully, your cousin
Fae Jensen


"Have you ever heard of either of those men, Smoke?"

"McCorkle. He came into that country twenty years or more ago. Started the Circle Double C. He's a hard man, but I never heard of him riding roughshod over a woman."

"How about this Dooley Hanks?"

Smoke shook his head. "The name sort of rings a bell. But it isn't ringin' very loud."

"When will you be leaving, honey?"

He turned his brown eyes on her, eyes that were usually cold and emotionless. Except when he looked at her. "I haven't said I was going."

"I'll be fine, Smoke. We've got some good hands and some good neighbors. You don't have to worry about me or the babies." She held up the letter. "They're blood kin, honey."

He slowly nodded his head. "I'll get things squared away around the Sugarloaf, and probably pull out in about three days." He smiled. "If you just insist that I go."

She poked him in the ribs and ran laughing out of the room.


"That's him," the little boy said to his friend, visiting from the East. "That's the one ever'body writes about in them penny dreadfuls. That's Smoke Jensen."

Smoke tied his horse to the hitchrail in front of the Big Rock Guardian and went inside to speak with Haywood Arden, owner and editor.

"He sure is mean-lookin'," the boy from back East said. "And he really does wear them guns all whopper-jawed, don't he?"

8

The first thing Haywood noticed was Smoke wearing two guns, the left hand .44 worn butt forward for a cross-draw, the right hand .44 low and tied down.

"Expecting trouble, Smoke?"

"Not around here. Just getting used to wearing them again. I've got to take a trip, Haywood. I don't know how long I'll be gone. Probably most of the spring and part of the summer. I know Sheriff Carson is out of town, so I'd be beholden if you'd ask him to check in with Sally from time to time. I'm not expecting any trouble out there; Preacher Morrow and Bountiful are right over the ridge and my hands would fight a grizzly with a stick. I'd just feel better if Monte would drop by now and then."

"I'll sure do it, Smoke." He had a dozen questions he'd like to ask, but in the West, a man's business was his own.

Smoke stuck out his hand. "See you in a few months, Haywood. Give Dana my best."

Haywood watched the tall, broad-shouldered, ruggedly handsome man stroll up the boardwalk toward the general store. Smoke Jensen, the last mountain man. The hero of dozens of dime novels. The fastest gun in the West. A man who never wanted the title of gunfighter, but who at sixteen years of age was taken under the tutelage of an old he-coon named Preacher. The old mountain man had taught the boy well, and the boy had grown into one of the most feared and respected men in the West.

No one really knew how many outlaws and murderers and gunslingers and highwaymen had fallen under Smoke's thundering .44's. Some said fifty, others said two hundred. Smoke himself didn't really know for sure.

But Haywood knew one thing for a fact: if Smoke Jensen had strapped on his guns, and was going on a journey, it would darn sure be interesting when he reached his destination.

Interesting and deadly.


The next morning Smoke saddled a tough mountain-bred horse named Dagger—the outline of a knife was on the animal's left rump—checked his canvased and tied-down supplies on the pack horse, and went back into the cabin.

The twins were still sleeping as their father slipped into their rooms and softly kissed each child's cheek. He stepped back out into the main room of the cabin—the den, as Sally called it.

"Sally, I don't know what I'm riding into this time. Or how long I'll be gone."

She smiled at him. "Then I'll see you when you get back."

They embraced, kissed, and Smoke stepped out the door, walking to the barn. With the pack horse rope in his left hand, Smoke lifted his right hand in farewell, picked up the reins, and pointed Dagger's nose toward the north.

Sally watched him until he was out of sight, then with a sigh, turned and walked into the cabin, quietly closing the door behind her.

Smoke had dressed warmly, for it was still early spring in the high lonesome, and the early mornings and nights were cold. But as the sun touched the land with its warming rays, he would shed his heavy lined jacket and travel wearing a buckskin jacket, made for him by the squaws of Indian friends.

He traveled following a route that kept the Rocky Mountains to his left and the Medicine Bow Mountains to his right. He crossed the Continental Divide and angled slightly west. He knew this country, and loved it. Preacher had first shown this country to him, back in the late sixties, and Smoke had fallen in love with it. The columbine was in early bloom, splashing the countryside in blue and lavender and white and purple.

Smoke's father, Emmett Jensen, was buried at Brown's Hole, up near the Utah line, in the northwest corner of Colorado. Buried lying atop thousands and thousands of dollars in gold. No one except Smoke and Preacher knew that, and neither one of them had any intention of spreading it about.

Old Preacher was in his early eighties, at least, but it had filled Smoke with joy and love to learn that he was still alive.

Cantankerous old billy-goat!

On his third night out, Smoke made camp halfway between Rabbit Ears Pass and Buffalo Pass, in the high-up country of the Rockies. He had caught some trout just before dusk dropped night on the land and was frying them in a dollop of lard when he saw Dagger's ears come up.

Smoke set the frying pan away from the flames, on a part of the circle of stones around the flames, and slipped back a few feet from the fire and put a hand on his Winchester .44.

"Hallo, the fire!" the voice came out of the darkness. "I'm friendly as a little wolf cub but as hongry as a just woke-up bar."

Smoke smiled. But his hand did not leave his Winchester. "Then come on in. I'll turn no hungry man away from a warm fire and a meal."

The stranger came out of the brush, keeping one hand in view, the other hand tugging at the lead rope which was attached to a reluctant donkey. "I'm aheadin' for the tradin' post on the Illinois," he said, stripping the gear from the donkey's back and hobbling the animal so it could graze and stay close. "Ran slap out of food yesterday and ain't seen no game atall."

"I have plenty of fish and fried potatoes and bread," Smoke told him. "Spread your blanket and sit." Smoke poured him a tin cup of coffee.

"Kind of you, stranger. Kind. I'm called Big Foot." He grinned and held up a booted foot. "Size fourteen. Been up in Montana lookin' for some color. Got snowed in. Coldest damn place I ever been in my life." He hooked a piece of bread and went to gnawing.

"I run a ranch south of here. The Sugarloaf. Name's Jensen."

Big Foot choked on his bread. When he finally got it swallowed, he took a drink of coffee. "*Smoke* Jensen?" he managed to gasp.

"Yes."

"Aunt Fanny's drawers!"

Smoke smiled and slid the skillet back over the flames, dumping in some sliced potatoes and a few bits of some early wild onions for flavor. "Where'bouts in Montana?"

"All around the Little Belt Mountains. East of the Smith River."

"Is that anywhere close to Gibson?"

"Durn shore is. And that's a good place to fight shy of, Smoke. Big range war goin' on. Gonna bust wide open any minute."

"Seems to me I heard about that. McCorkle and Hanks, right?"

"Right on the money. Dooley Hanks has done hired Lanny Ball, and McCorkle put Jason Bright on the payroll. I reckon you've heard of them two?"

"Killers. Two-bit punks who hire their guns."

Big Foot shook his head. "You can get away with sayin' that, but not me. Them two is poison fast, Smoke. They's talk about that Mex gunhawk, Diego, comin' in. He's 'pposed to be

11

bringing in half a dozen with him. Bad ones."

"Probably Pablo Gomez is with him. They usually double-team a victim."

"Say! You're right. I heard that. They gonna be workin' for Hanks."

Smoke served up the fish and potatoes and bread and both men fell to it.

When the edges had been taken off their hunger, Smoke asked, "Town had to be named for somebody ... who's Gibson?"

"Well, it really ain't much of a town. Three, four stores, two saloons, a barber shop, and a smithy. I don't know who Gibson is, or was, whatever."

"No school?"

"Well, sort of. Got a real prissy feller teachin' there. Say! His name's Jensen, too. Parnell Jensen. But he ain't no kin to you, Smoke. Y'all don't favor atall. Parnell don't look like nothin'!"

Parnell was his uncle's middle name.

"But Parnell's sister, now, brother, that is another story."

Smoke dropped in more lard and more fish and potatoes. He sopped up the grease in his tin plate with a hunk of bread and waited for Big Foot to continue.

"Miss Fae would tackle a puma with a short switch. She ain't no real comely lass, but that ain't what's keepin' the beaux away. It's that damn temper of her'n. Got her a tongue you could use for a skinnin' knife. I seen and heared her lash out at that poor brother of her'n one time that was plumb pitiful. Made my old donkey draw all up. He teaches school and she runs the little ranch they got. Durnest mixed-up mess I ever did see. That woman rides astraddle! Plumb embarrassin'!"

Big Foot ate up everything in sight, then picked up the skillet and sopped it out with a hunk of bread. He poured another cup of coffee and with a sigh of contentment, leaned back and rolled a smoke. "Mighty fine eats, Smoke. Feel human agin."

"Where you heading, Big Foot?"

"Kansas. I'm givin' 'er up. I been prowlin' this countryside for twenty-five years, chasin' color. Never found the motherlode. Barely findin' enough color to keep body and soul alive. My brother's been pesterin' me for years to come hep work his hog farm. So that's where I'm headin'. Me and Lucy over yonder. Bes' burro I ever had. I'm gonna retie her; just let

12

'er eat and get fat. You?"

"Heading up to Montana to check out some land. I don't plan on staying long."

"You fight shy of Gibson, now, Smoke. They's something wrong with that town."

"How do you mean that?"

"Cain't hardly put it in words. It's a feel in the air. And the people is crabby. Oh, most go to church and all that. But it's . . . well, they don't like each other. Always bickerin' about this and that and the other thing. The lid's gonna blow off that whole county one of these days. It's gonna be unpleasant when it do."

"How about the sheriff?"

"He's nearabouts a hundred miles away. I never put eyes on him or any of his deputies. Ain't no town marshal. Just a whole bunch of gunslicks lookin' hard at one another. When they start grabbin' iron, it's gonna be a sight to see."

Big Foot drank his coffee and lay back with a grunt. "And I'll tell you something else: that Fae Jensen woman, her spread is smack in the middle of it all. She's got the water and the graze, and both sides wants it. Sharp tongue and men's britches an' all . . . I feel sorry for her."

"She have hands?"

"Had a half a dozen. Down to two now. Both of them old men. Hanks and McCorkle keep runnin' off anyone she hires. Either that or just outright killin' them. Drug one young puncher, Hanks's men did. Killed him. But McCorkle is not a really mean person. He just don't like Hanks. Nothin' to like. Hanks is evil, Smoke. Just plain evil."

# TWO

Come the dawning, Smoke gave Big Foot enough food to take him to the trading post. They said their goodbyes and each went their own way: one north, one east.

Smoke pondered the situation as he rode, trying to work out a plan of action. Since he knew only a smattering of what was going on, he decided to go in unknown and check it out. He took off his pistols and tucked them away in his supplies. He began growing a mustache.

Just inside Wyoming, Smoke came up on the camp of half a dozen riders. It took him but one glance to know what they were: gunhawks.

"Light and set," one offered, his eyes appraising Smoke and deciding he was no danger. He waved toward the fire. "We got beef and beans."

"Jist don't ask where the meat come from," a young man said with a mean grin.

"You talk too much, Royce," another told him. "Shut up and eat." He looked at Smoke. "Help yourself, stranger."

"Thanks." Smoke filled a plate and squatted down. "Lookin' for work. Any of you boys know where they're hirin'?"

"Depends on what kind of work you're lookin' for," a man with a long scar on the side of his face said.

"Punchin' cows," Smoke told him. "Breakin' horses. Ridin' fence. Whatever it takes to make a dollar."

Smoke had packed away his buckskin jacket and for a dollar had bought a nearly wornout light jacket from a farmer, frayed at the cuffs and collar. He had deliberately scuffed his boots and dirtied his jeans.

"Can't help you there," the scar-faced man said.

Smoke knew the man, but doubted the man knew him. He

had seen him twice before. His name was Lodi, from down Texas way, and the man was rattlesnake quick with a gun.

"How come you don't pack no gun?" Royce asked.

Smoke had met the type many times. A punk who thought he was bad and liked to push. Royce wore two guns, both tied down low. Fancy guns: engraved .45 caliber Peacemakers.

"I got my rifle," Smoke told him. "She'll bang seventeen times."

"I mean a short gun," Royce said irritably.

"One in the saddlebags if I need it. I don't hunt trouble, so I ain't never needed it."

One of the other gunhands laughed. "You got your answer, Royce. Now let the man eat." He cut his eyes to Smoke. "What be your name?"

"Kirby." He knew his last name would not be asked. It was not a polite question in the West.

"You look familiar to me."

"I been workin' down on the Blue for three years. Got the urge to drift."

"I do know the feelin'." He rose to his boots and started packing his gear.

These men, with the possible exception of Royce, were range-wise and had been on the owlhoot trail many times, Smoke concluded. They would eat in one place, then move on several miles before settling in and making camp for the night. Smoke quickly finished his beef and beans and cleaned his plate.

They packed up, taking everything but the fire. Lodi lifted his head. "See you, puncher."

Smoke nodded and watched them ride away. To the north. He stayed by the fire, watching it burn down, then swung back into the saddle and headed out, following their trail for a couple of miles before cutting east. He crossed the North Platte and made camp on the east side of the river.

He followed the Platte up to Fort Fred Steele, an army post built in 1868 to protect workers involved in the building of the Union Pacific railroad. There, he had a hot bath in a wooden tub behind a barber shop and resupplied. He stepped into a cafe and enjoyed a meal that he didn't have to cook, and ate quietly, listening to the gossip going on around him.

There had been no Indian trouble for some time; the Shoshone and the Arapahoe were, for the most part, now settled in at the Wind River Reservation, although every now and then some whiskeyed-up bucks would go on the prowl.

15

They usually ended up either shot or hanged.

Smoke loafed around the fort for a couple of days, giving the gunhands he'd talked with ample time to get gone farther north.

And even this far south of the Little Belt Mountains, folks knew about the impending range war, although Smoke did not hear any talk about anyone here taking sides.

He pulled out and headed for Fort Caspar, about halfway between Fort Fetterman and Hell's Half Acre. The town of Casper would become reality in a few more years.

At Fort Caspar, Smoke stayed clear of a group of gunslicks who were resupplying at the general store. He knew several in this bunch: Eddie Hart, Pooch Matthews, Golden. None of them were known for their gentle, loving dispositions.

It was at Fort Caspar that he met a young, down-at-the-heels puncher with the unlikely handle of Beans.

"Bainbridge is the name my folks hung on me," Beans explained with a grin. "I was about to come to the conclusion that I'd just shoot myself and get it over with knowin' I had to go through the rest of my life with everybody callin' me Bainbridge. A camp cook over in the Dakotas started callin' me Beans. He didn't have no teeth, and evertime he called my name, it come out soundin' like Beans-Beans. So Beans it is."

Beans was one of those types who seemed not to have a care in the world. He had him a good horse, a good pistol, and a good rifle. He was young and full of fire and vinegar . . . so what was there to worry about?

Smoke told him he was drifting on up into Montana. Beans allowed as how that was as good a direction as any to go, so they pulled out before dawn the next day.

With his beat-up clothes and his lip concealed behind a mustache and his hair now badly in need of a trim, Smoke felt that unless he met someone who really knew him, he would not be recognized by any who had only bumped into him casually.

"You any good with that short gun?" Smoke asked.

"Man over in Utah didn't think so. I rattled my hocks shortly before the funeral."

Now, there was two ways to take that. "Your funeral or his?"

"He was a tad quicker, but he missed."

'Nuff said.

On the third night out, Beans finally said what he'd been mullin' about all day. "Kirby . . . there's something about you that just don't add up."

16

"Oh?"

"Yeah. Now, to someone who just happened to glance over at you and ride on, you'd appear to be a drifter. Spend some time on the trail with you, and a body gets to thinkin'."

Smoke stirred the beans and laid the bacon in the pan. He poured them both coffee and waited.

"You got coins in your pocket and greenbacks in your poke. That saddle don't belong to no bum. That Winchester in your boot didn't come cheap. And both them horses are wearin' a brand like I ain't never seen. Is that a circle double snake or what?"

"Circle Double-S." As his spread had grown, Smoke had changed his brand. S for Smoke, S for Sally. It was registered with the brand commission.

"There ain't no 'S' in Kirby." Beans noted.

"Maybe my last name is Smith."

"Ain't but one 'S' there."

"You do have a point." Beans was only pointing out things that Smoke was already aware of. "How far into Montana are you planning on going?"

"Well," Beans grinned, "I don't know. Taggin' along with you I found that the grub's pretty good."

"You're aware of the impending range war in Montana?"

"There's another thing that don't ring true, Kirby. Sometimes you talk like a schoolteacher. Now I know that don't necessarily mean nothin' out here, but it do get folks to thinkin'. You know what I mean?"

Smoke nodded and turned the bacon.

"And them jeans of yours is wore slick on the right side, down low on the leg. You best get you some other britches or strap that hogleg back on."

"You don't miss much, do you, Beans?"

"My folks died with the fever when I was eight. I been on my own ever since. Goin' on nineteen years. Startin' out alone, that young, a body best get savvy quick."

"My real name is Kirby, Beans."

"All right."

"You didn't answer my question about whether you knew about the range war?"

"I heard of it, yeah. But I don't hire my gun. Way I had it figured, with most of the hands fightin', them rich ranchers is gonna need somebody just to look after the cattle." He grinned. "That's me!"

"I'd hate to see you get tied up in a range war, Beans, 'cause

17

sooner or later, you're gonna have to take a stand and grab iron."

"Yeah, I know. But I don't never worry about bridges until I come to them. Ain't that food about fitten to eat?"

They were lazy days, and the two men rode easy; no reason to push. Smoke was only a few years older than Beans— chronologically speaking; several lifetimes in experience—and the men became friends as they rode.

Spring had hit the high country, and the hills and valleys were blazing in God's colors. The men entered Johnson County in the Wyoming Territory, rode into Buffalo, and decided to hunt up a hot bath; both were just a bit on the gamey side.

After a bath and a change of clothes, Smoke offered to buy the drinks. Beans, with a grin, pointed out the sign on the barroom wall: "Don't forget to write your mother, boys. Whether you are worth it or not, she is thinking of you. Paper and inveelopes free. So is the picklled eggs. The whiskey ain't."

"You got a ma, Kirby?"

"Beans, *everybody* has a mother!" Smoke grinned at the man.

"I mean . . . is she still alive?" He flushed red.

"No. She died when I was just a kid, back in Missouri."

"I thought I smelled a Missouri puke in here." The voice came from behind them.

Smoke had not yet tasted his whiskey. He placed the shot glass back on the bar as the sounds of chairs being pushed back reached him. He turned slowly.

A bear of a man sat at a table. Even sitting down he was huge. Little piggy eyes. Mean eyes. Bully was invisibly stamped all over him. His face looked remarkably like a hog.

"You talking to me, Pig-Face?" Smoke asked.

Big Pig stood up and held open his coat. He was not wearing a gun. Smoke opened his jacket to show that he was not armed.

Beans stepped to one side.

"I think I'll tear your head off," Big Pig snorted.

Smoke leaned against the bar. "Why?"

The question seemed to confuse the bully. Which came as no surprise to Smoke. Most bullies could not be classified as being anywhere close to mental giants.

"For fun!" Big Pig said.

Then he charged Smoke, both big hands balled into fists that

18

looked like hams. Smoke stepped to one side just at the last possible split second and Big Pig crashed into the bar. His bulk and momentum tore the rickety bar in half and sent Big Pig hurling against the counter. Whiskey bottles and beer mugs and shot glasses were splintered from the impact. The stench of raw whiskey and strong beer filled the smoky barroom.

Hollering obscenities and roaring like a grizzly with a sore paw, Big Pig lumbered and stumbled to his feet and swung a big fist that would've busted Smoke's head wide open had it landed.

Smoke ducked under the punch and sidestepped. The force of Big Pig's forward motion sent him staggering and slipping across the floor. Smoke picked up a chair and just as Big Pig turned around, Smoke splintered the wooden chair across his teeth.

Big Pig's boots flew out from under him and he went crashing to the floor, blood spurting from smashed lips and cuts on his face. But Smoke saw that Pig was a hard man to keep down. Getting to his feet a second time, Pig came at a rush, wide open. Smoke had already figured out that the man was no skilled slugger, relying on his enormous strength and his ability to take punches that would have felled a normal man.

Smoke hit him flush on the beak with a straight-from-the-shoulder right. The nose busted and the blood flew. Big Pig snorted away the pain and blood and backhanded Smoke, knocking him against a wall. Smoke's mouth filled with the copper taste of blood.

Yelling, falsely sensing that victory was his, Pig charged again. Smoke dropped to his knees and drove his right fist straight up into the V of Big Pig's legs.

Pig howled in agony and dropped to the floor, both hands cupping his injured parts. Still on his knees, Smoke hit the man on the side of the jaw with everything he could put into the punch. This time, Big Pig toppled over, down, but still a hell of a long way from being out.

Spitting out blood, Smoke got to his feet and backed up, catching his breath, readying himself for the next round that he knew was coming.

Big Pig crawled to his feet, glaring at Smoke. But his eyes were filled with doubt. This had never happened to him. He had never lost a fight; not in his entire life.

Smoke suddenly jumped at the man, hitting him with both fists, further pulping the man's lips and flattening his snout.

Pig swung and Smoke grabbed the thick wrist with both hands and turned and slung the man, spinning Big Pig across the room. Pig crashed into the wall and went right through it, sailing across the warped boardwalk and landing in a horse trough.

Smoke stepped through the splintered hole in the wall and walked to the trough. He grabbed Big Pig's head and forced it down into the water, holding him there. Just as it appeared the man would drown, Smoke pulled the head out, pounded it with his fists, then grabbed the man by his hair and once more forced the head under water.

Finally, Big Pig's struggling ceased. Smoke wearily hauled him out of the water and left him draped half in, half out of the trough. Big Pig was breathing, but that was about all.

Smoke sat down on the edge of the boardwalk and tried to catch his breath.

The boardwalk gradually filled with people, all of them staring in awe at Smoke. One man said, "Mister, I don't know who you are, but I'd have bet my spread that you wouldn't have lasted a minute against old Ring, let alone whip him."

Smoke rubbed his aching leg. "I'd hate to have to do it again."

Beans squatted down beside Smoke. When he spoke his voice was low. "Kirby, I don't know who you really are, but I shore don't never want to make you mad."

Smoke looked at him. "Hell, I'm not angry!" He pointed to the man called Ring. "He's the one who wanted to fight, not me."

"Lord, have mercy!" Beans said. "All this and you wasn't even mad."

Ring groaned and heaved himself out of the horse trough.

Smoke picked up a broken two-by-four and walked over to where Ring lay on the soaked ground. "Mister Ring, I want your attention for a moment. If you have any thoughts at all about getting up off that ground and having a go at me, I'm going to bust your head wide open with this two-by-four. You understand all that?"

Ring rolled over onto his back and grinned up at Smoke. One eye was swollen shut and his nose and lips were a mess. He held up a hand. "Hows 'bout you and me bein' friends. I shore don't want you for an enemy!"

# Three

The three of them pulled out the next morning, Ring riding the biggest mule Smoke had ever seen.

"Satan's his name," Ring explained. "Man was going to kill him till I come along. I swapped him a good horse and a gun for him. One thing, boys: don't never get behind him if you've got a hostile thought. He'll sense it and kick you clear into Canada."

There was no turning Ring back. He had found someone to look up to in Smoke. And Smoke had found a friend for life.

"I just can't handle whiskey," Ring said. "I can drink beer all day long and get mellow. One drink of whiskey and I'll turn mean as a snake."

"I figured you were just another bully," Beans said.

"Oh, no! I love everybody till I get to drinkin' whiskey. Then I don't even like myself."

"No more whiskey for you, Ring," Smoke told him.

"Yes, sir, Mister Kirby. Whatever you say is fine with me."

They were getting too far east, so when they left Buffalo, they cut west and crossed the Bighorn Mountains, skirting north of Cloud Peak, the thirteen-thousand-foot mountain rearing up majestically, snow-capped year round. Cutting south at Granite Pass, the men turned north, pointing their horses' noses toward Montana Territory.

"Mister Kirby?" Ring asked.

"Just Kirby, Ring. Please. Just Kirby."

"OK . . . Kirby. Why is it we're going to Montana?"

"Seeing the sights, Ring."

"OK. Whatever you say. I ain't got nothin' but time."

"We might find us a job punchin' cows," Beans said.

"I don't know nothin' about cows," Ring admitted. "But I can make a nine-pound hammer sing all day long. I can work the mines or dig a ditch. There ain't a team of horses or mules that I can't handle. But I don't know nothin' about cows."

"You ever done any smithing?" Smoke asked.

"Oh, sure. I'm good with animals. I like animals. I love puppy dogs and kitty cats. I don't like to see people mistreat animals. Makes me mad. And when I get mad, I hurt people. I seen a man beatin' a poor little dog one time back in Kansas when I was passin' through drivin' freight. That man killed that little dog. And for no good reason."

"What'd you do?" Smoke asked him.

"Got down off that wagon and broke his back. Left him there and drove on. After I buried the little dog."

Beans shuddered.

"Dogs and cats and the like can't help bein' what they are. God made them that way. If God had wanted them different, He'd have made 'em different. Men can think. I don't know about women, but men can think. Man shouldn't be cruel to animals. It ain't right and I don't like it."

"I have never been mean to a dog in my life," Beans quickly pointed out.

"Good. Then you're a nice person. You show me a man who is mean to animals, and I'll show you a low-down person at heart."

Smoke agreed with that. "You born out here, Ring?"

"No. Born in Pennsylvania. I killed a man there and done time. He was a no-good man. Mean-hearted man. He cheated my mother out of her farm through some legal shenanigans. Put her on the road with nothin' but the clothes on her back. I come home from the mines to visit and found my mother in the poor farm, dying. After the funeral, I looked that man up and beat him to death. The judge gimme life in prison."

"You get pardoned?" Beans asked.

"No. I got tired of it and jerked the bars out of the bricks, tied the guard up, climbed over the walls and walked away one night."

"Your secret is safe with us," Smoke assured him.

"I figured it would be."

They forded the Yellowstone and were in Montana Territory, but still had a mighty long way to go before they reached Gibson.

Smoke and Beans had both figured out that Ring was no great shakes when it came to thinking, but he was an incredibly gentle man—as long as you kept him away from the whiskey. Birds would come to him when he held out his arms. Squirrels would scamper up and take food from his fingers. And he almost cried one day when he shot a deer for food. He left the entrails for the wolves and the coyotes and spent the rest of the journey working on the hide, making them all moccasins and gloves.

Ring was truly one of a kind.

He stood six feet six inches and weighed three hundred pounds, very little of it fat. He could read and write only a little, but he said it didn't matter. He didn't have anyone to write to noways, and nobody ever wrote to him.

At a small village on the Boulder, Smoke resupplied and they all had a hot bath. Ring was so big he made the wooden tub look like a bucket.

But Smoke had a bad feeling about the village; not about the village itself, but at what might be coming at them if they stayed. Smoke had played on his hunches before; they had kept him alive more than once. And this one kept nagging at him.

After carefully shaving, leaving his mustache intact, he went to his pack horse and took out his .44's, belting them around his lean hips, tying down the right hand gun. He carefully checked them, wiping them clean with a cloth and checking the loads. He usually kept the chamber under the hammer empty; this time he loaded them both up full. He stepped out from behind the wooden partition by the wooden tubs and walked into the rear of the store, conscious of the eyes of Beans and Ring on him; they had never seen him wear a short gun, much less two of them, one butt forward for a cross draw.

"Five boxes of .44's," Smoke told the clerk.

"You plannin' on startin' a war?" the clerk said, sticking his mouth into something that didn't concern him.

Smoke's only reply was to fix his cold brown eyes on the man and stare at him. The clerk got the message and turned away, a flush on his face.

He placed the ammunition on the counter and asked no more questions. Smoke bought three cans of peaches and paid for his purchases. He walked out onto the shaded porch, Ring and Beans right behind him. The three of them sat down and opened the peaches with their knives, enjoying a midmorning sweet-syruped snack.

"Don't see too many people wearin' twin guns thataway," Beans observed, looking at Smoke's rig.

"Not too many," Smoke agreed, and ate a peach.

"Riders coming," Ring said quietly. "From the south."

The men sat on the porch, eating peaches, and watching the riders come closer.

"You recognize any of them?" Smoke tossed the question out.

Beans took it. "Nope. You?"

"That one on the right is Park. Gunfighter from over in the Dakotas. Man next to him is Tabor. Gunhawk from Oklahoma. I don't know the others."

"They know you?" Ring asked.

"They know of me." Smoke's words were softly spoken.

"By the name of Kirby?"

"No."

The five dusty gunhands reined up and dismounted. A ferret-faced young man ducked under the hitchrail and paused by the porch, staring at Smoke. His eyes drifted to Smoke's twin guns.

The other gunhawks were older, wiser, and could read sign. They were not being paid to cause trouble in this tiny village, therefore they would avoid trouble if at all possible.

The kid with the acne-pocked face and the big Colts slung around his hips was not nearly so wise. He deliberately stepped on Smoke's boot as he walked past.

Smoke said nothing. The four older men stood to one side, watching, keeping their hands away from the butts of their guns.

Ferret-face laughed and looked at his friends, jerking a thumb toward Smoke. "There ain't much to him."

"I wouldn't bet my life on it," Park said softly. To Smoke, "Don't I know you?"

Smoke stood up. At the approach of the men, he had slipped the leather hammer-thongs from his guns. "We've crossed rails a time or two. If this punk kid's a friend of yours, you might better put a stopper on his mouth before I'm forced to change his diapers."

The kid flushed at the insult. He backed up a few yards, his hands hovering over the butts of his fancy guns. "They call me

Larado. Maybe you've heard of me?"

"Can't say as I have," Smoke spoke easily. "But I'm glad to know you have a name. That's something that everybody should have."

"You're makin' fun of me!"

"Am I? Maybe so."

"I think I'll just carve another notch on my guns," Larado hissed.

"Yeah? I had you pegged right then. A tinhorn."

"Draw, damn you!"

But Smoke just stood, smiling at the young man.

Two little boys took that time to walk by the store; perhaps they were planning on spending a penny for some candy. One of them looked at Smoke, jerked a dime novel out of the back of his overalls, and stared at the cover. He mentally shaved off Smoke's mustache. His mouth dropped open.

"It's really him! That's Smoke Jensen!"

All the steam went out of Larado. His sigh was audible. He lifted his hands and carefully folded them across his chest, keeping his hands on the outside of his arms.

Beans and Ring sat in their chairs and stared at their friend.

"You some distance from Colorado, Smoke," Tabor said.

"And you're a long way from Oklahoma," Smoke countered.

"For a fact. You headin' north or south?"

"North."

"I never knowed you to hire your guns out."

"I never have. It isn't for sale this trip, either."

"But you do have a reputation for buttin' in where you ain't wanted," Park added his opinion.

"I got a personal invitation to this party, Park. But if you feel like payin' the fiddler, you can write your name on my dance card right now."

"I ain't got nothin' agin you, Smoke. Not until I find out which side you buckin' leastways. McCorkle or Hanks?"

"Neither one."

The gunslicks exchanged glances. "That don't make no sense," one of the men that Smoke didn't know said.

"You got a name?"

"Dunlap."

"Yeah, I heard of you. You killed a couple of Mexican sheepherders and shot one drunk in the back down in Arizona. But I'm not a sheepherder and I'm not drunk."

Dunlap didn't like that. But he had enough sense not to pull iron with Smoke Jensen.

"You was plannin' on riding in with nobody knowin' who you were, wasn't you?" Tabor asked.

"Yes."

"Next question is why?"

"I guess that's my business."

"You right. I reckon we'll find out when we get to Gibson."

"Perhaps." He turned to Beans and Ring. "Let's ride."

After the three men had ridden away, toward the north, one of the two gunhands who had not spoken broke his silence.

"I'm fixin' to have me a drink and then I'm ridin' over to Idaho. It's right purty this time of year."

Larado, now that Smoke was a good mile away, had reclaimed his nerve. "You act like you're yeller!" he sneered.

But the man just chuckled. "Boy, I was over at what they's now callin' Telluride some years back, when a young man name of Smoke Jensen come ridin' in. He braced fifteen of the saltiest ol' boys there was at that time. Les' see, that was back in, oh, '72, I reckon." He looked directly at Larado. "And you bear in mind, young feller, that he kilt about ten or so gettin' to that silver camp. He kilt all fifteen of them so-called fancy gunhandlers. Yeah, kid, he's *that* Smoke Jensen. The last mountain man. Since he kilt his first Injun when he was about fifteen years old, over in Kansas, he's probably kilt a hundred or more white men—and that's probably figurin' low. There ain't nobody ever been as fast as he is, there ain't never gonna be nobody as fast as he is.

"And I know you couldn't hep notice that bear of a man with him? That there is Ring. Ring ain't never followed no man in his life afore today. And that tells me this: Smoke has done whipped him fair and square with his fists. And if I ain't mistaken, that young feller with Smoke and Ring is the one from over in Utah, round Moab. Goes by a half a dozen different names, but one he favors is Beans.

"Now, boys, I'm a fixin' to have me a drink and light a shuck. 'Cause wherever Smoke goes, they's soon a half a dozen or more of the randiest ol' boys this side of hell. Smoke draws 'em like a magnet does steel shavin's. I had my say. We partin' company. Like as of right now!"

\* \* \*

26

Down in Cheyenne, two old friends came face-to-face in a dingy side-street barroom. The men whoopped and hollered and insulted each other for about five minutes before settling down to have a drink and talk about old times.

Across the room, a young man stood up, irritation on his face. He said to his companion, "I think I'll go over there and tell them old men to shut up. I'm tared of hearin' them hoot and holler."

"Sit down and close your mouth," his friend told him. "That's Charlie Starr and Pistol Le Roux."

The young man sat down very quickly. A chill touched him, as if death had brushed his skin.

"I thought them old men was *dead!*" he managed to croak after slugging back his drink.

"Well, they ain't. But I got some news that I bet would interest them. I might even get to shake their hands. My daddy just come back from haulin' freight down in Colorado. You wanna go with me?"

"No, sir!"

The young man walked over to where the two aging gunfighters were sitting and talking over their beers. "Sirs?"

Charlie and Pistol looked up. "What can I do for you?" Le Roux said.

The young man swallowed hard. This was real flesh and blood legend he was looking at. These men helped tame the West. "You gentlemen are friends with a man called Smoke Jensen, aren't you?"

"You bet your boots!" Charlie smiled at him.

"My daddy just come home from haulin' freight down to a place called Big Rock. He spoke with the sheriff, a man called Monte Carson. Smoke's in trouble. He's gone up to some town in Montana Territory called Gibson to help his cousin. A woman. He's gonna be facin' forty or fifty gunhands; right in the middle of a range war."

Pistol and Charlie stood up as of one mind. The young man stared in astonishment. God, but they were both big and gray and gnarled and old!

But the guns they wore under their old jackets were clean and shiny.

"I wish we could pay you," Charlie said. "But we're gonna have to scratch deep to get up yonder."

The young man stuck out his hand and the men shook it.

Their hands were thickly calloused. "There's a poke of food tied to my saddle horn. Take it. It's all I can do."

"Nice of you," Pistol said. "Thankee kindly."

The men turned, spurs jingling, and were gone.

The silver-haired man pulled off his boot and looked at the hole in the sole. He stuck some more paper down into the boot. "Hardrock, today is my birthday. I just remembered."

"How old are you, about a hundred?"

"I think I'm sixty-seven. And I know you two year older than me."

"Happy birthday."

"Thankee."

"I ain't got no present. Sorry."

Silver Jim laughed. "Hardrock, between the two of us we might be able to come up with five dollars. Tell you what. Let's drift up to Montana Territory. I got a friend up in the Little Belt Mountains. Got him a cabin and runs a few head of cattle. Least we can eat."

"Silver Jim . . . he *died* about three years ago."

"Ummm . . . that's right. He did, didn't he. Well, the cabin's still there, don't you reckon?"

"Might be. I thought of Smoke this mornin'. Wonder how that youngster is?"

"Did you now? That's odd. I did, too."

"I thought about Montana, too."

The two old gunfighters exchanged glances, Silver Jim saying, "I just remembered I had a couple of double eagles I was savin' for hard times."

"Is that right? Well . . . me, too."

"We could ride back to that little town we come through this morning and send a message through the wires to Big Rock."

The old gunslingers waited around the wire office for several hours until they received a reply from Monte Carson in Big Rock.

"Let's get the hell to Montanee!" Silver Jim said.

# Four

"I thought you would be a much older man," Ring remarked after they had made camp for the evening.

It was the first time Smoke's real identity had been brought up since leaving the little village.

Smoke smiled and dumped the coffee into the boiling water. "I started young."

"When was you gonna tell us?" Beans asked.

"The same time you told me that you was the Moab Gunfighter."

Beans chuckled. "I wasn't gonna get involved in this fight. But you headin' that way . . . well, it sorta peaked my interest."

"My cousin is in the middle of it. She wrote me at my ranch. You can't turn your back on kin."

"Y'all must be close."

"I have never laid eyes on her in my life. I didn't even know she existed until the letter came." He told them about his conversations with Big Foot.

"This brother of hers sounds like a sissy to me," Beans said.

"He does for a fact," Smoke agreed. "But I've found out this much about sissies: they'll take and take and take, until you push them to their limits, and then they'll kill you."

The three of them made camp about ten miles outside of Gibson, on the fringes of the Little Belt Mountains.

"There is no point in any of us trying to hide who we are," Smoke told the others. "As soon as Park and the others get in town, it would be known. We'll just ride in and look the place over first thing in the morning. I'm not going to take a stand in this matter unless the big ranchers involved try to run over Fae . . . or unless I'm pushed to it."

The three topped the hill and looked down at the town of Gibson. One long street, with vacant lots separating a few of the stores. A saloon, one general store, and the smithy was on one side of the street, the remainder of the businesses on the other side. Including a doctor's office. The church stood at the far end of town.

"We'd better be careful which saloon—if any—we go into," Beans warned. "For a fact, Hanks's boys will gather in one and McCorkle's boys in the other."

"I don't think I'll go into either of them," Ring said. "This is the longest I've been without a drink in some time. I like the feeling."

"Looks like school is in session." Smoke lifted the reins. "You boys hang around the smithy's place while I go talk to Cousin Parnell. Let's go."

They entered the town at a slow walk, Ring and Beans flanking Smoke as they moved up the wide street. Although it was early in the day, both saloons were full, judging by the number of horses tied at the hitchrails. A half a dozen or more gunslicks were sitting under the awnings of both saloons. The men could feel the hard eyes on them as they rode slowly up the street. Appraising eyes. Violent eyes; eyes of death.

"Ring," they heard one man say.

"That's the Moab Kid," another said. "But who is that in the middle?"

"I don't know him."

"I do," the voice was accented. Smoke cut his eyes, shaded by the wide brim of his hat. Diego. "That, amigos, is Smoke Jensen."

Several chair legs hit the boardwalk, the sound sharp in the still morning air.

The trio kept riding.

"Circle C on the west side of the street," Beans observed.

"Yeah." Smoke cut his eyes again. "That's Jason Bright standing by the trough."

"He is supposed to be very, very fast," Ring said.

"He's a punk," Smoke replied.

"Lanny Ball over at the Hangout," Beans pointed out.

"The Pussycat and the Hangout," Ring said with a smile.

30

"Where do they get the names?"

They reined up at the smith's place; a huge stable and corral and blacksmithing complex. Beans and Ring swung down. Smoke hesitated, then stepped down.

"Changed my mind," he told them. "No point in disturbing school while it's in session. We'll loaf around some; stretch our legs."

"I'm for some breakfast," Ring said. "Let's try the Cafe Eats."

Smoke told the stable boy to rub their horses down, and to give each a good bait of corn. They'd be back.

They walked across the wide street, spurs jingling, boots kicking up dust in the dry street, and stepped up onto the boardwalk, entering the cafe.

It was a big place for such a tiny town, but clean and bright, and the smells from the kitchen awakened the taste buds in them all.

They sat down at a table covered with a red-and-white checkered cloth and waited. A man stepped out of the kitchen. He wore an apron and carried a sawed-off double-barreled ten gauge express gun. "You are velcome to eat here at anytime ve are open," he announced, his German accent thick. "My name is Hans, and I own dis establishment. I vill tell you what I have told all the rest: there vill be no trouble in here. None! I operate a nice quiet family restaurant. People come in from twenty, terty miles avay to eat here. Start trouble, und I vill kill you! Understood?"

"We understand, Hans," Smoke said. "But we are not taking sides with either McCorkle or Hanks. I do not hire my guns and neither does Beans here." He jerked his thumb toward the Moab Kid. "And Ring doesn't even carry a short gun."

"Uummph!" the German grunted. "Den dat vill be a velcome change. You vant breakfast?"

"Please."

"Good! I vill start you gentlemen vith hot oatmeal vith lots of fresh cream and sugar. Den ham and eggs and fried potatoes and lots of coffee. Olga! Tree oatmeals and tree breakfasts, Liebling."

"What'd he call her?" Beans whispered.

"Darling," Ring told him.

Smoke looked up. "You speak German, Ring?"

31

"My parents were German. Born in the old country. My last name is Kruger."

The oatmeal was placed before them, huge bowls of steaming oatmeal covered with cream and sugar. Ring looked up. *"Danke."*

The two men then proceeded to converse in rapid-fire German. To Beans it sounded like a couple of bullfrogs with laryngitis.

Then, to the total amazement of Smoke and Beans, the two big men proceeded to slap each other across the face several times, grinning all the time.

Hans laughed and returned to the kitchen. "Y'all fixin' to fight, Ring?" Beans asked.

Ring laughed at the expression on their faces. "Oh, no. That is a form of greeting in certain parts of the old country. It means we like each other."

"That is certainly a good thing to know," Smoke remarked drily. "In case I ever take a notion to travel to Germany."

The men fell to eating the delicious oatmeal. When they pushed the empty bowls away, Hans was there with huge platters of food and the contest was on.

*"Guten appetit,* gentlemans."

"What'd he say?" Beans asked Ring.

"Eat!" He smiled. "More or less."

Olga stepped out of the kitchen to stand watching the men eat, a smile on her face. She was just as ample as Hans. Between the two of them they'd weigh a good five hundred pounds. Another lady stepped out of the kitchen. Make that seven hundred and fifty pounds.

When they had finished, as full as ticks, Ring looked up and said, *"Prima! Grobartig!"* He lifted his coffee mug and toasted their good health. *"Auf Ihre Gesundheit!"*

Olga and the other lady giggled.

"I didn't hear nobody sneeze." Beans looked around.


Ring stayed in the restaurant, talking with Hans and Olga and Hilda and drinking coffee. Beans sat down in a wooden chair in front of the place, staring across the street at the gunhawks who were staring at him. Smoke walked up to the church that doubled as a schoolhouse. The kids were playing out front so he figured it was recess time.

The children looked at him, a passing glance, and resumed their playing. Smoke walked up the steps.

Smoke stood in the open doorway, the outside light making him almost impossible to view clearly from the inside. He felt a pang of . . . some kind of emotion. He wasn't sure. But there was no doubt: he was looking at family.

The schoolteacher looked up from his grading papers. "Yes?"

"Parnell Jensen?"

"Yes. Whom do I have the pleasure of addressing?"

Smoke had to chew on that for a few seconds. "I reckon I'm your cousin, Parnell. I'm Smoke Jensen."


Parnell gave Smoke directions to the ranch and said he would be out at three-thirty. And he would be prompt about it. "I am a very punctilious person," Parnell added.

And a prissy sort too, Smoke thought. "Uh-huh. Right." He'd have to remember to ask somebody what punch-till-eous meant.

He was walking up the boardwalk just as the thunder of hooves coming hard reached him. The hooves drummed across the bridge at the west end of town and didn't slow up. A dozen hard-ridden horses can kick up a lot of dust.

Smoke had found out from Parnell that McCorkle's spread was west and north of town, Hanks's spread was east and north of town. Fae's spread, and it was no little spread, ran on both sides of the Smith River; for about fifteen miles on either side of it. McCorkle hated Hanks, Hanks hated McCorkle, and both men had threatened to dam up the Smith and dry Fae out if she didn't sell out to one of them.

"And then what are they going to do?" Smoke asked.

"Fight each other for control of the entire area between the Big Belt and the Little Belt Mountains. They've been fighting for twenty years. They came here together in '62. Hated each other at first sight." Parnell flopped his hand in disgust. "It's just a dreadful situation. I wish we had never come to this barbaric land."

"Why did you?"

"My sister wanted to farm and ranch. She's always been a tomboy. The man who owned the ranch before us, hired me—I was teaching at a *lovely* private institution in Illinois, close to

33

Chicago—and told Fae that he had no children and would give us the ranch upon his death. I think more to spite McCorkle and Hanks than out of any kindness of heart."

Smoke leaned against a storefront and watched as King Cord McCorkle—as Parnell called him—and his crew came to a halt in a cloud of dust in front of the Pussycat. When the dust had settled, Jason Bright stepped off the boardwalk and walked to Cord's side, speaking softly to him.

Parnell's words returned: "I have *always* had to look after my sister. She is so *flighty*. I wish she would marry and then I could return to civilization. It's so primitive out here!" He sighed. "But I fear that the man who gets my sister will have to beat her three times a day."

Cord turned his big head and broad face toward Smoke and stared at him. Smoke pegged the man to be in his early forties; a bull of a man. Just about Smoke's height, maybe twenty pounds heavier.

Cord blinked first, turning his head away with a curse that just reached Smoke. Smoke cut his eyes to the Hangout. Diego and Pablo Gomez and another man stood there. Smoke finally recognized the third man. Lujan, the Chihuahua gunfighter. Probably the fastest gun—that as yet had built a reputation— in all of Mexico. But not a cold-blooded killer like Diego and Pablo.

Lujan tipped his hat at Smoke and Smoke lifted a hand in acknowledgment and smiled. Lujan returned the smile, then turned and walked into the saloon.

Smoke again felt eyes on him. Cord was once more staring at him.

"You there! The man supposed to be Smoke Jensen. Git down here. I wanna talk to you."

"You got two legs and a horse, mister!" Smoke called over the distance. "So you can either walk or ride up here."

Pablo and Diego laughed at that.

"Damned greasers!" Cord spat the words.

The Mexicans stiffened, hands dropping to the butts of their guns.

A dozen gunhands in front of the Pussycat stood up.

A little boy, about four or five years old, accompanied by his dog, froze in the middle of the street, right in line of fire.

Lujan opened the batwings and stepped out. "We—all of us—have no right to bring bloodshed to the innocent people of

34

this town." His voice carried across the street. He stepped into the street and walked to the boy's side. "You and your dog go home, muchacho. Quickly, now."

Lujan stood alone in the street. "A man who would deliberately injure a child is not fit to live. So, McCorkle, it is a good day to die, is it not?"

Smoke walked out into the street to stand by Lujan's side. A smile creased the Mexican's lips. "You are taking a side, Smoke?"

"No. I just don't like McCorkle, and I probably won't like Hanks either."

"So, McCorkle," Lujan called. "You see before you two men who have not taken a side, but who are more than willing to open the *baile*. Are you ready?"

"Make that three people," Beans's voice rang out.

"Who the hell are you?" McCorkle shouted.

"Some people call me the Moab Kid."

"Make that four people," Ring said. He held his Winchester in his big hands.

"*Funf!*" Hans shouted, stepping out into the street. He held the sawed-off in his hands.

The window above the cafe opened and Olga leaned out, a pistol with a barrel about a foot and a half long in her hand. She jacked back the hammer to show them all she knew how to use it. And would.

"All right, all right!" Cord shouted. "Hell's bells! Nobody was going to hurt the kid. Come on, boys, I'll buy the drinks." He turned and bulled his way through his men.

At the far end of the street, Parnell stepped back from the open doorway and fanned himself vigorously. "*Heavens!*" he said.

35

# Five

"Almost come a showdown in town this morning, Boss," Dooley Hanks's foreman said.

Hanks eyeballed the man. "Between who?"

Gage told his boss what a hand had relayed to him only moments earlier.

Hanks slumped back in his chair. "Smoke Jensen," he whispered the word. "I never even thought about Fae and Parnell bein' related to him. And the Moab Kid and Lujan sided with him?"

"Or vicey-versy."

"This ain't good. That damn Lujan is poison enough. But add Smoke Jensen to the pot . . . might as well be lookin' the devil in the eyeballs. I don't know nothin' about Ring, except he's unbeatable in a fight. And the Moab Gunfighter has made a name for hisself in half a dozen states. All right, Gage. We got to get us a backshooter in here. Send a rider to Helena. Wire Danny Rouge; he's over in Missoula. Tell him to come a-foggin'."

"Yes, sir."

"Where's them damn boys of mine?"

"Pushin' cattle up to new pasture."

"You mean they actually doin' some work?"

Gage grinned. "Yes, sir."

Hanks shook his head in disbelief. "Thank you, Gage."

Gage left, hollering for a rider to saddle up. Hanks walked to a window in his office. He had swore he would be kingpin of this area, and he intended to be just that. Even if he bankrupted himself doing it. Even if he had to kill half the people in the area attaining it.

\*     \*     \*

Cord McCorkle had ridden out of town shortly after his face-down with Smoke and Lujan and the others. He did not feel that he had backed down. It was simply a matter of survival. Nobody but a fool willingly steps into his own coffin.

His hands would have killed Smoke and Lujan and the others, for a fact. But it was also hard fact that Cord would have gone down in the first volley . . . and what the hell would that have proved?

Nothing. Except to get dead.

Cord knew that men like Smoke and Lujan could soak up lead and still stay on their feet, pulling the trigger. He had personally witnessed a gunfighter get hit nine times with .45 slugs and before he died still kill several of the men he was facing.

Cord sat on the front porch of his ranch house and looked around him. He wanted for nothing. He had everything a man could want. It had sickened him when Dooley had OK'd the dragging of that young Box T puncher. Scattering someone's cattle was one thing. Murder was another. He was glad that Jensen had come along. But he didn't believe anyone could ever talk sense into Hanks.

Smoke, Ring, and Beans sat their horses on the knoll overlooking the ranch house of Fae and Parnell Jensen. Fae might well be a bad-mouthed woman with a double-edged tongue, but she kept a neat place. Flowers surrounded the house, the lawn was freshly cut, and the place itself was attractive.

Even at this distance, a good mile off, Smoke could see two men, with what he guessed was rifles in their hands, take up positions around the bunkhouse and barn. A woman—he guessed it was a woman, she was dressed in britches—came out onto the porch. She also carried a rifle. Smoke waved at her and waited for her to give them some signal to ride on in.

Finally the woman stepped off the porch and motioned for them to come on.

The men walked their horses down to the house, stopping at the hitchrail but not dismounting. The woman looked at Smoke. Finally she smiled.

"I saw a tintype of your daddy once. You look like him. You'd be Kirby Jensen."

"And you'd be Cousin Fae. I got your letter. I picked up these galoots along the way." He introduced Beans and Ring.

37

"Put your horses in the barn, boys, and come on into the house. It's about dinnertime. I got fresh doughnuts; 'bear-sign' as you call them out here."

Fae Jensen was more than a comely lass; she was really quite pretty and shapely. But unlike most women of the time, her face and arms were tanned from hours in the sun, doing a man's work. And her hands were calloused.

Smoke had met Fae's two remaining ranch hands, Spring and Pat. Both men in their early sixties, he guessed. But still leather-tough. They both gave him a good eyeballing, passed him through inspection, and returned to their jobs.

Over dinner—Sally called it lunch—Smoke began asking his questions while Beans skipped the regular food and began attacking a platter of bear-sign, washed down with hot strong western coffee.

How many head of cattle?

Started out with a thousand. Probably down to less than five hundred now, due to Hanks and McCorkle's boys running them off.

Would she have any objections to Smoke getting her cattle back?

She looked hard at him. Finally shook her head. No objections at all.

"Ring will stay here at the ranch and start doing some much needed repair work," Smoke told her. "Beans and me will start working the cattle, moving them closer in. Then we'll get your other beeves back. Tell me the boundaries of this spread."

She produced a map and pointed out her spread, and it was not a little one. It had good graze and excellent water. The brand was the Box T; she had not changed it since taking over several years back.

"If you'll pack us some food," Smoke said, "me and Beans will head out right now; get the lay of the land. We'll stay out a couple of days—maybe longer. This situation is shaping up to be a bad one. The lid could blow off at any moment. Beans, shake out your rope and pick us out a couple of fresh horses. Let's give ours a few days' rest. They've earned it."

"I'll start putting together some food," Fae said. She looked at Smoke. "I appreciate this. More than you know."

"Sorry family that don't stick together."

They rode out an hour later, Smoke on a buckskin a good seventeen hands high that looked as though it could go all day

38

and all night and still want to travel.

The old man who had given the spread to Fae had known his business—Smoke still wondered about how she'd gotten it. He decided to pursue that further when he had the time.

About ten miles from the ranch, they crossed the Smith and rode up to several men working Box T cattle toward the northwest.

They wheeled around at Smoke's approach.

"Right nice of you boys to take such an interest in our cattle," Smoke told a hard-eyed puncher. "But you're pushing them the wrong way. Now move them back across the river."

"Who the hell do you think you are?" the man challenged him.

"Jensen."

The man spat on the ground. "I like the direction we're movin' them better." He grabbed iron.

Smoke drew, cocked, and fired in one blindingly fast move. The .44 slug took the man in the center of his chest and knocked him out of the saddle. He tried to rise up but did not have the strength. With a groan, he fell back on the ground, dead. Beans held a pistol on the other McCorkle riders; they were all looking a little white around the mouth.

"Jack Waters," Smoke said. "He's wanted for murder in two states. I've seen the flyers in Monte's office."

"Yeah," Beans said glumly. "And he's got three brothers just as bad as he is. Waco, Hatley, and Collis."

"You won't last a week on this range, Jensen," a mouthy McCorkle rider said.

Smoke moved closer to him and backhanded the rider out of his saddle. He hit the ground and opened his mouth to cuss. Then he closed his mouth as the truth came home. Jensen. *Smoke* Jensen.

"All of you shuck outta them gun belts," Beans ordered. "When you've done that, start movin' them cattle back across the river."

"Then we're going to take a ride," Smoke added. "To see Cord."

While the Circle Double C boys pushed the cattle back across the river, Smoke lashed the body of Jack Waters across his saddle and Beans picked up the guns, stuffing guns, belts, and all into a gunny sack and tying it on his saddle horn. The riders returned, a sullen lot, and Smoke told them to head out for the ranch.

A hand hollered for Cord to come out long before Smoke and Beans entered the front yard. "Stay in the house," Cord told his wife and daughter. "I don't want any of you to see this."

Beans stayed in the saddle, a Winchester .44 across his saddle horn. Smoke untied the ropes and slung Jack Waters over his shoulder, and Jack was not a small man. He walked across the lawn and dumped the body on the ground, by Cord's feet.

Cord was livid, his face flushed and the veins in his neck standing out like ropes. He was breathing like an enraged bull.

"We caught Jack and these other hands on Box T Range, rustling cattle. Now you know the law out here, Cord: we were within our rights to hang every one of them. But I gave them a chance to ride on. Waters decided to drag iron."

Cord nodded his head, not trusting his voice to speak.

"Now, Cord," Smoke told him, "I don't care if you and Hanks fight until you kill each other. I don't think either of you remember what it is you're fighting about. But the war against the Box T is over. Fae and Parnell Jensen have no interest in your war, and nothing to do with it. *Leave . . . them . . . alone!*"

Smoke's last three words cracked like whips; several hardnosed punchers winced at the sound.

"You all through flappin' your mouth, Jensen?" Cord asked.

"No. I want all the cattle belonging to Fae and Parnell Jensen rounded up and returned. I'm not saying that your hands ran them all off. I'm sure Hanks and his boys had a hand in it, too. And I'll be paying him a visit shortly. Get them rounded up and back on Box T Range."

"And if I don't—not saying I have them, mind you?"

Smoke's smile was not pretty. "You ever heard of Louis Longmont, McCorkle?"

"Of course, I have! What's he have to do with any of this?"

"He's an old friend of mine, Cord. We stood shoulder to shoulder several years back and cleaned up Fontana. Then last year, he rode with me to New Hampshire . . . you probably read about that."

Cord nodded his head curtly.

"He's one of the wealthiest men west of the Mississippi, Cord. And he loves a good fight. He wouldn't blink an eye to spend a couple of hundred thousand putting together an army to come in here and wipe your nose on a porcupine's backside."

From in the house, Smoke heard a young woman's laughter and an older woman telling her to shush!

The truth was, Louis was in Europe on an extended vacation and Smoke knew it. But sometimes a good bluff wins the pot.

Cord had money, but nothing to compare with Louis Longmont . . . and he also knew that Smoke had married into a a great deal of money and was wealthy in his own right. He sighed heavily.

"I can't speak for Hanks, Jensen. You'll have to face him yourself. But as for me and mine . . . OK, we'll leave the Box T alone. I don't have their cattle. I'm not a rustler. My boys just scattered them. But I'm damned if I'll help you round them up. You can come on my range and look; any wearing the Box T brand, take them."

Smoke nodded and stuck out his hand. Cord looked startled for a few seconds, then a very grudging smile cut his face. He took the hand and gripped it briefly.

Smoke turned and mounted up. "See you."

Beans and Smoke swung around and rode slowly away from the ranch house.

"My back is itchy," Beans said.

"So is mine. But I think he's a man of his word. I don't think he'll go back on his word. Least I'm a poor judge of character if he does."

They rode on. Beans said, "My goodness me. I plumb forgot to give them boys their guns back."

"Well, shame on you, Beans. I hate to see them go to waste. We'll just take them back to Fae and she can keep them in reserve. Never know when she might need them. You can swap them for some bear-sign."

"What about hands?"

"We got to hire some, that's for sure. Fae's got to sell off some cattle for working capital. She told me so. So we've got to hire some boys."

"Durned if I know where. And there's still the matter of Dooley Hanks."

Fae would hire some hands, sooner than Smoke thought. But they would be about fifty years from boyhood.

41

# Six

They made camp early that day, after rounding up about fifty head of Box T cattle they found on Cord's place. They put them in a coulee and blocked the entrance with brush. They would push them closer to home in the morning.

They suppered on the food Fae had fixed for them and were rolled up in their blankets just after dark.

Smoke was the first one up, several hours before dawn. He coaxed life back into the coals by adding dry grass and twigs, and Beans sat up when the smell of coffee got too much for him to take. Beans threw off his blankets, put on his hat, pulled on his boots, and buckled on his gun belt. He squatted by the fire beside Smoke, warming his hands and waiting for the cowboy coffee to boil.

"Town life's done spoiled me," Beans griped. "Man gets used to shavin' and bathin' every day, and puttin' on clean clothes every mornin'. It ain't natural."

Smoke grinned and handed him a small sack.

"What's in here?"

"Bear-sign I hid from you yesterday."

Beans quit his grousing and went to eating while Smoke sliced the bacon and cut up some potatoes, adding a bit of wild onion for flavor.

"The problem of hands has got me worried," Beans admitted, slurping on a cup of coffee. "Ain't no cowboy in his right mind gonna go to work for the Box T with all this trouble starin' him in the face."

"I know." Smoke ladled out the food onto tin plates. "But I think I know one who just might do it, for thirty and found, just for the pure hell of it. I'll talk to him this afternoon if I can.

First we have to see Hanks."

"You got a lot of damn nerve, Jensen," the foreman of the D-H spread told him. "Mister Hanks don't wanna see you."

"You tell him I'm here and I'll wait just as long as it takes."

Gage stared into the cold eyes of the most respected and feared gunfighter in all the West. He sighed, shook his head, and finally said, "All right, mister. I'll tell him you insist on seein' him. But I ain't givin' no guarantees."

Hanks and McCorkle could pass for brothers, Smoke thought, as he squatted under the shade of a tree and watched as Dooley left the house and walked toward him. Both of them square-built men. Solid. Both of them in their early to mid forties.

Dooley did not offer to shake hands. "Speak your piece, Jensen."

Smoke repeated what he'd told Cord, almost word for word, including the bit about Louis Longmont. Grim-faced, Hanks stood and took it. He didn't like it, but he took it.

"Maybe I'll just wait you out, Jensen."

"Maybe. But I doubt it. You're paying fighting wages, Dooley. To a lot of people. You're like most cattlemen, Dooley: you're worth a lot of money, but most of it is standing on four hooves. Ready scratch is hard to come up with."

Dooley grunted. Man knew what he was talking about, all right. "You won't get between me and McCorkle?"

"I don't care what you two do to each other. The area would probably be better off if you'd kill each other."

"Plain-spoken man, ain't you?"

"I see no reason to dance around it, Dooley. What'd you say?"

Something evil moved behind Dooley Hanks's eyes. And Smoke didn't miss it. He did not trust this man; there was no honor to be found in Dooley Hanks.

"I didn't rustle no Box T cattle, Jensen. We just scattered them all to hell and gone. You're free to work my range. You find any Box T cattle, take them. You won't be bothered, and neither will Miss Fae or any punchers she hires." He grinned, and it was not a pleasant curving of the lips. He also had bad breath. "*If* she can find anyone stupid enough to work for her. Now get out of my face. I'm sick of lookin' at you."

"The feeling is quite mutual, Hanks." Smoke mounted up and rode away.

"I don't trust that hombre," Beans said. "He's got more twists and turns than a snake."

"I got the same feeling. See if you can find some of Fae's beef and start pushing them toward Box T graze. I'm going into Gibson."


"You're serious?"

"Oh, yes," Smoke told him. "Thirty and found, and you'll work just like any other cowboy."

The man threw back his head and laughed; his teeth were very white against his deeply tanned face. He tossed his hat onto the table in Hans's cafe.

"All right," he said suddenly. "All right, Smoke, you have a deal. I was a vaquero before I turned to the gun. I will ride for the Box T."

Smoke and Lujan shook hands. Smoke had always heard how unpredictable the man was, but once he gave his word, he would die keeping it.

Lujan packed up his gear and pulled out moments later, riding for the Box T. Smoke chatted with Hans and Olga and Hilda for a few moments—Hilda, as it turned out, was quite taken with Ring—and then he decided he'd like a beer. Smoke was not much of a drinker, but did enjoy a beer or a drink of whiskey every now and then.

Which saloon to enter? He stood in front of the cafe and pondered that for a moment. Both of the saloons were filled up with gunhands. "Foolish of me," he muttered. But a cool beer sounded good. He slipped the leather thongs from the hammers of his guns and walked over to the Pussycat and pushed open the batwings, stepping into the semi-gloom of the beery-smelling saloon.

All conversation stopped.

Smoke walked to the bar and ordered a beer. The barkeep suddenly got very nervous. Smoke sipped his beer and it was good, hitting the spot.

"Jack Waters was a friend of mine," a man spoke, the voice coming from the gloom of the far end of the saloon.

Smoke turned, his beer mug in his left hand.

His right thumb was hooked behind his big silver belt

buckle, his fingers only a few inches from his cross-draw .44.

He stood saying nothing, sipping at his beer. He paid for the brew, damned if he wasn't going to try to finish as much of it as possible before he had to deal with this loudmouth.

"Ever'body talks about how bad you are, Jensen," the bigmouth cranked his tongue up again. "But I ain't never seen none of your graveyards."

"I have," the voice came quietly from Smoke's left. He did not know the voice and did not turn his head to put a face to it.

"Far as I'm concerned," the bigmouth stuck it in gear again, "I think Smoke Jensen is about as bad as a dried-up cow pile."

"You know my name," Smoke's words were softly offered. "What's your name?"

"What's it to you?"

"Wouldn't be right to put a man in the ground without his name on his grave marker."

The loudmouth cursed Smoke.

Smoke took a swallow of beer and waited. He watched as the man pushed his chair back and stood up. Men on both sides of him stood up and backed away, getting out of the line of fire.

"My name's John Cheave, Jensen. I been lookin' for you for nearabouts two years."

"Why?" Smoke was almost to the bottom of his beer mug.

"My brother was killed at Fontana. By you."

"Too bad. He should have picked better company to run with. But I don't recall any Cheave. What was he, some two-bit thief who had to change his name?"

John Cheave again cursed Smoke.

Smoke finished his beer and set the mug down on the edge of the bar. He slipped his thumb from behind his belt buckle and let his right hand dangle by the butt of his .44.

John Cheave called Smoke a son of a bitch.

Smoke's eyes narrowed. "You could have cussed me all day and not said that. Make your grab, Cheave."

Cheave's hands dipped and touched the butts of his guns. Two shots thundered, the reports so close together they sounded as one. Smoke had drawn both guns and fired, rolling his left hand .44. It was a move that many tried, but few ever perfected; and more than a few ended up shooting themselves in the belly trying.

John Cheave had not cleared leather. He sat down in the chair he had just stood up out of and leaned his head back, his wide, staring eyes looking up at the ceiling of the saloon. There were two bloody holes in the center of his chest. Cheave opened his mouth a couple of times, but no words came out.

His boots drummed on the floor for a few seconds and then he died, his eyes wide open, staring at and meeting death.

"I seen it, but I don't believe it," a man said, standing up. He tossed a couple of dollars on the table. "Cheave come out of California. Some say he was as fast as John Wesley Hardin. Count me out of this game, boys. I'm ridin'."

He walked out of the saloon, being very careful to avoid getting too close to Smoke.

The sounds of his horse's hooves faded before anyone else spoke.

"The barber doubles as the undertaker," Pooch Matthews said.

Smoke nodded his head. "Fine."

The bartender yelled for his swamper to fetch the undertaker.

"Impressive," a gunhawk named Hazzard said. "I have to say it: you're about the best I've ever seen. Except for one."

"Oh?"

Hazzard smiled. "Yeah. Me."

Smoke returned the smile and turned his back to the man, knowing the move would infuriate the gunhawk.

"Another beer, Mister Smoke?" the barkeep asked.

"No."

The barkeep did not push the issue.

Smoke studied the bottom of the empty beer mug, wondering how many more would fall under his guns. Although he knew this showdown would have come, sooner or later, one part of him said that he should not have come into the saloon, while another part of him said that he had a right to go wherever he damned well pleased. As long as it was a public place.

It was an old struggle within the man.

The barber came in and he and the swamper dragged the body out to the barber's wagon and chunked him in. The thud of the body falling against the bed of the wagon could be heard inside the saloon.

"I believe I will have that beer," Smoke said. While the barkeep filled his mug, Smoke rolled one of his rare cigarettes and lit up.

The saloon remained very quiet.

The barkeep's hand trembled just slightly as he set the foamy mug in front of Smoke.

Several horses pulled up outside the place. McCorkle and Jason Bright and several of Cord's hands came in. They walked to a table and sat down, ordering beer.

"What happened?" Smoke heard Cord ask.

"Cheave started it with Jensen. He didn't even clear leather."

"I thought you was going to stay out of this game, Jensen?" McCorkle directed the question to Smoke's back.

Smoke slowly turned, holding the beer mug in his left hand. "Cheave pushed me, Cord. I only came in here for a beer."

"Man's got a right to have a drink," Cord grudgingly conceded. "I seen some Box T cattle coming in, Jensen. They was grazin' on range 'bout five, six miles out of town. On the west side of the Smith."

"Thanks." And with a straight face, he added, "I'll have Lujan and a couple of others push them back to Box T Range."

"Lujan!" Jason Bright almost hollered the word.

"Yes. He went to work for the Box T a couple of hours ago."

A gunslick that Smoke knew from the old days, when he and Preacher were roaming the land, got up and walked toward the table where Cord was sitting. "I figure I got half a month's wages comin' to me, Mister McCorkle. If you've a mind to pay me now, I'd appreciate it."

With a look of wry amusement on his face, Cord reached into his pocket and counted out fifty dollars, handing it to the man. "You ridin', Jim?"

"Yes, sir. I figure I can catch up with Red. He hauled his ashes a few minutes ago."

Cord counted out another fifty. "Give this to Red. He earned it."

"Yes, sir. Much obliged." He looked around the saloon. "See you boys on another trail. This one's gettin' crowded." He walked through the batwings.

"Yellow," Hazzard said disgustedly, his eyes on the swinging and squeaking batwings. "Just plain yellow is all he is."

Cord cut his eyes. "Jim Kay is anything but yellow, Hazzard. I've known him for ten years. There is a hell of a lot of difference between being yellow and bettin' your life on a busted flush." He looked at Smoke. "There bad blood between

47

you and Jim Kay?"

Smoke shook his head. "Not that I'm aware of. I've known him since I was just a kid. He's a friend of Preacher."

Cord smiled. "Preacher pulled my bacon out of the fire long years back. Only time I ever met him. I owe him. I often wonder what happened to him."

"He's alive. But getting on in years."

Cord nodded his head, then his eyes swept the room. "I'll say it now, boys; we leave the Box T alone. Our fight is with Dooley Hanks. Box T riders can cross our range and be safe doin' it. They'll be comin' through lookin' for the cattle we scattered. You don't have to help them, just leave them alone."

A few of the gunslicks exchanged furtive glances. Cord missed the eye movement. Smoke did not. The gunfighters that Smoke would have trusted had left the area, such as Jim Kay and Red and a few others. What was left was the dregs, and there was not an ounce of honor in the lot.

Smoke finished his beer. "See you, Cord."

The rancher nodded his head and Smoke walked out the door. Riding toward the Box T, Smoke thought: You better be careful, McCorkle, 'cause you've surrounded yourself with a bunch of rattlesnakes, and I don't think you know just how dangerous they are.

# Seven

The days drifted on, filled with hard honest work and the deep dreamless sleep of the exhausted. Smoke had hired two more hands, boys really, in their late teens. Bobby and Hatfield. They had left the drudgery of a hardscrabble farm in Wisconsin and drifted west, with dreams of the romantic West and being cowboys. And they both had lost all illusions about the romantic life of a cowboy very quickly. It was brutally hard work, but at least much of it could be done from the back of a horse.

True to his word, Lujan not only did his share, but took up some slack was well. He as a skilled cowboy, working with no wasted motion, and he was one of the finest horsemen Smoke had ever seen.

One hot afternoon, Smoke looked up to see young Hatfield come a-foggin' toward him, lathering his horse.

"Mister Smoke! Mister Smoke!" he yelled. "I ain't believing this. You got to come quick to the house."

He reined up in a cloud of dust and Smoke had to wait until the dust settled before he could even see the young man to talk to him.

"Whoa, boy! Who put a burr under your blanket?"

"Mister Smoke, my *daddy* read stories about them men up to Miss Fae's house when he was a boy. I thought they was all dead and buried in the grave!"

"Slow down, boy. What men?"

"Them old gunfighters up yonder. Come on." He wheeled his horse around and was gone at a gallop.

Lujan pulled up. "What's going on, amigo?"

"I don't know. Come on, let's find out."

Fae was entertaining them on the front porch when Smoke

and Lujan rode up. Smoke laughed when he saw them.

Lujan looked first at the aging men on the porch, and then looked at Smoke. When he spoke, there was disapproval in his voice. "It is not nice to laugh at the old, my friend."

"Lujan, I'm not laughing at them. These men are friends of mine. As well known as we are, we're pikers compared to those old gunslingers. Lujan, you're looking at Silver Jim, Pistol Le Roux, Hardrock, and Charlie Starr."

"*Dios mio!*" the Mexican breathed. "Those men *invented* the fast draw."

"And don't sell them short even today, Lujan. They can still get into action mighty quick."

"I wouldn't doubt it for a minute," Lujan said, dismounting.

"If I'd known you old coots were going to show up, I'd have called the old folks home and had them send over some wheelchairs," Smoke called out.

"Would you just listen to the pup flap his mouth," Hardrock said. "I ought to get up and spank him."

"Way your knees pop and crack he'd probably think you was shootin' at him," Pistol laughed.

The men shook hands and Smoke introduced them to Lujan.

Charlie Starr sized the Mexican up. "Yeah, I seen you down along the border some years back. When them Sabler Brothers called you out. Too bad you didn't kill all five of them."

"Wasn't two down enough?" Lujan asked softly, clearly in awe of these old gunslingers.

"Nope," Silver Jim said. "We stopped off down in Wyoming for supplies. Store clerk said the Sabler boys had come through the day before, heading up thisaway. Ben, Carl, and Delmar."

Lujan sighed. "Many, many times I have wished I had never drawn my pistol in anger that first time down in Cuauhtemoc." He smiled. "Of course, the shooting was over a lovely lady. And of course, she would have nothing to do with me after that."

"What was her name?" Hatfield asked.

Lujan laughed. "I do not even remember."


The old gunfighters were all well up in years—Charlie Starr being the youngest—but they were all leather-tough and could still work many men half their age into the ground.

And the news that the Box T had hired the famed gunslingers was soon all over the area. Some of Cord McCorkle's hired guns thought it was funny, and it would be even funnier to tree one of the old gunnies and see just what he'd do. The gunfighter they happened to pick that morning was the Louisiana Creole, Pistol Le Roux.

Ol' Pistol and Bobby were working some strays back toward the east side of the Smith when the three gunhawks spotted Pistol and headed his way. Just to be on the safe side, Pistol wheeled his horse to face the men and slipped the hammer thong off his right hand Colt and waited.

That one of the men held a coiled rope in his right hand did not escape the old gunfighter. He had him a hunch that these pups were gonna try to rope and drag him. A hard smile touched his face. That had been tried before. Several times. Ain't been done yet.

"Well, well," the hired gun said, riding up. "What you reckon we done come across here, boys?"

"Damned if I know," another said with a nasty grin. "But it shore looks to me like it needs buryin'."

"Yeah," the third gunny said, sniffing the air. "It's done died and gone to stinkin'."

"That's probably your dirty drawers you smellin', punk," Pistol told him. "Since your mammy ain't around to change them for you."

The man flushed, deep anger touching his face. Tell the truth, he hadn't changed his union suit in a while.

"I think we'll just check the brands on them beeves," they told Pistol.

"You'll visit the outhouse if you eat regular, too," Pistol popped back. "And you probably should, and soon, 'cause you sure full of it."

"Why, you godda—" He grabbed for his pistol. The last part of the obscenity was cut off as Pistol's Colt roared, the slug taking the would-be gunslick in the lower part of his face and driving through the base of his throat.

Pistol had drawn and fired so fast the other two had not had time to clear leather. Now they found themselves looking down the long barrel of Pistol's Peacemaker. The dying gunny moaned and tried to talk; the words were unintelligible, due in no small measure to the lower part of his jaw being missing.

"Shuck out of them gun belts," Pistol told them, just as Bobby came galloping up to see what the shooting was all about. "Usin' your left hands," Pistol added.

Gun belts hit the ground.

"Dismount," Pistol told them. "Bobby, git that rope."

"Hey!" one of the gunnies said. "We was just a-funnin' with you, that's all."

"I don't consider bein' dragged no fun. And that's what you was gonna do, right?"

"Aw, no!"

Pistol's Colt barked and the bootheel was torn loose from the gunny's left boot. "Wasn't it, boy?" Pistol yelled.

On the ground, holding his numbed foot, the gunny nodded his head. "Yeah. We all make mistakes."

"Git out of them clothes," Pistol ordered. "Bare-butted nekkid. Do it!"

Red-faced, the men stood before Pistol, Bobby, and God in their birthday suits.

"Tie 'em together, Bobby. But give them room to walk. They got a long way to hoof it."

The gunny on the ground jerked and died.

The bare-butted men tied, their hands behind their backs, Pistol looped the rope around his saddle horn and gave the orders. "Move out. Head for your bunkhouse, boys. Git goin'."

"What about Pete?" one hollered.

"He'll keep without gettin' too gamy. Now *move!*"

It was a good hour's walk back to the Circle Double C ranch house, and the gunnies hoofed it all the way. They complained and moaned and hollered and finally begged for relief from their hurting, bleeding feet. They shut up when Pistol threatened to drag them.

"Pitiful," Pistol told him. "Twice the Indians caught me and made me run for it, bare-butt nekkid. Miles and miles and miles. With them just a-whoopin' and a-hollerin' right behind me. You two are a disgrace."

Cord stood by the front gate and had to smile at the sight as the painful parade came to a halt. He had ordered his wife and daughter not to look outside. But of course they both did.

The naked men collapsed to the ground.

"Mister McCorkle, my name is Le Roux. They call me Pistol. Now, sir, I was minding my own business, herdin' cattle like I'm paid to do, when three of your hands come up and was gonna put a loop around me and drag me. One of them went for his gun. He was a tad slow. You'll find him dead by that big stand of cottonwoods on the Smith. He ain't real purty to look at. Course, he wasn't all that beautiful when he was livin'. I brung these wayward children back home. You want to spank them, that's your business. Good day, sir."

Pistol and Bobby swung their horses and headed back to Box T Range.

Cord looked at the naked men and their bloody feet and briar-scratched ankles and legs. "Get their feet taken care of, pay them off, and get them out of here," he instructed his foreman. He looked at the gunslicks on his payroll. "Pete was one of your own. Go get him and bury him. And stay the hell away from Box T riders." He pointed to the naked and weary and footsore men on the ground. "One man did that. One . . . old . . . man. But that man, and those other old gunfighters over at the Box T came out here in the thirties and forties as mountain men. Tough? You bet your life they're tough. When they do go down for the last time, they'll go out of this world like cornered wolves, snarling and ripping at anything or anyone that confronts them. Leave them alone, boys. If you feel you can't obey my orders, ride out of here."

The gunfighters stared at Cord. All stayed. As Cord turned his back to them and walked toward his house, he had a very bad feeling about the outcome of this matter, and he could not shake it.

"It's stupid!" Sandi McCorkle said to her friend. "They don't even know why they hate each other."

Rita Hanks nodded her head in agreement. "I'm going to tell you something, Sandi. And it's just between you and me. I don't trust my father, or my brothers."

Sandi waited for her friend to continue.

"I think Daddy's gone crazy." She grimaced. "I think my brothers have always been crazy. They've never been . . . well, just right; as far as I'm concerned. They're cruel and vicious."

"What do you think your dad is going to do?"

"I don't know. But he's up to something. He sent a hand out last week to Helena. Then yesterday this ratty-faced-looking guy shows up at the ranch. Danny Rouge. Has a real fancy rifle. Carries it in a special-made case. I think he's a back-shooter, Sandi."

The two young women, both in their late teens, had been forbidden by their fathers to see each other, years back. Of course, neither of them paid absolutely any attention to those orders. But their meetings had become a bit more secretive.

"Do you want me to tell Daddy about this, Rita?"

"No. He'd know it came from me and then you'd get in

trouble. I think we'd better tell Smoke Jensen."

Sandi giggled. "I'd like to tell him a thing or two—in private. He's about the best-looking man I've ever seen."

"He's also married with children," Rita reminded her friend. "But he sure is cute. He's even better looking than the covers of those books make him out to be. Have you seen the Moab Kid?"

"Yes! He's *darling!*"

The two young women talked about men and marriage for a few minutes. It was time for them to be married; pretty soon they'd be pegged as old maids. They both had plenty of suitors, but none lasted very long. The young women were both waiting for that "perfect man" to come riding into their lives.

"How in the world are we going to tell Smoke Jensen about this back-shooter?"

"I don't know. But I think it's our bounden duty to tell him. People listen to him."

"That Bobby's been gettin' all red-eared everytime he gets around me," Sandi said. "I think maybe he could get a message to Smoke and he'd meet us."

"Worth a try. We'll take us a ride tomorrow over to the Smith and have a picnic and wait. Maybe he'll show up."

"Let's do it. I'll see you at the pool about noon."

The young women walked to their buggies. Both buggies were equipped with rifle boots and the boots were full. A pistol lay on the seat of each buggy. Both Sandi and Rita could, would, and had used the weapons. With few exceptions, ranch-born-and-raised western women were no shrinking violets. They lived in a violent time and had to be prepared to fight. Although most western men would not bother a woman, there were always a few who would, even though they knew the punishment was usually a rope.

Very little Indian trouble now occurred in this part of Montana; but there was always the chance of a few bucks breaking from the reservations to steal a few horses or take a few scalps.

With a wave, the young women went their way, Sandi back to the Circle Double C, Rita back to D-H. Neither noticed the two men sitting their horses in the timber. The men wore masks and long dusters.

"You ready?" one asked, his voice muffled by the bandana tied round his face.

"I been ready for some of that Rita. Let's go."

# Eight

Silver Jim found the overturned buggy while out hunting strays. The horse was nowhere in sight. He noticed that the Winchester .44 Carbine was a good twenty feet from the overturned buggy. He surmised that whoever had been in this rig had pulled the carbine from its boot and was makin' ready to use it. Then he found the pistol. He squatted down and sniffed at the barrel. Recently fired.

He stood up and emptied his Colt into the air; six widely spaced shots. It took only a few minutes for Smoke and Lujan to reach him.

"That is Senorita Hanks's buggy," Lujan said. "I have seen her in it several times."

"Stay with it, boys," Smoke said. "Look around. I'll ride to the D-H."

He did not spare his horse getting to the ranch, reining up to the main house in a cloud of dust and jumping off. "Switch my saddle," he told a startled hand. He ran up the steps to face a hard-eyed Dooley Hanks. "Silver Jim found Miss Hanks's buggy just north of our range. By that creek. Overturned. No sign of Miss Hanks. But Silver Jim said her pistol had been fired. I left them looking for her and trying to cut some trail."

The color went out of Dooley's face. Like most men, his daughter was the apple of his eye. "I'm obliged. Let's ride, boys!" he yelled.

Already, one of his regular hands was noosing a rope.

Within five minutes, twenty-five strong, Dooley led his hands and his hired guns out at a gallop. The wrangler had switched Smoke's saddle to a mean-eyed mustang and was running for his own horse.

Smoke showed the mustang who was boss and then cut across country, taking the timber and making his own trail, going where no large group of riders could. He reached the overturned buggy just a couple of minutes before Dooley and his men.

"Silver Jim cut some sign," Bobby told him. "Him and Lujan took off thataway. Told me to stay here."

Dooley and his party reined up and Dooley jumped off his horse. Smoke pointed to the pistol, still where Silver Jim had found it.

"That's hers," the father said, a horrified look in his eyes. "I give it to her and taught her how to use it."

"Look!" Bobby pointed.

Heads turned. Silver Jim was holding a girl in his arms, Lujan leading the horse, some of its harness dragging the ground.

The cook from the D-H came rattling up in a wagon, Mrs. Hanks on the seat beside him. "I filled it with hay, Boss," he told Dooley. "Just in case."

Dooley nodded.

Smoke took the girl from Silver Jim and carried her to the wagon and to her mother. She had been badly beaten and her clothing ripped from her. One of her eyes was closed and discolored and blood leaked from a corner of her mouth. Silver Jim had wrapped her in a blanket.

"How did you . . . I mean," Dooley shook his head. "Had she been . . . ?"

"I reckon," Silver Jim said solemnly. "Her clothes and . . . underthings was strewn over about a half a mile. Looks like they was rippin' and tearin' as they rode. Two men took her, a third joined them over yonder on that first ridge." He pointed. "He'd been waitin' for some time. Half a dozen cigarette butts on the ground."

"She say who done this?" Dooley's voice was harsh and terrible sounding.

"No, senor," Lujan said. "She was unconscious when we found her."

"Shorty!" Dooley barked. "Go fetch that old rummy we call a doctor. If he ain't sober, dunk him in a horse trough until he is. Ride, man!"

Smoke had walked to the wagon bed and was looking at the young woman, her head cradled in her mother's lap. He noticed a crimson area on the side of her head. "Bobby, bring me my canteen, hurry!"

He wet a cloth and asked Mrs. Hanks to clean up the bloody spot.

"Awful bump on her head," the mother said, her voice calm but the words tight.

"For sure she's got a concussion," Smoke said. "Maybe a fractured skull. Cushion her head and drive real slow, Cookie. She can't take many bumps and jars."

Smoke and his people stood and watched the procession start out for the ranch. Dooley had sent several of his men to follow the trail left by the rapists. "Bring them back alive," he told them. "I want to stake them out." He turned his mean and slightly maddened eyes toward Smoke. "Ain't that what you done years back, Jensen?"

"That's what I did."

The man's gone over the edge, Smoke thought. This was all it took to push him into that shadowy, eerie world of madness.

"They're going to find out what we didn't tell them, Smoke," Lujan said. "The trail leads straight to Circle Double C Range."

"And one of them horses has a chip out of a shoe. It'll be easy to identify." Silver Jim said.

Smoke thought about that. "Almost too easy, wouldn't you think."

"That thought did cross my mind," the old gunfighter acknowledged, rolling a cigarette.

"I better get over there." Smoke swung into the saddle and turned the mustang's head.

He looped the reins around the hitchrail and walked up to the porch, conscious of a lot of hard eyes on him as he knocked on the door.

A very lovely young woman opened the door and smiled at him. "Why, Mister Jensen. How nice. Please come in."

Smoke removed his hat and stepped inside the nicely furnished home just as Cord stepped into the foyer. "Trouble, Cord. Bad trouble." He looked at Sandi.

"Go sit with your mother, girl," the father said.

Sandi smiled sweetly and leaned up against the wall, folding her arms under her breasts.

Cord lifted and spread his big hands in a helpless gesture. "Boys are bad enough, Smoke, but girls are impossible."

Smoke told them both, leaving very little out. He did not mention anything about the chipped shoe; not in front of Sandi. Nor did he say anything about the trail leading straight to Circle C Range.

"I've got to get over there," Sandi said, turning to fetch her shawl.

"No." Smoke's hard-spoken word stopped her, turning her around. "There is nothing you can do over there. Rita is unconscious and will probably remain so for many hours. Dooley is killing mad and likely to go further off the deep end. And those who . . . abused Rita are still out there. Your going over there would accomplish nothing and only put you in danger."

She locked rebellious eyes with Smoke. Then she slowly nodded her head. "You're right, of course. Thank you for pointing those things out. I'll go tell Mother."

Smoke motioned Cord out onto the porch where they could talk freely, in private. He leveled with Cord.

"Damn!" the man cursed, balling his fists. "If the men who done it are here, we'll find them and hold them for the law . . . or hang them," he added the hard words. "No matter what I feel about Hanks himself, Rita and my Sandi have been friends for years. Rita and her momma is the two reasons I haven't gone over there and burned the damn place down. I've known for years that Dooley was crazy; and his boys is twice as bad. They're cruel mean."

"I've heard that from other people."

"It's true. And good with short guns, too. Very good. As good and probably better than most of the hired hands on the payroll." He met Smoke's eyes. "There's something you ought to know. Dooley has hired a back-shooter name of Danny Rouge."

"I know of him. Looks like a big rat. But he's pure poison with a rifle."

Cord looked toward the bunkhouse, where half a dozen gunhands were loafing. "Worthless scum. I was gonna let them go. Now I don't know what to do."

Smoke could offer no advice. He knew that Cord knew that if Dooley even thought his daughter's attackers came from the Circle Double C, he would need all the guns he could muster. They were all sitting on a powder keg, and it could go up at any moment.

A cowboy walked past the big house. "Find Del for me," Cord ordered. "Tell him to come up here."

"Yes, sir."

"You want me to stick around and help you?" Smoke asked.

Cord shook his head. "No. But thanks. This is my snake. I'll kill it."

"I'll be riding, then. If you need help, don't hesitate to send word. I'll come."

Smoke was riding out as the foreman was walking up.

Smoke rode back to the site of the attack. His people had already righted the buggy and hitched up the now calmed horse.

"I'll take it over to the D-H," Smoke offered. "I've got to get my horse anyway."

"I'll ride with you," Lujan said.

"What are we supposed to do?" Silver Jim asked. "Sit here and grow cobwebs? We'll all ride over."

Bobby had returned to chasing strays and pushing them toward new pasture.

The foreman of the D-H, Gage, met them halfway, leading Smoke's horse. "You boys is all right," he said. "So I'll give it to you straight. Don't come on D-H Range no more. I mean, as far as I'm concerned, me and the regular hands, you could ride over anytime; but Dooley has done let his bread burn. He's gone slap nuts. Sent a rider off to wire for more gunhands; they waitin' over at Butte. Lanny Ball found where them tracks led to McCorkle Range and that's when Dooley went crazy. His wife talked him out of riding over and killing Cord today. But he's gonna declare war on the Circle Double C and anybody who befriends them. So I guess all bets is off, boys. But I'll tell you this: me and the regular boys is gonna punch cows, and that's it . . . unless someone tries to attack the house. I'm just damn sorry all this had to happen. I'll be ridin' now. You boys keep a good eye on your backtrail. See you."

"Guess that tears it," Smoke said, after Gage had driven off in the buggy, his horse and the horse Smoke had borrowed tied to the back. "Let's get back to the ranch. Fae and Parnell need to be informed about this day."

Rita regained consciousness the following day. She told her father that she never saw her attackers' faces. They kept masks

59

and hoods on the entire time she was being assaulted.

Cord McCorkle sent word that Dooley was welcome to come help search his spread from top to bottom to find the attackers.

Dooley sent word that Cord could go to hell. That he believed Cord knew who raped and beat his daughter and was hiding them, protecting them.

"I tried," Cord said to Smoke. "I don't know what else I can do."

The men were in town, having coffee in Hans's cafe.

Parnell had wanted to pack up and go back east immediately. Fae had told him, in quite blunt language, that anytime he wanted to haul his ashes, to go right ahead. She was staying.

Beans and Charlie Starr had stood openmouthed, listening to Fae vent her spleen. They had never heard such language from the mouth of a woman.

Parnell had packed his bags and left the ranch in a huff, vowing never to return until his sister apologized for such unseemly behavior and such vile language.

That set Fae off again. She stood by the hitchrail and cussed her brother until his buggy was out of sight.

Lujan and Spring walked up.

"They do this about once a month," Spring said. "He'll be back in a couple of days. I tell you boys what, workin' for that woman has done give me an education I could do without. Someone needs to sit on her and wash her mouth out with soap."

"Don't look at me!" Lujan said, rolling his dark eyes. "I'd rather crawl up in a nest of rattlesnakes."

"Get back to work!" Fae squalled from the porch, sending the men scrambling for their horses.


"There they are," Smoke said quietly, his eyes on three men riding abreast up the street.

"Who?" Cord asked.

"The Sabler Brothers. Ben, Carl, and Delmar. They'll be gunning for Lujan. He killed two of their brothers some years back."

"Be interesting to see which saloon they go in."

"You takin' bets?"

"Not me. I damn sure didn't send for them."

60

The Sabler boys reined up in front of the Hangout.

"It's like they was told not to come to the Pussycat," Cord reflected.

"They probably were. No chipped shoes on any of your horses, huh?"

"No. But several were reshod that day; started before you came over with the news. It's odd, Smoke. Del is as square as they come; hates the gunfighters. But he says he can account for every one of them the morning Rita was raped. He says he'll swear in a court of law that none of them left the bunkhouse-main house area. I believe him."

"It could have been some drifters."

"You believe that?"

"No. I don't know what to believe, really."

"I better tell you: talk among the D-H bunch—the gunslicks—is that it was Silver Jim and Lujan and the Hatfield boy."

Smoke lifted his eyes to meet Cord's gaze. Cord had to struggle to keep from recoiling back. The eyes were ice-house cold and rattler deadly. "Silver Jim is one of the most honorable men I have ever met. Lujan was with me all that morning. Both Hatfield and Bobby are of the age where neither one of them can even talk when they get around women; besides he was within a mile of me and Lujan all morning. Whoever started that rumor is about to walk into a load of grief. If you know who it is, Cord, I'd appreciate you telling me."

"It was that new bunch that came in on the stage the day after it happened. They come up from Butte at Hanks's wire."

"Names?"

"All I know is they call one of them Rose."

Lujan came galloping up, off his horse before the animal even stopped. He ran into the cafe. "Smoke! Hardrock found Young Hatfield about an hour ago. He'd been tortured with a running iron and then dragged. He ain't got long."

# Nine

Doc Adair, now sober for several days, looked up as Smoke and Cord entered the bedroom of the main ranch house. He shook his head. "Driftin' in and out of consciousness. I've got him full of laudanum to ease the pain. They burned him all over his body with a hot iron, then they dragged him. He isn't going to make it. He wouldn't be a whole man even if he did."

No one needed to ask what he meant by that. Those who did this to the boy had been more cruel than mean.

Bobby was fighting back tears. "Me and him growed up together. We was neighbors. More like brothers than friends."

Fae put her arm around the young man and held him, then, at a signal from Smoke, led him out of the bedroom. Smoke knelt down beside the bed.

"Can you hear me, Hatfield?"

The boy groaned and opened his one good eye. "Yes, sir, Mister Smoke." His voice was barely a whisper, and filled with pain.

"Who did this to you?"

"One of them was called . . . Rose. They called another one Cliff. I ain't gonna make it, am I, Mister Smoke?"

Smoke sighed.

"Tell me . . . the truth."

"The doc says no. But doctors have been wrong before."

"When they burned my privates . . . I screamed and passed out. I come to and they . . . was draggin' me."

His words were becoming hard to understand and his breathing was very ragged. Smoke could see one empty eye socket. "Send any money due me to . . . my ma. Tell her to buy something pretty . . . with it. Watch out for Bobby. He's . . .

62

He don't look it, but he's . . . cat quick with a short gun. Been . . . practicin' since we was about . . . six years old. Gettin' dark. See you, boys."

The young man closed his good eye and spoke no more. Doc Adair pushed his way through to the bed. After a few seconds, he said, "He's still alive, but just. A few more minutes and he'll be out of his pain."

Smoke glanced at Lujan. "Lujan, go sit on Bobby. Hogtie him if you have to. We'll avenge Hatfield, but it'll be after the boy's been given a proper burial."

Grim-faced, and feeling a great deal more emotion than showed on his face, the Mexican gunfighter nodded and left the room.

Hatfield groaned in his unconsciousness. He sighed and his chest moved up and down, as if struggling for breath. Then he lay still. Doc Adair held a small pocket mirror up to the boy's mouth. No breath clouded the mirror. The doctor pulled the sheet over Hatfield's face.

"I'll start putting a box together," Spring spoke from the doorway. "Damn, but I liked that boy!"


The funeral was at ten o'clock the following morning. Mr. and Mrs. Cord McCorkle came, accompanied by Sandi and a few of their hands. Doc Adair was there, as was Hans and Hilda and Olga. Olga went straight to Ring's side and stood there during the services.

No one had seen Bobby that morning. He showed up at the last moment, wearing a black suit—Fae had pressed it for him—with a white shirt and black string tie. He wore a Remington Frontier .44, low and tied down. He did not strut and swagger. He wore it like he had been born with it. He walked up to Smoke and Lujan and the others, standing in a group.

"Bobby just died with Hatfield," he told them. "My last name is Johnson. Turkey Creek Jack Johnson is my uncle. My name is Bob Johnson. And I'll be goin' into town when my friend is in the ground proper and the words said over him."

"We'll all go in, Bob," Smoke told him.

The preacher spoke his piece and the dirt was shoveled over Hatfield's fresh-made coffin.

"Cord, I'd appreciate it if you and yours would stay here

with Fae and Parnell until we get back."

"We'll sure do it, Smoke. Take your time. And shoot straight," he added.

The men headed out. Four aging gunfighters with a string of kills behind them so long history has still not counted them. One gunfighter from south of the border. Smoke Jensen, from north of the border. The Moab Kid and a boy/man who rode with destiny on his shoulders.

They slowed their horses as they approached Gibson, the men splitting up into pairs, some circling the town to come in at different points.

But the town was nearly deserted. Hans's cafe had been closed for the funeral. The big general store—run by Walt and Leah Hillery, a sour-faced man and his wife—was open, but doing no business. The barber shop was empty. There were no horses standing at the hitchrails of either saloon. Smoke walked his horse around the corral and then looked inside the stable. Only a few horses in stalls, and none of them appeared to be wet from recent riding.

The men gathered at the edge of town, talked it over, and then dismounted; splitting up into two groups, one group on each side of the street.

Smoke pushed open the batwings of the Hangout and stepped inside. The place was empty except for the barkeep and the swamper. The bartender, knowing that Smoke had on his warpaint, was nervously polishing shot glasses and beer mugs.

"Ain't had a customer all morning, Mister Smoke," he announced. "I think the boys is stayin' close to the bunkhouse."

Smoke nodded at the man and stepped back out onto the boardwalk, continuing on his walking inspection.

He met with Beans. "Nothing," the Moab Kid said. "Town is deserted."

"They are not yet ready to meet us," Lujan said, walking up.

"We're wasting time here. We've still got cattle to brand and more to move to higher pasture. There'll be another day. Let's get back to work."

The days passed uneventfully, the normal day-to-day routine of the ranch devouring the men's time. Parnell, just as Old Spring had called it, moved back to the ranch and he and Fae

64

continued their bickering. Rita improved, physically, but she was not allowed off the ranch. And to make sure that she did not try any meetings with Sandi, her father assigned two men to watch her at all times.

Bob Johnson was a drastically changed young man. Bobby was gone. The boy seldom smiled now, and he was always armed. Smoke and Charlie Starr had watched him practice late one afternoon, when the day's work on the range was over.

"He's better than good," Charlie remarked. "He's cursed with being a natural."

He did not have to explain that. Smoke knew only too well what the gunfighter meant. With Bob, it was almost as if the gun was a physical extension of his right arm. His draw was oil-smooth and his aim was deadly accurate. And he was fast . . . very fast.

Old Pat rode out to the branding site in the early morning of the sixth day after Hatfield's burying.

"Hans just sent word, Smoke. Them Waters Brothers come into town late yesterday and they brought a half dozen hardcases with them."

"Hans know who they are?"

"He knowed two of 'em. No-Count George Victor and Three-Fingers Kerman. Other four looked meaner than snakes, Hans said. 'Bout an hour later, four more guns come in on the stage. Wore them big California spurs."

"Of course they went straight to the Hangout?" Charlie asked.

"Waters's bunch did. Them California gunslicks went on over to the Pussycat. McCorkle's hirin' agin."

Smoke cursed, but he really could not blame Cord. Every peace effort he had made to Hanks had been turned down with a violent outburst of profanity from Dooley. And Hanks's sons were pushing and prodding each time they came into town. Sonny, Bud, and Conrad Hanks had made their brags that they were going to kill Cord's boys, Max, Rock, and Troy. They were all about the same age and, according to Cord, all possessing about the same ability with a short gun. Cord's boys were more level-headed and better educated—his wife had seen to that. Hanks's boys were borderline stupid. Hanks had seen to that. And they were cruel and vicious.

"We're gonna be pulled into this thing," Hardrock remarked. "Just sure as the sun comes up. There ain't no way we can miss it. Sooner or later, we're gonna run up on them no-goods that done in Young Hatfield. And whether we do it together, or Young Bob does the deed, we'll have chosen a side."

"I'm curious as to when that back-shootin' Danny Rouge is gonna uncork," Pistol said. "I been prowlin' some; I ain't picked up no sign of his ever comin' onto Box T Range."

"Hanks hasn't turned him loose yet." Smoke fished out the makings and rolled him a cigarette, passing the sack and the papers around. He was thoughtful for a moment. "I'll tell you all what's very odd to me: these gunhawks are drawing fighting wages, but they have made no move toward each other. I think there's something rotten in the potato barrel, boys. And I think it's time I rode over and talked it out with Cord."

"You would have to bring that to my attention," Cord said, a glum look on his face. "I hadn't thought of that. But by George, you may be right. I hope you're not," he quickly added, "but there's always a chance. Have you heard anything more about Rita's condition?"

"Getting better, physically. Hanks keeps her under guard at the ranch."

"Same thing I heard. Sandi asked to see her and Dooley said he wouldn't guarantee her safety if she set foot on D-H Range. He didn't out and out threaten her—he knows better than that—but he came damn close. His sons and my sons are shapin' up for a shootin', though. And I can't stop them. I want to, but I don't know how, short of hogtyin' my boys and chainin' them to a post."

"How many regular hands do you have, Cord?"

"Eight, counting Del. I always hire part-timers come brandin' time and drives."

"So that's twelve people you can count on, including yourself and your sons."

"Right. Cookie is old, but he can still handle a six-gun and a rifle. You think the lid is going to fly off the pot, don't you, Smoke?"

"Yes. But I don't know when. Do you think your wife and Sandi would go on a visit somewhere until this thing is over?"

"*Hell*, no! If I asked Alice to leave she'd hit me with a skillet. God only knows what Sandi would do, or say," he added drily.

"Her mouth doesn't compare to Fae's, but stir her up and you've got a cornered puma on your hands."

"How about those California gunhands that just came in?"

"I don't trust them any more than I do the others. But I felt I had to beef up my gunnies."

"I don't blame you a bit. And I may be all wrong in my suspicions."

"Sad thing is, Smoke, I think you're probably right."

Smoke left McCorkle's ranch and headed back to the Box T. Halfway there, he changed his mind and pointed his horse's nose toward Gibson. Some of the crew was running out of chewing tobacco. He was almost to town when he heard the pounding of hooves. He pulled over to the side of the road and twisted in the saddle. Four riders that he had not seen before. He pulled his Winchester from the boot, levered in a round, and eared the hammer back, laying the rifle across his saddle horn. He was riding Dagger, and knew the horse would stand still in the middle of a cyclone; he wouldn't even look up from grazing at a few gunshots.

The riders reined in, kicking up a lot of unnecessary dust. Smoke pegged them immediately. Arrogant punks, would-be gunslicks. Not a one of them over twenty-one. But they all wore two guns tied down.

"You there, puncher!" one hollered. "How far to Gibson?"

"I'm not standing in the next county, sonny, and I'm not deaf, either."

"You 'bout half smart, though, ain't you?" He grinned at Smoke. "You know who you're talkin' to?"

"Just another loud-mouthed punk, I reckon."

The young man flushed, looked at his friends, and then laughed. "You're lucky, cowboy. I feel good today, so I won't call you down for that remark. I've killed people for less. I'm Twain."

"Does that rhyme with rain or are you retarded?"

"Damn you!" Twain yelled. "Who do you think you are, anyways?"

"Smoke Jensen."

Twain's horse chose that moment to dump a pile of road apples in the dirt. From the look on Twain's face, he felt like doing the same thing in his saddle. He opened and closed his mouth about a half dozen times.

His friends relaxed in their saddles, making very sure both

hands were clearly visible and kept well away from their guns.

"You keep on this road," Smoke told them. "Gibson's about four miles."

"Ah . . . uh . . . yes, sir!" Twain finally got the words out. "I . . . uh . . . we are sure obliged."

"You got any sense, boy, you won't stop. You'll just keep on ridin' until you come to Wyoming. But I figure that anybody who cuts kill-notches in the butt of their gun don't have much sense. Who you aimin' to ride for, boy?"

"Ah . . . the D-H spread."

Smoke sat his saddle and stared at the quartet. He stared at them so long they all four began to sweat.

"Is . . . ah . . . something the matter, Mister Smoke?" Twain asked.

"The rest of your buddies got names, Twain?"

"Ah . . . this here is Hector. That's Rod, and that's Murray."

"Be sure and tell that to the barber when you get to town."

"The . . . barber?" Hector asked.

"Yeah. He doubles as the undertaker." Smoke turned his back on the young gunhands and rode on toward town.

# Ten

Among the many horses tied to the hitchrails, on both sides of
the street, the first to catch Smoke's eyes was Bob's paint, tied
up in front of Hans's cafe. Smoke looped his reins and went in
for some coffee and pie. He wondered why so much activity
and then remembered it was Saturday. Parnell sat with Bob at a
table. They were in such heated discussion neither noticed as
Smoke walked up to their table. They lifted their eyes as he
pulled back a chair and sat down.

"Perhaps you can talk some sense into this young man's
head, Mister Jensen," Parnell pleaded. "He is going to call out
these Rose and Cliff individuals."

Smoke ordered apple pie and coffee and then said, "His
right, Parnell. I'd do the same was I standing in his boots."

Parnell was aghast. His mouth dropped open and he shook
his head. "But he's just a boy! I cannot for the life of me
understand why you didn't call the authorities after the
murder!"

"Because the law is a hundred miles away, Parnell. And out
here, a man handles his own problems without runnin'
whining to the law."

"I find it positively barbaric!"

Smoke ate some apple pie and sipped his coffee. Then he
surprised the schoolteacher by saying, "Yes, it is barbaric,
Parnell. But it's quick. Don't worry, there'll be plenty of
lawyers out here before you know it, and they'll be messin'
things up and writin' contracts so's that only another lawyer
can read them. That'll be good for people like you . . . not so
good for the rest of us. You haven't learned in the time you've
been here that out here, a man's word is his bond. If he tells

you he's sellin' you five hundred head of cattle, there will be five hundred head of cattle, or he'll make good any missing. Call a man a liar out here, Parnell, and it's a shootin' offense. Honorable men live by their word. If they're not honorable, they don't last. They either leave, or get buried. Lawyers, Parnell, will only succeed in screwing that all up." He looked at Bob. "You nervous, Bob?"

"Yes, sir. Some. But I figure I'll calm down soon as I face him."

"As soon as *we* face *them,* Bob," Smoke corrected. "Yes, you'll calm down. Ever killed a man, Bob?"

"No, sir."

Smoke finished his pie, wiped his mouth with the napkin, and waved for Olga to refill his cup. He sugared and stirred and sipped. "A man gets real calm inside, Bob. It's the strangest thing. You can hear a fly buzz a hundred yards off. And you can see everything so clearly. And the quiet is so much so it's scary. Dogs can be barking, cats fighting, but you won't hear anything except the boots of the man you're facing walking toward you."

"How old was you when you killed your first man, Smoke?" Bob asked.

"Fifteen, I think. Maybe fourteen. I don't remember."

"That must have been a terribly traumatic time for you," Parnell said.

"Nope. I just reloaded 'er up and went on. Me and Preacher. I killed some Indians before that . . . in Kansas I think it was. Pa was still alive then. They attacked us," he added. "I always got along with the Indians for the most part. Lived with them for a while. Me and Preacher. That was after Pa died. Drink your coffee, Bob. It's about time."

Smoke noticed the young man's hands were calm as he lifted the cup to his mouth, sipped, and replaced the cup in the saucer.

Parnell looked at the men, his eyes drifting back and forth. He had heard from his sister and from the old gunfighters at the ranch that Smoke was a devoted family man: totally faithful to his wife and a loving father. A marvelous friend. Yet for all of those attributes, the man was sitting here talking about killing with less emotion than he exhibited when ordering a piece of pie.

Parnell watched with a curious mixture of fascination and

revulsion as Smoke took his guns from leather, one at a time, and carefully checked the action, using the napkin to wipe them free of any dust that might have accumulated during his ride to town. He loaded up the usually empty chamber under the hammer.

Bob checked his Remington .44 and then pulled a short-barreled revolver out of his waistband and checked that, loading both guns full. He cut his eyes to Smoke. "Insurance," he said.

"Never hurts." Smoke pushed back his chair and stood up. "You know these people, Bob?"

"They been pointed out to me." He stood up.

"Their buddies are sure to join them. We're probably not going to have much time for plan-making. At the first twitch, we start shooting. Take the ones to your left. I'll take care of the rest."

"Yes, sir."

"Let's go."

Both men had noticed, out of the corners of their eyes, the horses lining both sides of the wide dusty street being cleared from the line of fire.

They stepped out of the cafe and stood for a moment on the boardwalk, hats pulled down low, letting their eyes adjust to the bright sunlight.

"Your play," Smoke said. "You call it."

"Rose!" Bob yelled. "Cliff! And any others who tortured and dragged Hatfield. Let's see if you got the backbone to face someone gun to gun."

Rose looked out the window of the Hangout. "Hell, it's that damn kid."

"And Smoke Jensen," he was reminded.

"Let's shoot 'em from here," Cliff suggested.

"No!" Lanny Ball stepped in. "They're callin' you out fair and square. If you ain't got the stomach for it, use the back door and cut and run . . . and don't never show your faces around here agin. I've killed a lot of men, and I've rode the owlhoot trail with a posse at my back. But I ain't never tortured nobody while they was trussed up like a hog. I may not be much, but I ain't no coward."

Only a few of the other gunhawks in the large saloon murmured their agreement, but those few were the best-known and most feared of their kind. It was enough to bring the sweat out on the faces of Cliff and Rose and the two others who had taken part in the dragging and torture of Hatfield.

When open warfare was finally called by Hanks, Lanny and the few other who still possessed a modicum of honor would back-shoot and snipe at any known enemy . . . that was the way of war. But when a man called you out to face him, you faced him, eyeball to eyeball.

With a low curse, Rose checked his guns and stepped out through the batwings, Cliff and the others behind him. It was straight-up noon, the sun a hot bubbling ball overhead. There were no shadows of advantage for either side.

Smoke and Bob had drifted down the boardwalk and now stood in the middle of the street, about ten feet apart, waiting.

Rose and Cliff and their two partners in torture stepped off the boardwalk and walked to the center of the street.

"Rose to my left," Bob said. "Cliff is to your right."

"Who are those other two?"

"I don't know their names."

"You two in the middle!" Smoke called, his voice carrying the two hundred odd feet between them. "You got names?"

"I'm Stanford and this here is Thomas!"

"You take Stanford, Bob. Thomas is mine." Smoke's voice was low.

"You ready?" Bob asked.

"I been ready."

Smoke and Bob started walking, their spurs softly jingling and their boots kicking up small pockets of dust with each step toward showdown.

"You boys watch this," Lanny told the others. "I doubt they's many of you ever seen Jensen in action. Don't make no mistakes about him. He's the fastest I ever seen. Some of you may want to change your minds about stayin' once you seen him."

"I do not have to watch him," Diego boasted. "I am better." He knocked back a shot of whiskey.

Several of the others in the saloon agreed.

Lanny smiled at their arrogance. Lanny might be many things, but he was not arrogant when it came to facing Smoke Jensen. He did not feel he was better than Smoke, but he did feel he was as good. When the time came for them to meet, as he knew it would, it would all come down to that first well-placed shot. Lanny knew that he would probably take lead when he faced Smoke, therefore he would delay facing him as long as possible.

"You shoulda heard that punk squall when we laid that hot runnin' iron agin him!" Thomas yelled over the closing distance. "He jerked and hollered like a baby. Squalled and bawled like a calf."

Neither Smoke nor Bob offered any comment in reply.

The loud silence and the artificial inner brightness consumed them both.

There was less than fifty feet between them when Rose made his move. He never even cleared leather. None of the four managed to get clear of leather before they began dancing and jerking under the impact of .44 slugs. Thomas took two .44 slugs in the heart and died on his feet. He sat down in the dirt, on his knees, his empty hands dangling in the bloody dirt.

Bob was nearly as fast as Smoke. His .44 Remington barked again and Stanford was turned halfway around, hit in the stomach and side just as Cliff experienced twin hammer-blows to his chest from Smoke's Colt and his world began to dim. He fell to the dirt in a slack heap, seemingly powerless to do anything except cry out for his mother. He was still hollering for her when he died, the word frozen in time and space.

"Jesus Christ!" a gunslick spoke from the saloon window. He picked up his hat from the table and walked out the back door. He had a brother over in the Dakotas and concluded that this was just a dandy time to go see how his brother and his family was getting along. Hell would be better than this place.

Smoke and Bob turned and walked to the Pussycat, reloading as they walked. Inside the coolness of the saloon, they ordered beer and sat down at a table, with a clear view of the street.

Neither of them spoke for several minutes. When the barkeep had brought their pitcher of beer and two mugs and returned to his post behind the long bar, Bob picked up his mug and held it out. "For Hatfield," he said.

"I'll drink to that," Smoke said, lifting his mug.

Parnell entered the saloon, walking gingerly, sniffing disdainfully at the beery odor. Smoke waved him over and kicked out a chair for him.

"You want something to drink?" the barkeep called.

"A glass of your best wine would be nice." Parnell sat down.

"Ain't got no wine. Beer and whiskey and sodee pop."

Parnell shook his head and the bartender went back to polishing glasses, muttering under his breath about fancy-pants easterners.

Outside, in the bloody street, the barber and his helper were scurrying about, loading up the bodies. Business certainly had taken a nice turn for the better.

Smoke noticed that Parnell seemed calm enough. "Not your first time to see men die violently, Parnell?"

"No. I've seen several shootings out here. All of them as unnecessary as the one I just witnessed."

"Justice was served," Smoke told him, after taking a sip of beer.

Parnell ignored that. "Innocent bystanders could have been killed by a stray bullet."

"That is true," Smoke acknowledged. "I didn't say it was the best way to handle matters, only that justice had been served."

"And now you've taken a definite side."

"If that is the way people wish to view it, yes."

"I have a good notion to notify the army about this matter."

"And you think they'd do what, Parnell? Send a company in to keep watch? Forget it. The army's strung out too thin as it is in the West. And they'd tell you that this is a civilian matter."

"What you're saying is that this . . . ugly boil on the face of civilization must erupt before it begins the healing process?"

"That's one way of putting it, yes. Dooley Hanks has gone around the bend, Parnell. I suspect he was always borderline nuts. The beating and rape of his daughter tipped him the rest of the way. He's insane. And he's making a mistake in trusting those gunslicks he's hired. That bunch can turn on a man faster than a lightning bolt."

"And McCorkle?"

"Same with that bunch he's got. Only difference is, Cord knows it. He's tried to make peace with Hanks . . . over the past few weeks. Hanks isn't having any of it. Cord had no choice but to hire more gunnies."

"And now . . . ?"

"We wait."

"You are aware, of course, about the rumor that it was really some of your people who beat and sexually assaulted Rita Hanks?"

"Some of that crap is being toted off the street now," Smoke

74

reminded the schoolteacher. "When Silver Jim and Lujan hear of it—I have not mentioned it to them—the rest of it will be planted six feet under. But I think that rumor got squashed a few minutes ago."

"And if it didn't, there will be more violence."

"Yes."

"Why are we so different, Cousin? What I'm asking is that we spring from the same bloodlines, yet we are as different as the sun and the moon."

"Maybe, Parnell, it's because you're a dreamer. You think of the world as a place filled with good, decent, honorable men. I see the world as it really is. Maybe that's it."

Parnell pushed back his chair and stood up. He looked down at Smoke for a few seconds. "If that is the case, I would still rather have my dreams than live with blood on my hands."

"I'd rather have that blood on my hands than have it leaking out of me," Smoke countered. "Knowing that I could have possibly prevented it simply by standing my ground with a gun at the ready."

"A point well put. I shall take my leave now, gentlemen. I must see to the closing of the school for the summer."

"See you at the ranch, Parnell."

Both Smoke and Bob had lost their taste for beer. They left the nearly full pitcher of beer on the table and walked out onto the boardwalk. Most of the gunnies had left the Hangout, heading back to the D-H spread. Lanny Ball stood on the boardwalk in front of the saloon, looking across the street at Smoke.

"He's a punk," Smoke said to Bob. "But a very fast punk. I'd say he's one of the best gunslicks to be found anywhere."

"Better than you?" Bob asked, doubt in the question.

"Just as good, I'd say. And so is Jason Bright."

Lanny turned his back to them and entered the saloon.

"Another day," Smoke muttered. "But it's coming."

# Eleven

Smoke was riding the ridges early one morning, looking for any strays they might have missed. He had arranged for a buyer from the Army to come in, in order to give Fae some badly needed working capital, and planned to sell off five hundred head of cattle. He saw the flash of sunlight off a barrel just a split second before the rifle fired. Smoke threw himself out of the saddle, grabbing his Winchester as he went. The slug hit nothing but air. Grabbing the reins, Smoke crawled around a rise and picketed the horse, talking to the animal, calming it.

He wasn't sure if he was on Box T Range, or D-H Range. It would be mighty close either way. If the gunman had waited just a few more minutes, Smoke might well be dead on the ground, for he had planned to ride in a blind canyon to flush out any strays.

Working his way around the rise of earth, Smoke began to realize just how bad his situation was. He was smack in the middle of a clearing, hunkering down behind the only rise big enough to conceal a human or horse to be found within several hundred yards.

And he found out just how good the sniper was when a hard spray of dirt slapped him in the face, followed closely by the boom of the rifle. Smoke could not tell the caliber of the rifle, but it sounded like a .44-40, probably with one of those fancy telescopes on it. He'd read about the telescopes on rifles, but had never looked through one mounted on a rifle, only seen pictures of them. They looked awkward to Smoke.

He knew one thing for an iron-clad fact: he was in trouble.

Whatever the gunman was using, he was one hell of a fine rifleman.

Hanks had cut loose his rabid dog: that rat-faced Danny Rouge.

What to do? He judged his chances of getting to the timber facing him and rejected a frontal run for it. He worked his way to his horse and removed his boots, slipping into a pair of moccasins he always carried. The fancy moccasins Ring had made were back at the house.

Smoke eased back to his skimpy cover and chanced a look, cursing as the rifle slammed again, showering him with dirt.

No question about it, he had to move, and soon. If he stayed here, and tried to wait Danny out—if it was Danny, and Smoke was certain it was—sooner or later the sniper would get the clean shot he was waiting for and Smoke would take lead. He'd been shot before and didn't like it at all. It was a very disagreeable feeling. Hurt, too.

Smoke looked around him. There was a drop-off about fifty yards behind him; a natural ditch that ran in a huge half circle, the southeast angle of the ditch running close to the timber. He studied every option available to him, and there weren't that many.

His horse would be safe, protected by the rise. If something happened to Smoke—like death—the horse would eventually pull its picket pin and return to the ranch.

Smoke checked his gun belt. All the loops were full. Returning to the horse, he stuffed a handful of cartridges into his jeans' pocket and slung his canteen after first filling his hat with water and giving the horse a good drink. Squatting down, he munched on a salt pork and biscuit sandwich, then took a long satisfying pull at the canteen. He patted the horse's neck.

"You stay put, fellow. I'll be back." I hope, he silently added.

Smoke took several deep breaths and took off running down the slope.

Smoke knew that shooting either uphill or downhill was tricky; bad enough with open sights. But with a telescope, trying to line up a running, twisting target would be nearly impossible. He hoped.

The gunman started dusting Smoke's running feet, but he was hurrying his shots, and missing. But coming close enough to show Smoke how good he was with a rifle.

Smoke hurled himself in the ditch, managed to stay on his feet, then dive for the cover of the ravine's wall. Now, Danny would have to worry about which side Smoke would pop up out of. Catching his breath, Smoke began working his way around, staying close to the earthen wall. He knew the distance was still too great for his .44, and besides that, he didn't want to give away his position.

77

Smoke took his time, smiling as the ravine curved closer to the timber and began narrowing as the timber loomed up on both sides. When he came to a brushy spot, Smoke carefully eased out of the ravine and slipped into the timber. His jeans were a tan color, his shirt a dark brown; he would blend in well with his surroundings.

He began closing the distance. Smoke had been taught well the ways of a woodsman; Preacher had been his teacher, and there was no finer woodsman to be found than the old mountain man.

He moved carefully while still covering a lot of ground, stopping often to check the terrain all around him. Danny not only looked like a big rat, the killer could move as furtively as a rodent.

Before making his run for it, Smoke had inspected the area on the ridges as carefully as possible—considering that he was being shot at—and kept Danny's position highlighted in his mind.

But Smoke was certain the sniper would have changed positions as soon as he made his run for it. Where to was the question.

He moved closer to where he had last seen the puff of smoke. When he was about a hundred yards from where he thought Danny had been firing from, Smoke made himself comfortable behind a tree and waited, every sense working overtime. He felt he could play the waiting game just as good, or better, than Danny.

He waited for a good twenty minutes, as motionless as a snake waiting for a passing rat. Then the rat he was waiting for moved.

It was only a very slight move, perhaps to brush away a pesky fly. But it was all Smoke needed. Very carefully, he raised his rifle and sighted in—he had been waiting with the hammer eared back—and pulled the trigger. The rifle slammed his shoulder and Smoke knew he had a clean miss on his target.

The gunman rolled away and came up shooting, shooting way fast. Maybe he had two rifles, one a short-barreled carbine, or maybe he was shooting one of those Winchester .44-40's with the extra rear sight for greater accuracy. If that was the case, the man was still one hell of a marksman.

Smoke caught a glimpse of color that didn't seem right in the timber and triggered off two fast rounds. This time he heard a squall of pain. He fired again and something heavy fell in the woods. A trick on the man's part? Maybe. Smoke settled back and waited.

He listened to the man cough, hard, racking coughs of pain. Then the man cursed him.

"Sorry, partner," Smoke called. "You opened this dance, now you pay the fiddler."

"You Injun bastard!" the man said with a groan. "I never even heard you come up on me."

Smoke offered no reply.

"I'm hit hard, man. I got the makins but my matches is all bloody. Least you can do is give me a light."

"You're gonna have lots of fire where you're goin', partner. Just give it a few minutes."

That got Smoke another round of cussing.

But Smoke was up and moving, working his way up the ridge to a vantage point which would enable him to look down on the wounded man. If he was as hard hit as he claimed.

The man was down, all right, Smoke could see that. And the front of his shirt was badly stained with blood. But it wasn't Danny Rouge.

It was a man he'd seen riding with Cord's hired guns.

What the hell was going on?

The man had stopped his moaning and was lying flat on his back, both hands in plain sight. He was not moving.

Smoke inched his way down the ridge to just above the gunman. He was dead. He had taken a round in his guts and one in his chest. Smoke had been right: it was a .44-.40, and a brand spanking new one from the looks of it.

It took him a few minutes to find the man's horse and get him roped belly-down across the saddle. He shoved the dead man's Winchester in the boot and led the animal down the ridge to his own horse. His horse shied away from the smell of blood and death, pulling his picket pin, and Smoke had to catch him and calm him down.

Now what to do with the McCorkle rider?

If the gunnies on Cord's payroll were playing both ends against the middle, it would not be wise to just ride over there with one of their buddies draped belly-down across his saddle. On the other hand, Cord had to be notified.

Smoke headed for the Box T. On the way, he ran into Hardrock and sent him over to the Circle Double C to get Cord.

The old gunfighter had looked close at the dead man.

"You know him, Hardrock?"

"Only by his rep. His name is Black. Call him Blackie. He's a back-shooter. Was."

"Keep this quiet at the ranch. Speak to only Cord."

"Right."

Smoke rode on over to the bunkhouse and relieved the horse of its burden and saddle, letting the animal water and feed and roll. Fae came out of the house, accompanied by her brother.

Smoke explained, ending with, "Something's up. I think we'd better get set for a hard wind."

"And a violent one," Parnell added, grimacing at the smell of the dead gunny.

"You better get a gun, Parnell," Smoke told him.

"I will not have one of those abominable things in my possession!"

"Suit yourself. But I have a hunch you're gonna change your mind before this is all over."

"Never!" Parnell stood his ground.

"Uh-huh" was all Smoke said in reply to that.

Parnell's sister had plenty to say about her brother. Smoke could but stand in awe and amazement at the words rolling from her mouth.

"I don't understand this," Cord said, after viewing the dead man.

"I didn't think you would. But the big question is this: was the sniper working as a lone wolf, perhaps just to gain a reputation for killing me, or was he part of a larger scheme?"

"Involving the gunhands from both ranches?"

"Yes."

Cord's sigh was loud in the hot stillness of Montana summer. "I don't know. My first thought is: yes. My next thought is: I've got to get Dooley to talk to me; bury the hatchet before this thing goes any further."

"Forget it," Smoke said bluntly. "The man is crazy. He's kill-crazy. I've heard he's making all sorts of wild claims and charges and plans. He's going to take over the whole area and be king. Keep a standing army of a hundred gunhawks—all sorts of wild talk."

"He's damn near got a hundred," Cord said glumly. "If what we're both thinking is true."

"Close to fifty if they all get together," Smoke added it up.

"And if I go back and fire all of those drawing fighting

wages . . . ?" Cord left it hanging.

"We'd know where they stand. And you and your family would probably be safer. But if we're wrong, it would leave you wide open, 'cause for sure the gunnies you fire would just hire on at the D-H."

Cord cursed softly for a few seconds. "I'm stuck between that much-talked-about rock and a hard place."

"Whichever way you decide to go, watch your back."

"Yeah." He looked at the blanket-covered body of the sniper. "What about him?"

"We'll bury him. And don't mention it, Cord. Just let the others wonder what happened—if there really is some sort of funny business going on."

"There is some grim humor in all of this, Smoke. If this thing goes on for any length of time, both Dooley and me will go broke paying fighting wages."

"Maybe that's what the gunhands want. Maybe that's why they're hanging back, for the most part."

Cord shook his big head. It appeared that the man's hair had grayed considerably since Smoke had first seen him, only a few weeks back. "This thing's turnin' out to have more maybe's and what-if's than a simple man can understand."

Smoke motioned for Charlie and Spring to come over. "Let's get him in the ground, boys. Well away from the house and unmarked. Spring, you can have that .44-40. It's a whale of a rifle. Dusted my butt proper," he added.

"I'll go through his pockets," Charlie said. "See if there is some address for his family."

Smoke nodded. "Take his horse and turn him loose. He'll find his way back to the ranch. We'll keep the rig. That'll add even more doubt in the minds of the gunslicks." He turned to Cord. "You 'bout caught up at your place, Cord?"

"Yeah. Why?"

"Pull a couple of your best men off the range. Keep them close by at all times. When you ride, take one of them with you and let the other stay around the house."

"Good idea. But at night I don't worry much." He smiled a father's smile. "Ever'time I look up, the Moab Kid is over there sparkin' my daughter."

Smoke chuckled. "She could do worse. Beans is a good man."

"At first, I told her she couldn't see him. That made about as much impression on her as a poot in a whirlwind. I finally told

81

her to go ahead and see him. She told me that she'd never stopped. Daughters!"

"You keepin' a tight rein on your boys?"

"I'm trying. Lord, I'm trying. I've got them working just as far away from D-H Range as possible. But they told me last night they think they're being watched. Stalked was the word Max used. That gives me an uneasy feelin'."

"It might be wise to pull them in and keep them around the house." He smiled. "Tell you what; do this: Tell the gunhands to start workin' the range."

Cord thought about that for a moment, then burst out laughing. "*Hell*, yes! That'll make them earn their pay and keep them away from the house."

"Or it'll put them on the road."

The men shook hands and Cord rode back to his ranch. Fae came to Smoke's side. "Now what?"

"We sell some cows to the Army. And wait."


The buyer for the Army had already looked over the cattle and agreed to a price. When he returned, a couple of days after Smoke's misunderstanding with the sniper, he brought drovers with him. Smoke and the buyer settled up the paperwork and the bank draft was handed over to Fae. The two men leaned up against a corral railing and talked.

"You know about the battle looking at us in the face, don't you?" Smoke asked.

"Uh-huh. And from all indications it's gonna be a real cutter."

"What would it take to get the Army involved?"

"Not a chance, Jensen. The Army's done looked this situation over and, unofficially, and I didn't say this, they decided to stay out of it. It'd take a presidential order to get them to move in here."

It was as Smoke had guessed. All over the fast-settling West little wars were flaring up; too many for the authorities or the Army to put down, so they were letting them burn themselves out. Here, they would be on their own, whichever way it went.

The buyer and his men moved the cattle out and the range was silent.

Smoke wondered for how long?

# Twelve

"You tellin' me you're not gonna work cattle?" Cord faced the gunslick.

"I'm paid to fight, not herd cattle," Jason Bright told him.

"You're not being paid to do either one after this moment. Pack your kit and clear out. Pick up your money at the house."

Jason's eyes became cloudy with hate. "And if I don't go?"

"Then one of us is going to be on the ground."

Jason laughed. "Are you challengin' me, old man?"

Cord was far from being an old man. At forty-five he was bull-strong and leather-tough. And while he was no fast gun, there was one thing he was good at. He showed Jason a hard right fist to the jaw.

Flat on his back, his mouth leaking blood, Jason grabbed for his gun, forgetting that the hammer thong was still on it. Cord stomped the gunfighter in the belly, reached down while Jason was gasping for breath, and jerked the gun out of leather, tossing it to one side. He backed up, his big hands balled into fists.

"Catch your breath and then get up, you yellow-bellied pup. Let's see how good you are without your gun."

A dozen gunhawks ran from the bunkhouse, stopping abruptly as Cord's sons, his daughter, his wife, and four regular hands appeared from both sides of the house and on the porch, rifles and sawed-off shotguns in their hands.

"It's going to be a fair fight, boys," Alice McCorkle said, her voice strong and calm. She held a double-barreled shotgun in her hands. "Between two men; and my husband is giving Mr. Bright a good ten or fifteen years in age difference. Boys, I was nineteen when I killed my first Indian. With this very shotgun. I've killed half a dozen Indians and two outlaws in my day, and anytime any of you want to try me, just reach for a gun or try to break up this fight—whichever way it's going—and I'll spread your guts all over this yard. Then I'll make your gunslinging buddies clean up the mess."

She lifted the shotgun, pointing the twin muzzles straight at Pooch Matthews.

"Lord, lady!" Pooch hollered. "I ain't gonna interfere."

"And you'll stop anyone who does, right, Mr. Matthews?"

"Oh, yes, ma'am!"

Jason was on his feet, his eyes shiny with hate as he faced Cord.

"Clean his plow, honey," Alice told her husband.

Cord stepped in and knocked Jason spinning, the gunfighter's mouth suddenly a bloody smear. Like so many men who lived by the gun and depended on a six-shooter to get them out of any problem, Jason had never learned how to use his fists.

Cord gave him a very short and very brutal lesson in fistfighting.

Cord gave him two short hard straight rights to the stomach then followed through with a crashing left hook that knocked the gunfighter to the ground. Normally, Cord would have kicked the man in the face and ended it. No truly tough man, who fights only when hard-pushed, does not consider that "dirty" or unfair fighting, but merely a way to get the fight over with and get back to work. In reality, there is no such thing as a "fair fight." There is a winner and a loser. Period.

But in this case, Cord just wanted the fight to last a while. He was enjoying himself. And really, rather enjoying showing off for his wife a little bit.

Cord dropped his guard while so pleased with himself and Jason busted him in the mouth.

Shaking his head to clear away the sparkling confusion, for Jason was no little man, Cord settled down to a good ol'-fashioned rough-and-tumble, kick-and-gouge brawl.

The two men stood boot to boot for a moment, hammering away at each other until finally Jason had to give ground and back up from Cord's bull strength. Jason was younger and in good shape, but he had not spent a lifetime doing brutally hard work, twelve months a year, wrestling steers and digging postholes and roping and branding and breaking horses.

Jason tried to kick Cord. Cord grabbed the boot and

dumped the gunhawk on the ground, on his butt. That brought several laughs from Jason's friends, all standing and watching and being very careful not to let their hands get too close to the butts of their guns.

Jason jumped to his boots, one eye closing and his nose a bloody mess, and swung at Cord. Cord grabbed the wrist and threw Jason over his hip, slamming him to the ground. This time Jason was not as swift getting to his feet.

Cord was circling, grinning at Jason, but giving the man time to clear his head and stand and fight.

But this time Jason came up with a knife he'd pulled out of his boot.

"No way, Jason!" Lodi yelled from the knot of gunslingers. "And I don't give a damn how many guns is on me. Drop that knife or I'll shoot you personal."

With a look of disgust on his face, Jason threw the knife to the ground.

Cord stepped in and smashed the man a blow to the jaw and followed that with a wicked slash to Jason's belly, doubling him over. Then he hit him twice in the face, a left and right to both sides of the man's jaw.

Jason hit the ground and did not move.

Cord walked to a water barrel by the side of the house and washed his face and soaked his aching hands for a moment. He turned and faced the gunslicks.

"I want Jason out of here within the hour. No man disobeys an order of mine. Any of you who want to stay, that's fine with me. But you'll take orders and you'll work the spread, doing whatever Del tells you to do. Make up your mind."

"Hell, Mister McCorkle . . ." a gunhawk said. He looked at the ladies. "I mean, heck. We come here to fight, not work cattle. No disrespect meant."

"None taken. But the war is over as far as I'm concerned. Any of you who want to ride out, there'll be no hard feelings and I'll have your money ready for you at the house."

All of them elected to ride.

"See me on the porch for your pay," Cord told them.

When the last gunslick had packed his warbag, collected his pay, and ridden out, Del sat down beside Cord on the front porch.

"Feels better around the place, Boss. But if them gunnies hire on with Hanks, we're gonna be hard up agin it."

"I know that, Del. Tell the men that from this day on, they'll be receiving fighting wages." He held up a warning finger. "We start nothing, Del. Nothing. We defend home range and no more. I won't ask that the men stay out of Gibson; only that they don't go in there looking for trouble. Send Willie riding over to the Box T and tell Smoke what I've done. He needs to know."

"Sure got the crap pounded out of you," Lanny said, looking at the swollen and bruised face of Jason Bright.

Jason lay on a bed in the bunkhouse of the D-H spread. "It ain't over," he mush-mouthed the words past swollen lips. "Not by no long shot, it ain't."

Dooley Hanks had eagerly hired the gunslicks. He was already envisioning himself as king. And he wanted to kill Cord McCorkle personally. In his maddened mind, he blamed Cord for everything. He'd worked just as hard as Cord, but had never gained the respect that most people felt toward McCorkle. And this just wasn't right. King Hanks. He sure liked the way that sounded.

"It's just going to make matters worse," Hanks's wife was telling their daughter.

Rita looked up from her packing. "Papa's crazy, Mother. He's crazy as a lizard. Haven't you seen the way he slobbers on himself? The way he sits on the porch mumbling to himself? Now he's gone and hired all those other gunfighters. Worse? For who? I'll tell you who: everybody. Everything from the Hound to the Sixteenmile is going to explode."

"And you think you'll be safer over at the Box T?"

"I won't be surrounded by crazy people. I won't be under guard all the time. I'll be able to walk out of the house without being watched. Are you gong to tell on me, Mother?"

She shook her head. "No. You're a grown woman, Rita. Your father has no right to keep you a prisoner here. But I don't know how you're going to pull this off."

Rita smiled. "I'll make it, Mother." She kissed her mother's cheek and hugged her. "This can't last forever. And I won't be that far away."

"Have you considered that your father might try to bring you back by force?"

"He might if I was going to Sandi's. I don't think he'll try

86

with Smoke Jensen."

The mother pressed some money into the daughter's hand. "You'll need this."

"Thank you, Mother. I'll pretend I'm going to bed early. Right after supper. Then I'll be gone."

After the mother had left the room, Rita laid out her clothes. Men's jeans, boots, a man's shirt. She had one of her brother's old hats and a work jacket to wear against the cold night. She picked up the scissors. Right after supper she would whack her hair short.

She believed it would work. It had to work. If she stayed around this place, she would soon be as nutty as her father and her crazy brothers.


"Peaceful," Cord said to Alice. "Like it used to be."

They sat on the front porch, enjoying the welcome coolness of early evening after the warm day.

"If it will only last, Cord."

"All we can do is try, honey. That's all a mule can do, is try."

"Tell me about this Smoke Jensen. I've met him, but never to talk with at length."

"He's a good man, I believe. A fair man. Not at all like I thought he'd be. He's one of those rare men that you look at and instantly know that this one won't push. I found that out very quickly." His last comment was dry, remembering that first day he'd yelled at Smoke, in Gibson, and the man had looked at him like he was a bug.

"It sounds like you have a lot of respect for the man."

"I do. I'd damn sure hate to have him for an enemy."

From inside the house, they heard the sounds of Sandi's giggling. She was entertaining her young man this evening, as she did almost every evening. The Moab Kid was fast becoming a fixture around the place.

Cord and Alice sat quietly, smiling as they both recalled their own courting days.


Smoke leaned against a corral railing and thought about Sally and the babies. He missed them terribly. One part of him wanted this little war to come to a head so he could go home. But another part of him knew that when it did start, there would be a lot of people who would never go home . . . except for six feet of earth. And he might well be one of them.

Charlie Starr walked up and the men stood in silence for a moment, enjoying the peaceful evening. Charlie was the first to break the silence.

"I'd like to have seen that fight 'tween Cord and Jason."

Smoke smiled, then the smile faded. "Jason won't ever forget it, though. The next time he sees Cord, Cord better have a gun in his hand."

"True."

They stood in silence for another few moments. Both men rolled an after-supper cigarette and lit up.

"You were in deep thought when I walked up, Smoke. What's on your mind?"

"Oh, I had a half dozen thoughts going, Charlie. I was thinking about my wife and our babies; how much I miss them. And, I was thinking just what it's going to take to blow the lid off this situation here."

"What don't concern me as much as when."

"Tonight."

Charlie looked at him. "What are you, one of them fortune-tellers?"

"I feel it in my guts, Charlie. And don't tell me you never jumped out of a saddle or spun and drew on a hunch."

"Plenty o' times. Saved my bacon on more than one occasion, too. That's what you're feelin'?"

"That's it." Smoke dropped his cigarette butt and ground it out with the heel of his boot. "It's always something you least expect, too."

"I grant you that for a fact. Like that time down in Taos this here woman crawled up in bed with me. Like to have scared the longhandles right off of me. Wanted me to save her from her husband. Didn't have a stitch on. I tell you what, that shook me plum down to my toenails."

"Did you save her?"

Charlie chuckled softly. "Yeah. 'Bout two hours later. I've topped off horses that wasn't as wild as she was."

# Thirteen

Rita had cropped her hair short, hating to do it, but she had always been a tomboy and, besides, it would grow back. She had turned off the lamp and now she listened at her bedroom door for a moment, hearing the low murmur of her mother talking to her father. The front door squeaked open and soon the sound of the porch swing reached her. She picked up her valise and swung out the window, dropping the few feet to the ground. She remained still for a long moment, checking all around her. She knew from watching and planning this that her guards were not on duty after nine o'clock at night. It had never occurred to her father that his daughter would attempt to run away.

Sorry, Pa, Rita thought. But I won't be treated like a prisoner.

Rita slipped away from the house and past the corral and barn. She almost ran right into a cowboy returning from the outhouse but saw him in time to duck into the shadows. He walked past her, his galluses hanging down past his knees. The door to the bunkhouse opened, flooding a small area with lamplight.

"Shut the damn door, Harry!" a man called.

The door closed, the area once more darkened. But something primeval touched Rita with an invisible warning. She remained where she was, squatting down in her jeans.

"It's clear," a man's voice said.

Rita recognized it as belonging to the shifty-eyed gunslinger called Park. And the men were only a few yards away.

Rita remembered something else, too: she had heard that voice before. The sudden memory was as hot and violent as the act that afternoon. While she was being raped.

Fury and cold hate filled the young woman. Her father's own men had done that to her. She thought about returning to the house and telling her father. She immediately rejected that. She had no proof. And her father would take one look at her close-cropped hair and lock her up tight, with twenty-four-hour guards.

She touched the short-barreled .44 tucked behind her belt. She was good with it, and wanted very badly to haul it out and start banging.

She fought back that feeling and waited, listening.

"When?" the other man asked.

"Keep your britches on," Park said. "Lanny gives the orders around here. But it'll be soon, he tole me so hisself."

"I'd like to take my britches off with Rita agin," the mystery man said with a rough chuckle.

And I'd like to stick this pistol . . . Rita mentally brushed away the very ugly thought. But it was a satisfying thought.

"You reckon Hanks is so stupid he don't realize what his boys is up to?"

"He's nuts. He don't realize them crazy boys of his'n would kill him right now if they thought they could get away with it."

Rita crouched in the darkness and wanted to cry. Not for herself or for her father—he had made the boys what they were today, simply by being himself—but for her mother. She deserved so much better.

"It better be soon, 'cause the boys is gettin' restless."

"It'll be soon. But we gotta do it all at once. All three ranches. There can't be no survivors to tell about it. They got to be kilt and buried all in one night. We can torture the widows till they sign over the spreads to us."

"We gonna keep the young wimmen alive for a time, ain't we? 'Specially that Fae Jensen. I want her. I want to show her a thing or two."

"I don't know. Chancy. Maybe too chancy. It's all up to Jason and Lanny."

"Them young wimmen would bring a pretty penny south of the border."

"Transport them females a thousand miles! You're nuts, Hartley."

"It was jist a thought."

"A bad one. Man, just think of it: the whole area controlled

90

by us. Thousands and thousands of acres, thousands of cattle. We could be respectable, and you want to mess it all up because of some swishy skirts. Sometimes I wonder about you, Hartley."

"I'm sorry. I won't bring it up no more."

"Fine."

The men walked off, splitting up before entering the bunkhouse.

Rita felt sick to her stomach; wanted to upchuck. Fought it back. Now more than ever, she had to make it to the Box T. She waited and looked around her, carefully inspecting each dark pocket around the ranch, the barn and the bunkhouse. She stood up and moved out, silently praying she wouldn't be spotted.

Once clear of the ranch complex, Rita began to breathe a little easier. She slung her valise by a strap and could move easier with it over her shoulder. She headed southwest, toward the Box T.

The restlessness of the horses awakened Smoke. He looked at his pocket watch. Four o'clock. Time to get up anyway. But the actions of the horses bothered him. Dressed and armed, he stepped out of the ranch house just as the bunkhouse door opened and Lujan stepped out, followed by the other men. Smoke met them in the yard. They all carried rifles.

"Spread out," Smoke told them. "Let's find out what's spooking the horses."

"Hello the ranch!" the voice came out of the darkness. A female voice.

"Come on in," Smoke returned the call. "Sing out!"

"Rita Hanks. I slipped away from the house about eight o'clock last night. You might not recognize me, 'cause I cut off my hair to try to fool anyone who might see me."

"Come on in, Rita," Smoke told her, then turned to Beans. "Wake up those in the house; if they're not already awake. Get some coffee going. As soon as Hanks finds out his girl is gone, we're going to have problems."

She was limping from her long walk, and she was tired, but still could not conceal her happiness at finally being free of her father. Over coffee and bacon and eggs, she told her story while Fae and Parnell and all the others gathered around in the big

91

house and listened.

When she was finished, she slumped in her chair, exhausted.

"I wondered why the gunnies were holding back," Hardrock said. "This tells it all."

"Yes," Lujan said. "But I don't think they came in here with that in mind. No one ever approached me with any such scheme. And both sides offered me fighting wages."

"I think this plan was just recently hatched, after several others failed. Rita's attack did not produce the desired effect; Hanks didn't attack Cord. Blackie failed to kill me. So they came up with this plan."

Smoke looked at Rita. The young woman was asleep, her head on the table.

"I'll get her to bed," Fae said. "You boys start chowing down. I think it's going to be a very long day."

"Yeah," Beans agreed. "'Cause come daylight, Hanks and his boys are gonna be on the prowl. If this day don't produce some shootin', my name ain't Bainbridge."

Silver Jim looked at him and blinked. "Bainbridge! No wonder they call you Beans. Bainbridge!"


Hanks knocked his wife sprawling, backhanding her. "You knew, damn you!" he yelled at her. "You heped her, didn't you? Don't lie to me, woman. You and Rita snuck around behind my back and planned all this."

Liz slowly got to her feet. A thin trickle of blood leaked from one corner of her mouth. She defiantly stood her ground. "I knew she was planning to leave, yes. But I didn't know when or how. You've changed, Dooley. Changed into some sort of a madman."

That got her another blow. She fell back against the wall and managed to grab the back of a chair and steady herself. She stared at her husband as she wiped her bloody mouth with the back of her hand.

"Where'd she go?" Hanks yelled the question. "Naw!" Dooley waved it off. "You don't have to tell me. I know. She went over to Cord's place, didn't she?"

"No, she didn't," Liz's voice had calmed, but her mouth hurt her when she spoke.

"You a damn liar!" Dooley raged. "A damn frog-eyed liar.

92

There ain't no other place she could have gone."

Outside, just off the porch, Lanny was listening to the ravings.

"This might throw a kink into things," Park spoke softly.

"Maybe not. This might be a way to get rid of Cord and his boys in a way that even if the law was to come in, they'd call it a fair shootin'. Man takes another man's kid in without the father's permission, that's a shootin' offense."

"I hadn't thought of that. You right."

"If she did go to the Double Circle C," Lanny added.

"Where else would she go? Her and that damn uppity Sandi McCorkle is good friends."

"Rita is no fool. She just might have gone over to the Box T. But we won't mention that. Just let Hanks play it his way."

"I'm gonna tell you something, woman," Hanks pointed a blunt finger at his wife. "I find out you been lyin' to me, I'm gonna give you a hidin' that you'll remember the rest of your life."

"That would be like you," she told him. "Whatever you don't understand, you destroy."

"What the hell does that mean?" Dooley screamed at her, slobber leaking out of his mouth, dribbling onto his shirt and vest.

She turned her back to him and started to leave the room.

"Don't you turn your back to me, woman! I done put up with just about all I'm gonna take from you."

She stopped and turned slowly. "What are you going to do, Dooley? Beat me? Kill me? It doesn't make any difference. Love just didn't die a long time ago. Your hatred killed it. Your hatred, your obsession with power. You allowed our sons to grow up as nothing more than ignorant savages. You . . ."

"Shut up, shut up, shut up!" Dooley screamed, spittle flying from his mouth. "Lies, all lies, woman. I'm ridin' to get my kid back. And when I get her back here, I'm gonna take a buggy whip to her backside. That's something I shoulda done a long time ago. And I just might take it in my head to use the same whip on you."

Liz stared hard at him. "If you ever hit me again, Dooley. I'll kill you." Dooley recoiled as if struck with those words. "And the same goes for Rita. But you've lost her. She'll never come back here; don't worry about that. I'll tell you where she's gone, Dooley. She's gone to the Box T."

"Lies! More lies from you. Cord planned with you all on this, and you know it. He's con-spired agin me ever since we come into this area. He'd do anything to get at me. He's jealous of me."

His wife openly laughed at that.

Dooley's face reddened and he took a step toward his wife, his hand raised. She backed up and picked up a poker from the fireplace.

"You were warned," she told him. "You try to hit me and I'll bash your head in."

He stood and cursed her until he ran out of breath. But she would not lower the poker and even in his maddened state he knew better than to push his luck.

"I'll deal with you later," he said, then turned and stalked out the door.

She leaned against the wall, breathing heavily, listening to him holler for his men to saddle up and get ready to ride. She did not put down the poker as long as he was on the front porch. Only when she heard him mount up and the thunder of hooves pound away did she lower the poker and replace it in the set on the hearth.

She walked outside to stand on the porch, waiting for the dust to settle from the fast-riding men. She noticed Gage and several of the other hands had not ridden with her husband.

The foreman walked over to the porch and looked up at the still attractive woman. There was open disgust in his eyes as he took in the bruises on her face.

"I ain't got no use atall for a man who hits a woman," Gage said.

"That's not the man I married, Gage."

"Yeah, it is, Liz. It's the same man I been knowin' for years. You just been deliberately blind over the years, that's all."

"Maybe so, Gage." She sighed. She knew, of course, that Gage had been in love with her for a long, long time. And her feelings toward the foreman had been steadily growing stronger with time. She cut her eyes toward him. "You're not riding with him?"

"Me and the boys punch cows, Liz. I made that plain to him the other day. He still has enough sense about him to know that someone has to work the spread."

"What would you say if I told you I was going to leave him?"

"Then me and you would strike out together, Liz."

94

She smiled. "And do what, Gage?"

"Get married. Start us a little spread a long ways from here."

"I'm a married woman, Gage. It's not proper to talk to a married woman like that."

"I don't see you turnin' around and walkin' off, Liz."

She looked hard at him. "Mister Hanks and I will be sharing separate bedrooms from now on, Gage. I would appreciate if you would stay close as much as possible."

"I would consider that an honor, Liz."

"Would you like to have some coffee, Gage?"

"I shore would."

"Make yourself comfortable on the porch, Gage. I'll go freshen up and hotten the coffee. I won't be a minute."

"Take your time, Liz. I'll be here."

She smiled. Her hair was graying and there were lines in her face. But to the foreman, she was as beautiful as the first day he'd laid eyes on her. "I'm counting on that, Gage."

# Fourteen

Cord heard the riders coming long before he or any of his men could spot them. It was a distant thunder growing louder with each heartbeat.

"Load up the guns, Mother," he told his wife. "I believe it's time." He walked to the dinner bell on the porch and rang it loudly, over and over. Del and four hands came on the run, carrying rifles, pistols belted around them.

"Stand with me on the porch, boys. Mother, get your shotgun and take the upstairs."

"I'm up here with a rifle, Daddy!" Sandi called.

"Good girl."

Rifles were loaded to capacity. Pistols checked. A couple of shotguns were loaded up and placed against the porch railing.

Thirty riders came hammering past the gate and up to the picket fence around the ranch house, Hanks in the lead.

"I don't appreciate this, Dooley," Cord raised his voice. "You got no call to come highballin' up to my place."

"I got plenty of call, Cord. Where's my daughter?"

Cord blinked. "How the hell do I know? I haven't seen her in days."

"You a damn liar, McCorkle!"

Cord unbuckled his gun belt and handed it to Dell. He swung his eyes back to Hanks. "You'll not come on my property and call me names, Dooley. Git out of that saddle and let's settle this feud man to man."

"Goddamn you! I want my daughter!"

"I ain't got your daughter! But what I will have is your apology for callin' me a liar."

"When hell freezes over, McCorkle!"

Two upstairs windows were opened. A shotgun and a rifle poked out. Sandi's voice said, "The first man to reach for a gun, I kill Lanny Ball." The sound of a hammer being eared back was very plain.

The sounds of twin hammers on a double-barreled shotgun was just as plain. "And I blow the two Mexicans out of the saddle," Alice spoke.

Diego and Pablo froze in their saddles.

"Dooley," Cord's voice was calm. "Would you like to step down and have some coffee with me? You can inspect the house and the barn and the bunkhouse . . . after you tell me your anger overrode your good sense when callin' me a liar."

Hanks's eyes cleared for a moment. Then he looked confused. "I know you ain't no liar, Cord. But where'd she go?" There was a pleading note in the man's voice.

"I don't know, Dooley. I didn't even know she was gone."

But the moment was gone, and Jason Bright and Lanny Ball and most of the others knew it. There would be no gunfire this day.

"The Box T," Dooley said. "Liz wasn't lyin'."

"Dooley," Cord said, "You go over there a-smokin', and if she is there, she's liable to catch a bullet. 'Cause Smoke Jensen and them others are gonna start throwin' lead just as soon you come into range."

"She's my daughter, dammit, Cord!" Some of the madness reappeared.

"She's also a grown woman," Alice called from the second floor.

Hanks slumped in his saddle. The fire had left him . . . for the moment. "She don't want my hearth and home, she can stay gone. I don't have no daughter no more." He looked at Cord. "It ain't over, Cord. Not between us. The time just ain't right. There'll be another day."

"Why, Dooley? Tell me that. Your spread is just as big as mine. I made peace with Fae Jensen. She ain't botherin' nobody. Let's us bury the hatchet and be friends. Then you can fire these gunslicks and we can get on with livin'."

Dooley shook his head. "Too late, Cord. It's just too late." He wheeled his horse and rode off, the gunnies following.

"Did you see his eyes, Boss?" Willie asked. "The man is plumb loco."

"I'm afraid you're right, Willie. Question is, when will it

take control of him . . . or rather, when will he lose control?"

"One thing for certain, Boss," Del said. "When he does go total nuts, we're all going to be right smack dab in the big fat middle of it."

"Something is rotten," Cord spoke softly. "Something is wrong with this whole setup."

"Riders coming, Boss," Fitz said.

As the dot on the landscape grew larger, Del squinted his eyes. "Smoke Jensen and the Moab Kid."

Sandi smiled and Alice said, "I'll make fresh coffee."

Beans sniffed the air. "Lots of dust in the air."

"I think Cord's had some visitors," Smoke replied. "Look at the hands gathered around the house."

The men swung down and looped the reins around the hitchrail. Cord shook hands with them both and introduced Smoke to those punchers he had not met.

"Fancy seeing you, Beans," Cord said, a twinkle in his eyes. "It's been so long since you've come callin'. Hours, at least."

Beans just grinned.

"Gather your men, Cord," Smoke told the man. "This is something that everybody should hear."

Cord's three sons had just ridden in. His other four punchers were out on the range. Everybody gathered around on the porch and listened as Smoke related what Rita had told him.

"Damn!" Max summed it up, then glanced at his mother, who was giving him a warning look for the use of profanity.

"Let's kick it around," Smoke said. "Anybody got any suggestions?"

"Take it to them 'fore they do it to us," Corgill said.

"No proof," Cord said. "Only the word of Rita and she didn't even see the men; just heard them talkin'."

"If we don't do something," Cal said, "we're just gonna be open targets, and they'll pick us off one at a time."

Cord shook his head. "Maybe, but I don't think so. I think they got to do everything all at once. At night. If what Rita says is true—and I ain't got no reason to doubt it—they'll split their people and hit us at the same time. And they can't leave any survivors."

"I've got people bunching the cattle and moving them to high graze," Smoke said. "They'll scatter some, but they can be rounded up. From now on, we stay close to the ranch house."

Cord nodded his head and looked at Willie. "Ride on out, Willie. Tell the boys to start moving them up toward summer graze. Get as much as you can done, and then you boys get on back here. We're gonna lose some to rustlers, for a fact. But it's either that or we all die spread out." He glanced at Smoke. "When do you think they'll hit us?"

Smoke shook his head. "Tonight. Next week. Next month. No way of knowing."

Cord did some fancy cussing, while his wife listened and looked on with a disapproving frown on her face. "We may end up taking to the hills and fighting defensively."

"I'm thinking that we will," Smoke agreed.

"You mean leave the house?" Sandi protested. "But they'll just move in!"

"Can't be helped, girl," her father told her. "We can always clean up and rebuild."

"Or just go on over and kill Dooley Hanks," Rock McCorkle said grimly.

"Rock!" his mother admonished.

Cord put a big hand on her shoulder. "It may come to that, Alice. God help me, I don't want it, but we may have no choice in the matter."

"Here comes Jake," Del said. "And he's a-foggin' it."

The puncher slowed up as he approached the house, to keep the dust down, and walked his horse up to the main house, dismounting.

"What's up, Jake?" the foreman asked.

"I just watched about fifteen guys cut across our range, comin' from the northeast. Hardcases, ever' one of them. They was headin' toward Gibson."

Alice handed the puncher a cup of coffee and a biscuit, then looked at her husband. He wore an increasingly grim expression.

"The damn easterners talk about law and order," Cord said. "Well, where is it when it comes down to the nut-cuttin'?"

Smoke pulled out his right hand Colt and held it up for all to see. "Right here, Cord. Right here."


"The Cat Jennings gang," Charlie said. He had been to town and back while Smoke was talking with the men and women of the Double Circle C. "He's been up in Canada raisin' Cain for the past few years."

"This here thing is shapin' up to be a power play," Pistol said.

"Yeah," Lujan agreed. "With us right in the middle of it."

"Damn near seventy gunslingers," Silver Jim mused. "And the most we can muster is twenty, and that's stretchin' it."

"One thing about it," Smoke stuck some small humor into a grim situation, "we've sure taken the strain off of a lot of other communities in the West."

"Yeah," Hardrock agreed. "Ever' outlaw and two-bit pistol-handler from five states has done con-verged on us. And it wouldn't do a bit of good to wire for the law. No badge-toter in his right mind would stick his face into this situation."

"Must be at least a quarter of a million dollars worth of re-ward money hanging over them boys' heads," Silver Jim said. "And that's something to think about."

"Yeah, it shore is," Pistol said. "Why, with just a little dab of that money, we could re-tire, boys." There was a twinkle in his hard eyes.

"Now, wait just a minute," Smoke said.

The old gunfighters ignored him. "You know what we could do," Charlie said. "We could start us up a re-tirement place for old gunslingers and mountain men."

"You guys are crazy!" Lujan blurted out the words. "You are becoming senile!"

"What's that mean?" Hardrock asked.

"It means we ain't responsible for our actions," Charlie told him.

"That's probably true," Hardrock agreed. "If we had any sense, none of us would be here." He looked at Lujan. "And that goes for you, too."

Lujan couldn't argue with that.

"Cat backed up from me a couple of times," Charlie said. "This time, I think I'll force his hand."

Smoke and Beans had stepped back, letting the men talk it out.

"Peck and Nappy is gonna be with him, for sure," Pistol said. "That damn Nappy got lead in a friend of mine one time. I been lookin' for him for ten year. And that Peck is just a plain no-good."

"No-Count George Victor's got ten thousand on his head," Silver Jim mused. "And he don't like me atall."

"Insane old men!" Lujan muttered.

"Well, I damn shore ain't gonna try to stop them," Beans made that very clear. "I ain't real sure I could take any of them . . . even if I was a mind to," he added.

Smoke stepped back in. "You boys ride for the Box T," he reminded them. "You took the lady's money to ride for the brand. Not to go off head-hunting. You all are needed here. Now when the shootin' starts, speaking for myself, you can have all the reward money."

"Same for me," Beans and Lujan agreed.

"Aw, hell, Smoke," Charlie said, a bit sheepishly. "We was just flappin' our gums. You know we're stickin' right here. But Cat Jennings is mine."

"And Peck and Nappy belong to me." Pistol's tone told them all to stand clear when grabbin'-iron time came.

"And No-Count George Victor is gonna be lookin' straight at me when I fill his belly full of lead," Silver Jim said.

Hardrock said, "Three-Fingers Kerman and Fulton kilt a pal of mine over to Deadwood some years back. Back-shot him. I didn't take kindly to that. So them two belongs to me."

"You men are incorrigible!" Parnell finally spoke.

"Damn right," Pistol said.

"Whatever the hell that means," Hardrock muttered.

Fae walked out to join them. "Rita's up, having breakfast."

"How's she feeling?" Smoke asked.

"Aside from some sore feet—she's not used to walking in men's boots—she's doing all right. I think she's pretty well resigned that her father is around the bend. I told her what you said about Dooley saying he no longer had a daughter. It hurt her. But not as much as I thought it would. I think she's more concerned about her mother."

"She should be. There is no telling what that crazy bastard is liable to do," Silver Jim summed it up.

# Fifteen

He had looked into their bedroom and came stomping out. "Where is all your clothes, Liz?" Dooley demanded, his voice hard.

"I moved them out. I no longer feel I am married to you, Dooley."

"You don't . . . *what?*"

"I don't love you anymore. I haven't for a long time. Years. I cringe when you touch me. I . . ."

He jumped at her and backhanded her, knocking her against a wall. She held back a yelp of pain. She didn't want Gage to come storming in, because she knew that she had absolutely no rights as a married woman. She owned nothing. Could not vote. And in a court of law, her husband's word was next to God's. And if Gage were to kill Dooley during a domestic squabble, he would hang.

She leaned against the wall, staring at Dooley as the front door opened, her sons stomping in.

Conrad, the youngest of the boys, grinned at her. "You havin' a good time while Pa's usin' you for a punchin' bag?"

Sonny and Bud laughed.

Dooley grabbed Liz by the arm and flung her toward the kitchen. "Git in there and fix me some dinner. I don't wanna hear no more mouth from you."

Liz walked toward the kitchen, her back straight. I won't put up with this any longer, she vowed. I'll follow Rita, just as quickly as I can.

A plan jumped into her head and she smiled at the thought. It might work. It just might work.

She began putting together dinner and working out the plan.

It all depended on what Gage said. And the other hands.


She had gone out to gather eggs in the henhouse. Dooley and her sons had left the house without telling her where they were riding off to. As usual. All the hired guns were in town, drinking. Gage had ambled over, as he always did, to carry her basket. She told him of her plan.

"I like it, Liz. Go in the house and pack a few things while ever'body is gone. I'll get the boys."

She stared at him, wide-eyed. "You mean . . . ?"

"Right now, Liz. Let's get gone from this crazy house 'fore Dooley gets back. Move, Liz!"

She went one way and Gage trotted to the bunkhouse. He sent the only rider in the bunkhouse out to tell the others to meet him at the McCorkle ranch.

"We quittin', Gage?"

"I am."

"I'm with you. And so will the others. Hep me pack up their stuff, will you. I'll tote it to them on a packhorse. How about ol' Cook?"

"He'll go wherever Liz goes. He came out here with them."

The hand cut his eyes at the foreman and grinned. "Ahh! OK, Gage."

Working frantically, the two men stuffed everything they could find into canvas and lashed it on a packhorse. "I'll tell Cook to hightail it. Move, Les. See you at the Circle Double C."

Ol' Cook was right behind Les. He packed up his warbag and swung into the saddle just as Liz was coming out of the house, a satchel in her hand.

"You want me to hitch up the buckboard, Gage?"

"No time, Cook."

"Wal, how's she fixin' to ride then? We ain't got no sidesaddle rigs."

"Astride. I done saddled her a horse."

Ol' Cook rolled his eyes. "Astride! Lord have mercy! Them sufferingetts is gonna be the downfall of us all." He galloped out.

Gage led her horse over to the porch. "Turn your head, Gage. I don't quite know how I'm going to do this. I have never sat astride in my life."

Gage turned his head.

"You may look now, Gage," she told him.

He had guessed at the stirrup length and got it right. She sure had a pretty ankle. "Hang on, Liz. We got some rough country and some hard ridin' to do."

"Wherever you ride, I'll be with you," she told him, adding, "Darling."

Gage blushed all the way down to his holey socks.

"I'll kill ever' goddamn one of them!" Dooley screamed. "I'll stake that damn Gage out over an anthill and listen to him scream." Dooley cussed until he was red-faced and out of breath.

"This ain't good," Jason said. "I'm beginnin' to think we're snake-bit."

"I don't know." Lanny scratched his jaw. "It gives the other side a few more guns, is all."

"Seven more guns."

"No sweat."

Inside the house, Dooley was still ranting and cussing and roaring about what he was going to do to Gage and to his wife. The men outside heard something crash against a wall. Dooley had picked up a vase and shattered it.

The sons were leaning against a hitchrail, giggling and scratching themselves.

"Them boys," Jason pointed out, "is as goofy as their dad."

"And just as dangerous," Lanny added. "Don't sell them short. They're all cat-quick with a gun."

"About the boys . . . ?"

"We'll just kill them when we've taken the ranches."

"Of course you can stay here, Liz," Alice told her. "And stop saying it will be a bother." She smiled. "You and Gage. I'm so happy for you."

"If we survive this," Liz put a verbal damper on the other woman's joy.

"We'll survive it. Oh, Liz!" She took the woman's hands into hers. "Do you remember how it was when we first settled here? Those first few years before all the hard feelings began. We fought outlaws and Indians and were friends. Then . . ." She bit back the words.

"I know. I've tried to convince myself it wasn't true. But it was and is. Even more so now. Dooley began to change. Maybe he was always mad; I don't know. I know only that I love Gage and have for a long, long time. From a distance," she quickly added. "I just feel like a great weight has been lifted from me."

"You rest for a while. I'll get supper started."

"Pish-posh! I'm not tired. And I want to do my share here. Come on. I've got a recipe for cinnamon apple pie that'll have Cord groaning."

Laughing, the two women walked to the kitchen.

Outside the big house, Cord briefed Gage and the other men from the D-H about the outlaws' plans.

Gage shuddered. "Kill the women! God, what a bunch of no-goods. Well, we got out of that snake pit just in time. Cord, me and boys will hep your crew bunch the cattle." He cut his eyes to Del. "You 'member that box canyon over towards Spitter Crick?"

Del nodded. "Yeah. It's got good graze and water that'll keep 'em for several weeks. That's a good idea. We'll get started first thing in the morning. Smoke said him and his boys will be over at first light to hep out. They done got their cattle bunched and safe as they could make 'em."

"I sent a rider over to tell them about y'all," Cord told him. "I 'magine Rita will be comin' over to stay with her momma. Smoke's already makin' plans to vacate the Box T. We both figure that'll be the first spread Dooley will hit, and Smoke ain't got the men to defend it agin seventy or more men."

"No, but them men that he's got was shore born with the bark on," Gage replied. "I'd shore hate to be in that first bunch that tackles 'em."

"They'll cut the odds down some, for sure," Del said. "You know," he reminisced, "I growed up hearin' stories about Pistol Le Roux and Hardrock and Silver Jim . . . and Charlie Starr. Lord, Lord! Till Smoke Jensen come along, I reckon he was the most famous gun-handler in all the West. Hardrock and Pistol and Silver Jim . . . why, them men must be nigh on seventy years old. But they still tough as wang leather and mean as cornered grizzlies. It just come to me that we're lookin' at history here."

"Let's just hope that we all live to read about it," Cord said drily.

"I think they'll try us tonight, Smoke," Charlie said. "My old bones is talkin' to me."

"I agree with you."

"I done tossed my blankets over yonder in that stand of trees," Pistol said, pointing. "I never did like to sleep all cooped up noways. I like to look at the stars."

"We'll all stay clear of the house tonight," Smoke said. "Fill your pockets with ammunition, boys, and don't take your boots off. I think tonight is gonna be interesting."

Bob was in the loft of the barn. Spring and Pat stayed in the bunkhouse, both of them armed with rifles. Lujan was in the barn, lower level. Pistol, Silver Jim, Charlie, and Hardrock were spread around the house. Smoke elected to stay close to the now-empty corral. The horses had been moved away to a little draw; Ring was with them. Beans had slipped into moccasins and was roaming. Parnell was in the house with the women. Rita and Fae were armed with rifles. Parnell refused to take a gun.

About a quarter of a mile from the ranch complex, Beans knelt down in the road and put his ear to the hard-packed earth. He smiled grimly, then stood up. "Coming!" he shouted to Silver Jim, who was the closest to him. "Sounds like a bunch of them, too."

Silver Jim relayed the message and then settled in, earing back the hammer on his Winchester.

Beans was the first to see the flames from the torches the gunnies carried. "They're gonna try to burn us out!" he yelled.

Then the hard-riding outlaw gunslingers were thundering past Beans's position. At almost point-blank range, Beans emptied his six-shooter into the mass of riders, then holstered his pistol and picked up his Winchester. He put five fast rounds into the outlaws, then shifted positions when the lead started flying around him.

Beans knew he'd hit at least three of the riders, and two of them were hard hit and on the ground.

Silver Jim got three clean shots off, with one outlaw on the ground and the other two just hanging on, gripping the saddle horn. Not dead, but out of action.

Bob took his time with his Winchester and emptied two saddles before Lujan hollered, "Another bunch coming behind us, Bob. Shift to the rear."

Smoke stood by the corral, a dim figure in the torchlit night, with both hands full of long-barreled Colts, and picked his

106

targets. His aim was deadly true. He knocked two to the ground and knew he'd hit several more before being forced to run for cover

A rider threw his torch through a window—only two windows were not shuttered, front and back, giving the women a place to fire from—and the torch landed on the couch. The couch burst into flames and Parnell went to work with buckets of water already filled against such an action. He managed to keep the fire confined to the couch.

The barn was not so lucky. While Lujan and Bob were fighting at the rear of the barn, a rider tossed a torch into the hay loft. That action got him a bullet from Smoke that cut his spine and shattered his heart, but there was no saving the barn. Bob and Lujan fought inside until it became too difficult to see and breathe and they had to run for cover amid a hail of lead.

The small band of defenders of the Box T were now having to fight against range-robbers on all sides. One outlaw made the mistake of finding the horses and thinking he was going to set them free.

One second he was in the saddle, the next second he was on the ground. The last thing he would remember hearing on this earth was a deep voice rumbling, "I do not like people who are mean to nice people."

Huge hands clamped around the man's head and with one quick jerk, Ring broke the gunny's neck and tossed him to one side, his head flopping from side to side. Ring got the rifle from the outlaw's saddle boot, made sure it was full, and waited for some more action.

The area around the ranch house was now brightly lighted from the flaming barn; too bright for the outlaws' taste, for the accuracy of the defenders was more than they had counted on.

"Let's go!" came the shout.

No one bothered to fire at or pursue the outlaws. All ran into the yard to form a bucket line to wet down the roof of the house so sparks from the burning barn could not set it on fire. The men worked frantically, for already there were smouldering spots on the roof.

It did not take long for the barn to go; soon there was nothing left except a huge mound of glowing coals.

The men sat down on the ground where they were, all of them suddenly tired as the adrenaline had slowed.

"Fae!" Parnell said. "Give up this madness. Let us leave this

107

barbaric country and return to civilization."

Fae walked toward him, her gloved hands balled into fists. Her face was sooty and her short hair disheveled and she was mad clear through. When she got within swinging distance she let him have it, giving him five in the mouth and dropping him to the ground.

Parnell lay flat on his butt, blood leaking out of a busted lip, looking up at his baby sister. He wore a hurt expression on his face. He blinked and said, "I suppose, Sister, that is your quaint way of saying no?"

Smoke and the others burst out laughing. The laughter spread and soon Fae and Rita were laughing. No one paid any attention to the bodies littering the yard and the areas all around the ranch complex.

Parnell sat up and rubbed his jaw. "I, for one, fail to see the humor in this grotesque situation."

That caused another round of laughter. They were still laughing as Ring walked up, leading several horses, one with the body of the neck-broke outlaw draped across the saddle.

"Crazy folks," Ring said. "But nice folks."

# Sixteen

"This ain't worth a damn!" Jason summed up the night's action. "Nine dead and six wounded. Couple more nights like this and we might as well hang it up."

"Shore got to change our plans," Lanny agreed. "We should have hit McCorkle first."

"Well, you can bet they all is gonna be on the alert after this night," No-Count Victor said. "Hell, let's just go on and kill that stupid Dooley and his sons and settle for this spread."

"No!" Lanny stopped that quick. "It's got to be the whole bag or nothing. Think about it. You think Cord and Smoke would let us stay in this area, on this spread? And what about Dooley's wife; you forgettin' about her?"

"I reckon so," Cat said sullenly.

Both Jason and Lanny had been admiring Cat's matched guns since he'd arrived. They were silver-plated, scroll-engraved, with ivory grips. Smith & Wesson .44's, top break for easier loading. They both coveted Cat's guns. Both of them had thought, more than once: When this is over, I'll kill him and take them fancy guns.

Honor extended only so far.

A wounded man moaned in restless unconsciousness on his bloody bunk. Before he had passed out, he had drunk a full bottle of laudanum to ease the pain in his chest. Pink froth was bubbling past his lips. Lung shot, and all knew he wasn't going to make it.

"You want me to shoot him, Jason?" Nappy asked.

"Naw. He'll be gone in a few hours. If he's still alive come the mornin', we'll put a piller over his face and end it thataway. It won't make so much noise."

\*　　\*　　\*

109

Smoke stepped out before first light, carrying his rifle, loaded full. It had come to him during the night, and if it came to the range-robbers, the small band of defenders would be in trouble. They could starve them out; a few well-placed snipers could keep them pinned down for days. He hated to tell Fae, but Smoke felt it would be best to desert the ranch and head for Cord's place. If they stayed here, it was only a matter of time before they were overrun.

He looked around the darkness. Before turning in, they had stacked the bodies of the outlaws against a wall of a ravine. At first light, they would go through their pockets in search of any clues to family or friends. They would then bury the men by collapsing dirt over the stiffening bodies. There would be no markers.

Smoke smelled the aroma of coffee coming from the bunkhouse, the good odors just barely overriding the smell of charred wood from the remnants of the barn. Smoke walked to the bunkhouse, faint lanternlight shining through the windows.

"Comin' in," he announced just before reaching the door.

"Come on," ol' Spring called. "Got hot coffee and hard biscuits."

Before Smoke poured his first cup of coffee of the day, he noticed the men had already packed their warbags and rolled their slim mattresses.

"You boys read my mind, hey?"

"Figured you'd be wantin' to pull out this mornin'," Hardrock said, gumming a biscuit to soften it. He had perhaps four teeth left in his mouth. "What about the cattle?"

Smoke took a drink of the strong cowboy coffee before replying. "Figured we'd drive them on over to Cord's."

"Them no-goods is gonna fire the cabin soon as we're gone," Silver Jim said. "After they loot it." He grinned nastily. "We all allow as to how we ought to leave a few surprises in there for them."

Smoke, squatting down, leaned back against the bunkhouse wall and smiled. "What you got in mind?"

Hardrock kicked a cloth sack by his bunk. The sack moved and buzzed. "I gleamed me a rattler nest several days back. 'Fore I snoozed last night I paid it a visit and grabbed me several. I figured I'd plant 'em in the house 'fore we left, in stra-teegic spots." He grinned. "You like that idee?"

"Oh, yeah!"

"Thought you would. Soon as Miss Fae and that goosy brother of her'n is gone we'll plant the rattlers."

Smoke chewed on yesterday's biscuit and took a swallow of coffee. "You reckon any varmits got to the bodies last night?"

"Doubtful," Charlie said. "Ring stayed out there, close by. Said he didn't much like them people but it wouldn't be fitten to let the coyotes and wolves chew on them. Strange man."

Pistol looked toward the dusty window. "Gettin' light enough to see. I reckon we better get to it whilst it's cool. Them ol' boys is gonna get plumb ripe when the sun touches 'em."

The men put on their hats, hitched up their britches, and turned out the lamps. "I'd hate to be an undertaker," Hardrock said. "Hope when I go I just fall off my horse in the timber."

"By that time, you'll be so old you won't be able to get in the saddle," Silver Jim needled him.

"Damn near thataways now," Hardrock fired back.


They kept the outlaws' guns and ammunition and put what money they had in a leather sack, to give to Fae. Then they caved in the ravine wall and stacked rocks over the dirt to keep the varmints from digging up the bodies and eating them. By the time they had finished, it was time for breakfast.

Fae and Rita had fixed a huge breakfast of bacon and eggs and oatmeal and biscuits. The men dug in, piling their plates high. Conversation was sparse until the first plates had been emptied. Eating was serious business; a man could talk anytime.

After eating up everything in sight—it wasn't polite to leave any food; might insult the cook—the men refilled their coffee cups, pushed back their chairs, and hauled out pipes and papers, passing the tobacco sack around.

"We're leaving, aren't we?" Fae asked, noticing how quiet the men were.

"Till this is over," Smoke told her. "It's a pretty location here, Cousin, but it'd be real easy for Hanks's men to pin us down."

"They'll destroy the house."

"Probably. But you can always rebuild. That beats gettin' buried here. Take what you just absolutely have to have. We

111

can stash the rest for you. Spring, you and Pat stay here and keep a sharp eye out. We'll go bunch the cattle and start pushing them toward Cord's range. We'll cross the Smith at the north bend, just south of that big draw. Let's go, boys."

The cattle were not happy to be leaving the lush grass of summer graze, but finally the men got the old mossyhorn lead steer moving and the others followed. Smoke and Hardrock rode back to the ranch house. Hardrock went to the bunkhouse to get his bag of goodies for the outlaws. Ring had bunched the horses and with Pat's help was holding them just off the road. Spring was driving the wagon. Both Rita and Rae were riding astride; Parnell was in his buggy. He had a fat lip from his encounter with his sister the night past. He didn't look at all happy.

"I'll catch up with y'all down the road," Hardrock told Smoke.

"What is in the sack?" Parnell inquired.

"Some presents for the range-robbers. It wouldn't be neighborly to just go off and not leave something."

Parnell muttered something under his breath about the strangeness of western people while Smoke grinned at him.

The caravan moved out, with Smoke riding with his rifle across his saddle horn. Smoke did not expect any trouble so soon after the outlaw attack the past night, but one never knew about the mind of Dooley Hanks. The man didn't even know his own mind.

The trip to the Smith was uneventful and Spring knew a place where the wagon and the buggy could get across with little difficulty. A couple of Cord's hands were waiting on the west side of the river to point the way for the cattle. Smoke rode on to the ranch with the women and Parnell. Cord met them in the front yard.

"The house and barn go up last night?" he asked. "We seen a glow."

"Just the barn. I imagine the house will be fired tonight." He smiled. "After they try to loot it. But Hardrock left a few surprises for them." He told the ranch owner about the rattlesnakes in the bureau drawers and in other places.

Cord's smile was filled with grim satisfaction. "They'll get exactly what they deserve. Your momma's in the house, Rita." He stared at her. "Girl, what *have* you done to your hair?"

"Whacked it off." Rita grinned. "You like my jeans, Mister Cord?"

Cord shook his head and muttered about women dressin' up in men's britches and ridin' astride. Rita laughed at him as Sandi came out onto the porch. She squealed and the young women ran toward each other and hugged.

"The women been cleaning out the old bunkhouse all mornin', Smoke. It ain't fancy, but the roof don't leak and the bunks is in good shape and the sheets and blankets is clean."

"Sounds good to me. I'll go get settled in and get back with you."

"Smoke?"

He turned around to face Cord. The man stuck out his big hand and Smoke took it. "Good to have you with us in this thing."


"They done pulled out!" Larado reported back to Jason and Lanny. "They moved the cattle toward the Smith this mornin'. I found where they caved a ravine in on top of them they kilt last night. And it looks like the house is nearabouts full of good stuff."

"One down," Lanny said with a grin. "Let's take us a ride over there and see what we can find in the house. If they left in a hurry, they prob'ly didn't pack much."

The range-robbers rode up cautiously, but already the place had that aura of desertion about it. Lanny and Jason were feeling magnanimous that morning and told the boys to go ahead, help themselves to whatever they could find in the house.

A dozen gunnies began looting the house.

"Hey!" Slim called. "This here box is locked. Gimme that there hammer over yonder on the sill." He hammered the lock off while others squatted down, close to him, ready to snatch and grab should the box be filled with valuables. Slim opened the lid. Two rattlesnakes lunged out, one of them taking Slim in the throat and the other nailing a bearded gunny on the cheek and hanging on, wrapping around the gunny's neck, striking again and again.

One outlaw dove through a window escaping the snakes; another took the back door off its hinges. A gunny known only as Red fell over the couch knocking a bureau over. A rattler slithered out of the opened drawer and began striking at the man's legs, while Red kicked and screamed and howled in agony.

Larado ran from the house in blind fear, running into Lanny who was running toward the house, Lanny fell back into Jason, and all three of them landed in the dust in a heap of arms and legs.

Ben Sabler rode up with his kin just in time to see Red crawl from the house and scream out his misery, the rattlesnake coiled around one leg, striking again and again at Red's stomach.

Ben did not hesitate. He jerked iron and shot Red in the head, putting him out of his agony, and then shot the snake, clipping its head off with deadly accuracy.

The bearded gunny staggered out the door, dying on his feet. Venom dripped from his face. He stood for a moment, and then fell like a tree, facefirst in the dirt. The rattler sidewinded toward Larado, who jerked out his pistol and emptied it into the rattler.

"Burn this damn place!" Lanny shouted.

"Slim's in there!"

Lanny looked inside. Slim was already beginning to swell from the massive amount of venom in his body. Lanny carefully backed out. "Slim's dead," he announced. "Damn Smoke Jensen. The bassard ain't human to do something lak this."

"I heard that he was from hell, myself," a gunny called Blaine said. He sat his horse and looked at the death house. "I knowed a man said Jensen took lead seven times one day some years back. Never did knock him down. He just kept on comin'."

"That ain't no story," Ben Sabler said. "I was there. I seen it."

Lanny looked at Ben. "I'll kill him. And that's a promise."

"I gotta see it." Ben didn't back down. "I seen his graveyards. I ain't never seen none of yours."

"Hang around," Lanny told him. He turned his back and shouted the order. "Burn this damn place to the ground!"

114

# Seventeen

They stood in the front yard and watched the smoke spiral up into the sky, caught by vortexes in the hot air and spinning upward until breaking up.

Parnell stood with clenched fists, his eyes on the dark smoke. "I say now, that was unnecessary. Quite brutish. And *that* makes me angry." He stalked away, muttering to himself.

Fae was on the porch, her face in her hands, crying softly.

"She's a woman after all," Lujan said, so softly only Smoke could hear.

Del worked the handle of the outside pump, wetting a bandana and taking it to Fae.

Fae looked at the foreman, surprise in her eyes, and tried a smile as she took the dampened bandana. "Thank you, Del."

"You're shore welcome, ma'am." He backed off a few feet.

"Lujan," Smoke said. "You and me and Beans. We hit them tonight."

"*Sí, señor.*" Lujan's teeth flashed in a smile. "I was wondering when you would have enough of being pushed."


By late afternoon, everyone at the Circle Double C knew the three men were going headhunting. But no one said a word about it. That might have caused some bad luck. And no one took umbrage at not being asked along. This was to be—they guessed—a hit-hard-and-quick-and-run-like-hell operation. Too many riders would just get in the way.

When Smoke threw a saddle on Dagger, the big mean-eyed horse was ready for the trail, and he showed his displeasure at not being ridden much lately by trying to step on Smoke's foot.

The men took tape from the medicine chest and taped

everything that might jingle. They took everything out of their pockets that was not necessary and looped bandoleers of ammunition across their chests. They were all dressed in dark clothing.

Just after dusk, Beans and Sandi went for a short walk while Smoke and Lujan squatted under the shade of a huge old tree by the bunkhouse and watched as Cord left the main house and walked toward them.

He squatted down beside them in the near-darkness of Montana's summer dusk. "Nice quiet evenin', boys."

"Indeed it is, senor." Lujan flashed his smile. His eyes flicked over to Beans and Sandi, now sitting in the yard swing. "A night for romance."

Cord grunted, but both men knew the rancher liked the young man called the Moab Kid. "Sandi would be inclined to give me all sorts of grief if anything was to happen to Beans."

When neither Smoke nor Lujan replied, Cord said, "Three against sixty is crappy odds, boys."

"Not the way we plan to fight," Smoke told him. "They'll be expecting a mass attack. Not a small surprise attack."

Again, the rancher grunted. It was clear that he did not like the three of them going head-hunting. "We can expect you back when?"

"Around dawn. But keep guards out, Cord. If we do as much damage as I think we will, Dooley is likely to ride against you this night."

"I'll double the guards."

Beans and Sandi had parted, with Sandi now on the lamplighted front porch. The Moab Kid was walking toward the three men at the tree. Faint light reflected off the double bandoleers of ammunition crisscrossing his chest.

All three men wore two guns around their waist; a third pistol rested in homemade shoulder holsters. They had each added another rifle boot; with two fully loaded Winchester .44 rifles and three pistols, that meant each man was capable of firing fifty-two times before reloading. And each man carried a double pouch over their saddlebags, each pouch containing a can of giant powder, already rigged with fuse and cap.

The men intended to raise a lot of hell at Dooley's D-H spread.

Smoke and Lujan rose to their boots.

Cord's voice was soft in the night. "See you, boys."

The three men walked toward their horses and stepped into the saddles. They rode toward the east, fast disappearing into the night.

116

The old gunslingers joined Cord by the tree. "Gonna be some fireworks this night," Silver Jim said. "Pistol, you 'member that time me and you and that half-breed Ute hit them outlaws down on the Powder River?"

Pistol laughed in the night. "Yeah. They was about twenty of them. We shore give them what-for, didn't we?"

"Was that the time y'all catched them gunnies in their drawers?" Hardrock asked.

"Takes something out of a man to have to fight in his longhandles. We busted right up into their camp. Stampeded their horses right over them, with us right behind the horses, reins in our teeth and both hands full of guns. Of course," he added with a smile, "that was when we all had teeth!"

The men rode slowly, saving their horses and not wanting to reach the ranch until all were asleep. They kept conversation to a minimum, riding each with their own thoughts. They did not need to be shared. Facing death was a personal thing, the concept that had to be worked out in each man's mind. None of the three considered themselves to be heroes; they were simply doing what they felt had to be done. The niceties of legal maneuvering were fast approaching the West, but it would be a few more years before they reached the general population. Until that time, codes of conduct would be set and enforced by the people, and the outcome would usually be very final.

The men forded the Smith, careful not to let water splash onto the canvas sacks containing the giant powder bombs. On the east side of the river, they pulled up and rested, letting their horses blow.

The men squatted down and carefully checked their guns, making sure they were loaded up full. Only after that was done did Lujan haul out the makings and pass the sack and papers around. The men enjoyed a quiet smoke in the coolness of Montana night and only then was the silence broken.

"We'll walk our horses up to that ridge overlooking Dooley's spread," Smoke spoke softly. "Look the situation over. If it looks OK, we'll ride slow-like and not light the bombs until we're inside the compound. Lujan, you take the new bunkhouse. Beans, you toss yours into the bunkhouse that was used by Gage and his boys. I'll take the main house." He picked up a stick and drew a crude diagram in the dirt, just visible in the moonlight. "We've got about a hundred and fifty rounds

117

between us all loaded up for the first pass. But let's don't burn them all up and get caught short.

"Beans, the corral is closest to your spot; rope the gates and pull 'em down. The horses will be out of there like a shot. We make one pass and then get the hell gone from there. We'll link up just south of that ridge. If we get separated, we'll meet back at the Smith, where we rested. I don't want to bomb the barn because of the horses in there. Ain't no point in hurtin' a good horse when we don't have to."

Lujan chuckled quietly. "I think when the big bangs go off, there will be no need for Beans to rope the gates. I think the horses will break those poles down in a blind panic and be gone."

"Let's hope so," Smoke said. "That'll give us more time to raise Cain."

"And," Beans said, "when them bombs go off, those ol' boys are gonna be so rattled they'll be runnin' in all directions. I'd sure like to have a pitcher of it to keep."

Lujan ground out his cigarette butt under a boot heel and stood up. "Shall we go make violent sounds in the night, boys?"

The men rode deeper into the night, drawing closer to their objective. It was unspoken, but each man had entertained the thought that if Dooley had decided to strike first this night, Cord would be three guns short. If that was the case, and they were hitting an empty ranch, Dooley would experience the sensation of seeing another glow in the night sky.

His own ranch.

The three men left their horses and walked up to the ridge overlooking the darkened complex of the D-H ranch. They all three smiled as their eyes settled on the many horses in the double corral.

Without speaking, Smoke pointed out each man's perimeter and, using sign language, told them to watch carefully. He gave the soft call of a meadowlark and Lujan and Beans nodded their understanding, then faded into the brush.

They watched for over an hour, each of them spotting the locations of the two men on watch. They were careless, puffing on cigarettes. Smoke bird-called them back in and they slipped to their horses.

"What'd you think?" Smoke tossed it out.

"Let's swing around the ridge and walk our horses as close in as we can," Beans suggested.

"Suits me," Lujan said.

"Let's do it."

They swung around the ridge and came up on the east side of the ranch, walking their horses very slowly, keeping to the grass to further muffle the sound of the hooves.

"They're either drunk or asleep," Beans whispered.

"With any kind of luck, we can put them to sleep forever," Lujan returned the whisper. He reached back for the canvas sack and took out a giant powder bomb, the others following suit.

They were right on the edge of the ranch grounds when a call went up. "Hey! They's something movin' out yonder!"

The three men scratched matches into flames and lit the fuses. Beans let out a wild scream that would have sent any self-respecting puma running for cover and the horses lunged forward, steel-shod hooves pounding on the hard-packed dirt road.

Smoke reached the house first, sending Dagger leaping over the picket fence. He hurled the bomb through a front window and circled around to the back, lighting the fuse on his second bomb and tossing it into an upstairs window. The front of the house blew, sending shards of glass and splintered pieces of wood flying just as Smoke was heading across the backyard, low in the saddle, his face almost pressing Dagger's neck. He was using his knees to guide the horse, the reins in his teeth and both hands filled with .44's.

The upstairs blew, taking part of the roof off just as the bunkhouses exploded. All the men knew that with these black powder bombs, as small as they were, unless a man was directly in the path of one, or within a ten-foot radius, chances of death were slim. Injury, however, was another matter.

The first blast knocked Dooley out of bed and onto the floor. The second blast in the house went off just as he was getting to his feet, trying to find his boots and hat and gun belt. That blast went off directly over his bedroom and caved in the ceiling, driving the man to his knees and tearing out the button-up back flap in his longhandles. A long splinter impaled itself to the hilt in one cheek of his bare butt, bringing a howl of pain from the man.

One of his sons fell through the huge hole in the ceiling and landed on his father's bed, collapsing the frame and folding the son up in the feather tick.

"Halp!" Bud hollered. "Git me outta here. Halp!"

Conrad came running, saw the hole in the ceiling too late, and fell squalling, landing on his father, knocking both men even goofier than they were already were.

Outside, Smoke leveled a six-shooter and fired almost point-blank at a gunny dressed in his longhandles, boots, and hat—with a rifle in his hands. Smoke's slug took the man in the center of the chest and dropped him.

Dagger's hooves made a mess of the man's face as Smoke charged toward a knot of gunnies, both his guns blazing, barking and snarling and spitting out lead.

He ran right through and over the gunnies, Dagger's hooves bringing howls of pain as bones were broken under the steel shoes.

Lujan knee-reined his horse into a mass of confused and badly shaken gunslicks. He fired into the face of one and the man's face was suddenly slick with blood. Turning his horse, Lujan knocked another gunslick sprawling and fired his left hand gun at another, the bullet taking the man in the belly.

Smoke was suddenly at his side, and both men looked around for Beans, spotting him, and with a defiant cry from Lujan's throat, the two men charged toward the Moab Kid. They circled the Kid, holstering their pistols and pulling Winchesters from the boots. The three of them charged the yard, firing as fast as they could work the levers of their seventeen-shot Winchesters. In the darkness, they could not be sure they hit anything, but as they would later relate, the action sure solved blocked bowel-movement problems any of the gunnies might be suffering from.

The horses from the corral were long gone, just as Lujan had predicted, stampeding in a mad rush and tearing down the corral gates after the explosion of the first bomb.

"Gimme a bomb!" Smoke yelled over the confusion.

At a full gallop, Beans handed him a bomb and Smoke circled the house, screaming like a painted-up Cheyenne, while Lujan and Beans reined up and began laying down a blistering line of fire. Smoke lit the bomb and tossed it in a side window.

"Let's go!" he yelled.

Screaming like young bucks on the warpath, the three men gave their horses full rein and galloped off into the dusty night. Smoke took one look back and grinned.

Dooley was getting to his feet for the third time when the bomb blew. The blast impacted with Dooley, turning him around and sending him, door, and what was left of his longhandles, right out the bedroom window. Dooley landed right on top of Lanny Ball, the door separating them, both of the men knocked out cold.

"Lemme out of here!" Bud squalled. "Halp! Halp!"

# Eighteen

There had been no pursuit. It would take the gunnies hours to round up their horses. But come the dawning, all three men knew the air would be filled with gunsmoke whenever and wherever D-H riders met with Circle Double C men.

Several miles from the house, the men stopped and loosened cinch straps on their horses, letting them rest and blow and have a little water, but not too much; this was no time for a bloated horse.

Smoke, Lujan, and Beans lay bellydown beside the little creek and drank alongside their horses, then sat down on the cool bank and rolled cigarettes, smoking and relaxing and unwinding. They had been very, very lucky this night, and they all knew it.

Suddenly, Beans started laughing and the laughter spread. Soon all three were rolling on the bank, laughing almost hysterically.

Gasping for breath, tears running down their tanned cheeks, the men gripped their sides and sat up, wiping their eyes with shirt sleeves.

"*Sabe Dios!*" Lujan said. "But I will never see anything so funny as that we witnessed tonight if I live to be a hundred!"

"Man," Beans chuckled, "I never knew them fellers was so ugly. Did you ever see so many skinny legs in all your life?"

"I saw Dooley blown slap out of the house," Smoke said. "He looked like he was in one piece, but I couldn't tell for sure. He was on a door, looked like to me. Landed on somebody, but I couldn't tell who it was, 'cept he wasn't wearing longjohns, had on one of those short-pants lookin' things some men have taken to wearing. Come to think of it, it did sorta resemble

Lanny Ball. He had his guns belted on over his drawers."

That set them off again, howling and rolling on the ground while their horses looked at the men as if they were a bunch of idiots.


After a few hours' sleep, Smoke rolled out of his blankets, noting that Lujan and Beans were already up. Smoke washed his face and combed his hair and was on his first cup of bunkhouse coffee—strong enough to warp a spoon—when Cord came in.

"I just got the word," the rancher said. "You and the boys played Billy-Hell last night over to the D-H. Doc Adair was rolled out about three this morning. So far there's four dead and two wounded who ain't gonna make it. Several busted arms and legs and heads. Dooley took a six-inch-long splinter in one side of his butt. Adair said the man has gone slap-dab nuts. Just sent off a wire to a cattle buyer to sell off a thousand head for money to hire more gunslicks . . . or rather, he sent someone in to send the wire. Dooley can't sit a saddle just yet." Try as he did, Cord could not contain his smile.

"Hell, Cord," Smoke complained. "There *aren't* any more gunfighters."

"Dad Estes," Cord said, his smile fading.

Smoke stood up from the rickety chair. "You have got to be kidding!"

"Wish I was. They been hiding out over in the Idaho wilderness. Just surfaced a couple of weeks ago on the Montana border."

"I haven't heard anything about Dad in several years. Not since the Regulators ran them out of Colorado."

Cord shook his head. "I been hearin' for some time they been murderin' and robbin' miners to stay alive. Makin' little forays out of the wildnerness and then duckin' back in."

"How many men are we talking about, Cord?"

Cord shrugged his shoulders. "Don't know. Twenty to thirty, I'd guess."

"Then all we're doing is taking two steps forward and three steps back."

"Looks like."

"Did you get a report on damage last night?"

"One bunkhouse completely ruined, the other one badly

damaged. The big house is pretty well shot, back and front. Smoke, Dooley has given the word: shoot us on sight. He says Gibson is his and for us to stay out of it."

"The hell I will!"

"That's the same thing everybody else around here told me . . . more or less."

"Well, it was funny while it lasted." Smoke's words were glum.

Cord poured a cup of coffee. "Personally, I'd like to have seen it. Beans and Lujan has been entertaining the crews for an hour. Did Lanny Ball really have his guns strapped on over his short drawers?"

Smoke laughed. "Yeah. That was right before the door hit him."

Both men shared a laugh. Cord said, "Would it do any good to wire for some federal marshals?"

"I can't see that it would. It would be our word against theirs. And they'd just back off until the marshals left, then we'd still have the same problem facing us. If I had the time, I could probably get my old federal commission back . . . but what good would it do? Dooley's crazy; the gunslicks he's buyin' are playing a double-cross and Dooley's so nuts you'd never convince him of it. I think we'd just better resign ourselves that we're in a war and take it from there."

"The wife says we need supplies in the worst way. We've got to go into town."

"Then we'll go in a bunch. This afternoon. We've got to show Dooley he doesn't run the town."

"Sorry, Mister McCorkle," Walt Hillery said primly. "I'm completely out of everything you want."

"You're a damn liar!" Cord flushed. "Hell, man, I can *see* most of what I ordered."

"All that has been bought by the D-H spread. They're coming in to pick it up this afternoon."

"Jake!" Cord yelled at his hand driving the wagon. "Pull it around back and get ready to load up."

"Now, see here!" Leah's voice was sharp. "You don't give us orders, Mister Big Shot!"

"Dooley's bought them," Smoke said quietly. He stood by a table loaded with men's jeans. He lifted his eyes to Walt. "You

123

should have stayed out of this, Hillery." He walked to the counter and dug in his jeans pocket, tossing half a dozen double eagles onto the counter. "That'll pay for what I pick out, and Cord's money is layin' right beside mine. If Dooley sets up a squall, you tell him to come see me. Load it up, Jake."

The sour-faced and surly Walt and Leah stood tight-lipped, but silent as Jake began loading up supplies.

"Grind the damn coffee, Walt," Cord ordered. "As a matter of fact, double my order. That way I won't have to look at your prissy face for a long time."

"I hope Mister Hanks kills you, McCorkle!" Leah hissed the verbal venom at him. "And I hope you die hard!"

Cord took the hard words without changing expression. "You never have liked me, Leah, and I never could understand why."

She didn't back down. "You don't have the mental capability to appreciate quality people, McCorkle . . . like Dooley Hanks."

"Quality people? What in the name of Peter and Paul are you talking about, Leah?"

But she would only shake her head.

"Money talks, Cord," Smoke told him. "Especially with little-minded people like these two fine citizens. They're just like Dooley: prideful, envious, spiteful, hateful . . . any and all of the seven deadly sins." He walked around the counter and stripped the shelf of all the boxes of .44 and .45 rounds. "Tally it up, storekeeper."

Cord walked around the general store, filling a large box with all the bandages and various balms and patent medicines he could find. "Might as well do it right," he muttered.

If dark looks of hate could kill, both Cord and Smoke would have died on the spot. Not another word was exchanged the rest of the time spent in the store except for Walt telling the men the amount of their purchases. All the supplies loaded onto the wagon, both Cord and Smoke experienced a sense of relief when they exited the building to stand on the boardwalk.

"Quality people?" Cord said, shaking his head, still not able to get over that statement.

"Forget them," Smoke said. "They're not worth worrying about. When this war is over, and we've won—and we will win, count on it—those two will be sucking up to you as if nothing had happened."

"What they'll do is do without my business," Cord said shortly.

The men walked over to Hans for a cup of coffee and a piece of pie. Beans and Lujan, with Charlie Starr and his old gunslinging buddies, had dropped into the Pussycat for a beer. There were half a dozen horses wearing the D-H brand, among others, at the hitchrail in front of the Hangout.

"You any good with that six-gun?" Smoke asked the rancher.

"Contrary to what some believe, I'm no fast gun. But I hit what I aim at."

"That counts most of all in most cases. I've seen so-called fast guns many, many times put their first shot in the dirt. They didn't get another shot." Then Smoke added, "Just buried."

They sipped their coffee and enjoyed the dried apple pie with a hunk of cheese on it. They both could sense the tension hanging in and around the small town; and both knew that a shooting was more than likely looking them in the face. It would probably come just before they tried to leave Gibson.

Nothing stirred on the wide street. Not one dog or cat could be seen anywhere. And it was very hot, the sun a bubbling ball in a very blue and very cloudless sky. A dust devil spun out its short frantic life, whipping up the street and then vanishing.

Hilda refilled their cups. "And how is Ring?" she inquired, blushing as she asked.

"Fine." Smoke smiled at her. "He sends his regards."

She giggled and returned to the kitchen.

Smoke looked at Cord as he scribbled in a small tally book most ranchers carried with them. "Eighteen dead," the rancher muttered. "Near as I can figure. May God have mercy on us."

"They'll be fifty or sixty dead before this is over. If Dooley doesn't pull in his horns."

"He won't. He's gone completely around the bend. And you know," Cord said thoughtfully, some sadness in his voice, "I don't even remember what caused the riff between us."

"That's the way it usually is. Your rider who talked to Doc Adair, he have any idea when Dad Estes and his bunch will be pulling in?"

"Soon as possible, I reckon. They'll ride hard gettin' over here. And I'd be willing to bet they'd already left the wilderness

125

and was waitin' for word; and I'd bet it was Jason or Lanny who put the bug about them into Dooley's ear."

"Probably right on both counts."

Both men looked up as several riders rode into town, reining up in front of the Hangout.

"You know them, Smoke?"

"Some of No-Count Victor's bunch."

"Daryl Radcliffe and Paul Addison are ze zwo in der front," Hans rumbled from behind the counter. "Day vas pointed out to me when day first come to zown."

"I've heard of them," Smoke said. "They're scum. Bottom of the barrel but good with a pistol."

"Maybe ve vill get lucky and day will all bite demselves und die from der rabies," Hans summed up the feelings of most in the town.

They all heard the back door open and close and Hans turned as Olga came to his side and whispered in his ear. She disappeared into the kitchen and Hans said, "Four men she didn't know have hitched dere horses at der far end of town and are valking dis vay. All of dem vearing zwo guns."

"Is that our cue?" Cord asked.

"I reckon. But I'm going to finish my pie and coffee first."

"You always this calm before a gunfight?"

"No point in getting all worked about it. Stay as calm as you can and your shootin' hand stays steady."

"Good way to look at it, I suppose." Cord finished his pie and took a sip of coffee. "I hate it that we have to do this in town. A stray bullet doesn't care who it hits."

Smoke drained his coffee cup and placed it carefully in the saucer. "It doesn't have to be on the street if you're game."

"I'm game for anything that'll keep innocent people from getting hurt."

"You ready?"

"As I'll ever be. Where are we going?"

"Like Daniel, into the lion's den. Or in this case, the Hangout. Let's see how they like it when we take it to them."

# Nineteen

Beans and Lujan and Charlie Starr and his old buddies were waiting on the boardwalk.

"The beer is on me, boys," Smoke told them. "We'll try the fare at the Hangout."

"I hope they have tequila," Lujan said. "They didn't a couple of weeks ago. I have not had a decent drink in months."

"They probably do by now, with Diego and Pablo hanging around in there. But the bottles might be reserved for them."

"If they have tequila, I shall have a drink," Lujan replied softly, tempered steel under the liltingly accented words.

The men pushed through the batwing doors and stepped inside the saloon. For all but Lujan and Cord, this was their first excursion into the Hangout. The men fanned out and quickly sized up the joint.

They realized before the first blink that they were outnumbered a good two to one. Surprise mixed with irritation was very evident on the faces of the D-H gunfighters. This move on the part of the Circle Double C had not been anticipated, and it was not to their liking. For in a crowded barroom, gunfights usually took a terrible toll due to the close range.

Smoke led the way to the bar, deliberately turning his back to the gunslicks. The barkeep looked as if he really had to go to the outhouse. "Beer for me and the Moab Kid and Mister McCorkle, please. And a bottle of whiskey for the boys and a bottle of tequila for Mister Lujan."

The barkeep looked at the "boys," average age about sixty-five, and nodded his head. "I got ever'thing 'cept the tequila. Them bottles is reserved for my regular customers."

127

"Put a bottle of tequila on the bar, partner," Smoke told him. "If a customer can see it, it's for sale."

"Yes, sir," the barkeep said, knowing he was caught between a rock and a hard place. But who the hell would have ever figured this bunch would come in *here?*

Smoke and his men could watch the room of gunfighters in the mirror behind the bar, and they could all see the D-H hired guns were very uncertain. It showed in their furtive glances at one another. Smoke kept a wary eye on Radcliffe and Addison, for they were known to be backshooters and would not hesitate to kill him should Smoke relax his guard for just a moment.

Several D-H guns had been standing at the bar. They had carefully moved away while Smoke was ordering the drinks.

"Diego finds out you been suckin' at his tequila bottle," a gunny spoke, "you gonna be dead, Lujan."

"One day is just as good as the next day to meet the Lord," Lujan replied, turning to face the man. "But since Diego is not present, perhaps you would like to attempt to fill his boots, *puerco.*"

"What'd you call me?" the man stood up.

Lujan smiled, holding his shot glass in his left hand. "A pig!"

Radcliffe and Addison and half a dozen others stood up, their hands dangling close to their guns.

The town's blacksmith pushed open the batwings, stood for a moment staring at the crowd and feeling the tension in the room. He slowly backed out onto the boardwalk. The sounds of his boots faded as he made his exit.

"No damn greasy Mex is gonna call me a pig!" the gunny shouted the words.

Lujan smiled, half turning as he placed the shot glass on the bar. He expected the D-H gunny to draw as he turned, and the man did. Lujan's Colt snaked into his hand and the beery air exploded in gunfire. The D-H gunny was down and dying as his hand was still trying to lift his pistol clear of leather.

Radcliffe and Addison grabbed for iron. Smoke's right hand dipped, drew, cocked, and fired in one smooth cat-quick movement. A second behind his draw, Cord drew and fired. Radcliffe and Addison stumbled backward and fell over chairs on their way to the floor.

The room erupted in gunsmoke, lead, and death as Beans and the old gun-handlers pulled iron, cocked it back, and let it bang.

Two D-H riders, with more sense than the others, jumped right through a saloon window, landing on the boardwalk and rolling to the street. They were cut in a few places, but that beat the hell out of being dead.

The bartender had dropped to the floor at the first shot. He came up with a sawed-off ten gauge shotgun, the hammers eared back, and pointed it at Pistol's head. Cord turned and shot the man in the neck. The bartender jerked as the bullet took him, the barrels of the shotgun pointed toward the ceiling. The shotgun went off, the stock driving back from the recoil, smashing into the man's mouth, knocking teeth out.

Cord felt a hammer blow in his left shoulder, a jarring flash of pain that turned him to one side for a painful moment and rendered his left arm useless. Regaining his balance and lifting his pistol, the rancher fired at the man who had shot him, his bullet taking the man in his open mouth and exiting out the man's neck.

Beans felt a burning sensation on his cheek as a slug grazed him, followed by the warm drip of blood. He jerked out his second pistol and added more gunsmoke and death to the mounting carnage.

Lujan twisted as a slug tore through the fleshy part of his arm. Cursing, he lifted his Colt and drove two fast rounds into the belly of the D-H gunhawk who stood directly in front of him, doubling the man over and dropping him screaming to the floor.

The barroom was thick with gunsmoke, making it almost impossible to see. The roaring of guns was near-deafening, adding to the screaming of the wounded and the vile cursing of those still alive.

Smoke jerked as a bullet burned his leg and another slug clipped the top of his ear, sending blood flowing down his face. He stumbled to one side and picked up a gun that had fallen from the lifeless fingers of a D-H gunslick. It was a short-barreled Colt Peacemaker .45. Smoke eared the hammer back and let it snarl as he knelt on the floor, his wounded leg throbbing.

The old gunfighters seemed invincible as they stood almost shoulder-to-shoulder, hands filled with .44's and .45's, all of them belching fire and smoke and lead. This was nothing new to them. They had been doing this since the days a man carried a dozen filled cylinders with him for faster reloading. They had stood in barrooms from the Mississippi to the Pacific Ocean, and from Canada to the Mexican border and fought it out, sometimes with a tin star pinned to their chests, sometimes close to the outlaw trail. This was as familiar to them as to a bookkeeper with his figures.

Several D-H hired guns stumbled through the smoke and the blood, trying to make it to the boardwalk, to take the fight into the streets. The first one to step through the batwings was flung back into the fray, his face missing. Hans had blown it off with a sawed-off shotgun. The second D-H gunny had his legs knocked out from under him from the other barrel of Hans's express gun.

Through the thick choking killing haze, Smoke saw a man known to him as Blue, a member of Cat Jennings's gang of no-goods and trash. Blue was pointing his Smith & Wesson Schofield .45 at Charlie.

He never got to pull the trigger. Smoke's Peacemaker roared and bucked in his hand and Blue felt, for a few seconds, the hot pain of frontier justice end his days of robbing and murdering.

The gunfire faded into silence, broken only by the moaning of wounded gunslingers.

"Coming in!" Hans shouted from the boardwalk.

"Come on, partner," Hardrock said, punching out empties and filling up his guns.

Hans stepped through the batwings and coughed as the arid smoke filled his nostrils. His eyes widened in shock at the human carnage on the floor. Widened further as he looked at the wounded men leaning up against the bar. "I vill get the doctor." He backed out and ran for Doc Adair's office.

While Charlie and Pistol kept their guns on the moaning gunslicks on the floor, Smoke and Lujan walked among them, silently determining which should first receive Adair's attentions and who would never again need attention.

Not in this life.

Smoke knelt down beside a young man, perhaps twenty years old. The young man had been shot twice in the stomach, and already his dark eyes were glazing over as death hovered near.

"You got any folks, boy?" Smoke asked.

"Mother!" the young man gasped.

"Where is she?"

"Arkansas. Clay County. On the St. Francis. Name's . . . name's Claire . . . Shelby."

"I'll get word to her," Smoke told him as that pale rider came galloping nearer.

"She always told me . . . I was gonna turn out . . . bad." The words were very weak.

"I'll write that your horse threw you and you broke your neck."

"I'd . . . 'preciate it. That'd make her . . . feel a bunch better." He closed his eyes and did not open them again.

"I thought you was gonna kiss him there for minute, Jensen," a hard-eyed gunslick mocked Smoke. The lower front of the man's shirt was covered with blood. He had taken several rounds in the gut.

"You got any folks you want me to write?" Smoke asked the dying man.

The gunslick spat at Smoke, the bloody spittle landing close to his boot.

"Suit yourself." Smoke stood up, favoring his wounded leg. He limped back to the bar and leaned against it, just as the batwings pushed open and Doc Adair and the undertaker came in.

Both of them stopped short. "Jesus God!" Adair said, looking around him at the body-littered and blood-splattered saloon.

"Business got a little brisk today, Doc," Smoke told him, accepting a shot glass of tequila from Lujan. "Check Cord here first." He knocked back the strong mescal drink and shuddered as it hit the pit of his stomach.

The doctor, not as old as Smoke had first thought—of course he'd been sober now for several weeks, and was now wearing clean clothes and had gone back to shaving daily—knew his business. He cleaned out the shoulder wound and bandaged it, rigging a sling for Cord out of a couple of bar towels. He then turned his attention to Lujan, swiftly and expertly patching up the arm.

Smoke had cut open his jeans, exposing the ugly rip along the outside of his leg. "It ought to be stitched up," Adair said. "It'll leave a bad scar if I don't."

"Last time my wife Sally counted, Doc, I had seventeen bullet scars in my hide. So one more isn't going to make any difference."

"So young to have been hit so many times," the doctor muttered as he swabbed out the gash with alcohol. Smoke almost lifted himself out of the chair as the alcohol cleaned the raw flesh. Adair grinned. "Sometimes the treatment hurts worse than the wound."

"You've convinced me," Smoke said as his eyes went misty, then went through the same sensation as Adair cleaned the wound in his ear.

"How 'bout us?" a gunfighter on floor bitched. "Ain't we gonna get no treatment?"

"Go ahead and die," Adair told him. "I can see from here that you're not going to make it."

Charlie and his friends had walked around the room, collecting all the guns and gun belts, from both the dead and the living.

"Always did want me a matched set of Remingtons," Silver Jim said. "Now I got me some. Nice balance, too."

"I want you to lookee here at this Colt double-action," Charlie said. "I'll just be hornswoggled. And she's a .44-.40, too. Got a little ring on the butt so's a body could run some twine through it and not lose your gun. Ain't that something, now. Don't have to cock it, neither. Just point it and pull the trigger." He tried it one-handed and almost scared the doctor half to death when Charlie shot out a lamp. "All that trigger-pullin'-the-hammer-back does throw your aim off a mite, though. Take some gettin' used to, I reckon."

"Maybe you 'pposed to shoot it with both hands," Hardrock suggested.

"That don't make no sense atall. There ain't no room on the butt for two hands. Where the hell would you put the other'n?"

"I don't know. Was I you, I'd throw the damn thing away. They ain't never gonna catch on."

"I'm a hurtin' something fierce!" a D-H gunhawk hollered.

"You want me to kick you in the head, boy?" Pistol asked him. "That'd put you out of your misery for a while."

The gunhawk shut his mouth.

Adair finished with Beans and went to work on the fallen gunfighters. "This is strictly cash, boys," he told them. "I don't give no credit to people whose life expectancy is as short as yours."

# Twenty

All was calm for several days. Smoke imagined that even in Dooley's half-crazed mind it had been a shock to lose so many gunslicks in the space of three minutes, and all that following the raid on Dooley's ranch. So much had happened in less than twenty-four hours that Dooley was being forced to think over very carefully whatever move he had planned next.

But all knew the war was nowhere near over. That this was quite probably the lull before the next bloody and violent storm.

"Dad Estes and his bunch just pulled in," Cord told Smoke on the morning of the fourth day after the showdown in the saloon. "Hans sent word they came riding in late last night."

"He'll be making a move soon then."

"Smoke, do you realize that by my count, thirty-three men have been killed so far?"

"And about twenty wounded. Yes. I understand the undertaker is putting up a new building just to handle it all."

"That is weighing on my mind, Smoke. I've killed in my lifetime, Smoke. I've killed three white men in about twenty years, but they had stole from me and were shooting at me. I've hanged one rustler." He paused.

"What are you trying to say, Cord?"

"We've got to end this. I'm getting where I can't sleep at night! That boy dying back yonder in the saloon got to me."

"I'm certainly open to suggestions, Cord. Do you think it didn't bother me to write that boy's mother? I don't enjoy killing, Cord. I went for three years without ever pulling a gun in anger. I loved it. Then until I got Fae's letter, I hadn't even worn both guns. But you know as well as I do how this little war

133

is going to be stopped."

Cord leaned against the hitchrail and took off his hat, scratching his head. "We force the issue? Is that what you're saying?"

"Do you want peace, Cord?"

"More than anything. Perhaps we could ride over and talk to . . . ?" He shook his head. "What am I saying? Time for that is over and past. All right, Smoke. All right. Let me hear your plan."

"I don't have one. And it isn't as if I haven't been thinking hard on it. What happened to your sling?"

"I took it off. Damn thing worried me. No plan?"

"No. The ranch, this ranch, must be manned at all times. We agreed on that. If not, it'll end up like Fae's place. And if we keep meeting them like we did back in town, they're going to take us. We were awfully lucky back there, Cord."

"I know. So . . . ?"

"I'm blank. Empty. Except for hit and run night fighting. But we'll never get as lucky as we did the other night. Count on that. You can bet that Dooley has that place heavily guarded night and day."

"Wait them out, then. I have the cash money to keep Gage and his boys on the payroll for a long time. But not enough to buy more gunslicks . . . if I could find any we could trust, that is."

"Doubtful. Must be half a hundred range wars going on out here, most of them little squabbles, but big enough to keep a lot of gunhawks working."

"I've written the territorial governor, but no reply as yet."

"I wouldn't count on one, either." Smoke verbally tossed cold water on that. "He's fighting to make this territory a state; I doubt that he'd want a lot of publicity about a range war at this time."

Cord nodded his agreement. "We'll wait a few more days; neither one of us is a hundred percent yet . . ." He paused as a rider came at a hard gallop from the west range.

The hand slid to a halt, out of the saddle and running to McCorkle. "Saddle me a horse!" he yelled to several punchers standing around the corral. "The boys is bringin' in Max, Mister Cord. Looks like Dooley done turned loose that back-shootin' Danny Rouge. Max took one in the back. He's still able to sit a saddle, but just barely. I'll ride into town and fetch

Doc Adair." He was gone in a bow-legged run toward the corral.

Cord's face had paled at the news of his oldest son being shot. "I'll have Alice get ready with hot water and bandages. She's a good nurse." He ran up the steps to the house.

Smoke leaned against the hitchrail as his eyes picked up several riders coming in slow, one on either side helping to keep the middle rider in the saddle. Smoke knew, with this news, all of Cord's willingness to talk had gone right out the window. And if Max died . . . ?

Smoke pushed away from the hitchrail and walked toward the bunkhouse. If Max died there would be open warfare; no more chance meetings between the factions involved. It would be bloody and cruel until one side killed off the other.

"Might as well get ready for it," Smoke muttered.


"All we can do is wait," Adair said. "I can't probe for the bullet 'cause I don't know where it is. It angled off from the entry point. It missed the kidney and there is no sign of excessive internal bleeding; so he's got a chance. But don't move him any more than you have to."

Smoke and several others stood listening as Doc Adair spoke with Cord and Alice.

"His chances . . . ?" Cord asked, his voice tired.

"Fifty-fifty." Adair was blunt. "Maybe less than that. Don't get your hopes up too high, Cord. Have someone close by him around the clock. We'll know one way or the other in a few days."


"Did you get him?" Dooley asked the rat-faced Danny Rouge.

"I got him." Danny's voice was high-pitched, more like a woman's voice.

"Good!" Dooley took a long pull from his whiskey bottle, some of the booze dribbling down his unshaven chin. "One less of that bastard's whelps."

He was still mumbling and scratching himself as Danny walked from the room and stepped outside. Dooley's sons were on the porch, sharing a bottle.

"Did he squall when you got him?" Sonny asked, his eyes bright from the cruelty within the young man.

"I 'magine he did," Danny told him. "But I couldn't hear him; I was a good half mile away." Danny stepped from the porch and walked toward the one bunkhouse that was still usable. With the coming in of Dad Estes and his bunch, tents had been thrown up all over the place, the ranch now resembling a guerrilla camp.

The other gunhawks avoided Danny. No one wanted anything to do with him, all feeling that there was something unclean about the young man, even though Danny was as fastidious as possible, considering the time and the place. He was considerate of his personal appearance, but his mind resembled anyone's concept of hell. Danny was a cold-blooded killer. He enjoyed killing, the killing act his substitute for a woman. He would kill anybody: man, woman, or child. It did not make one bit of difference to Danny. Just as long as the price was right.

He went to his bunk and carefully cleaned his rifle, returning it to the hard leather case. Then he stretched out on the bunk and closed his eyes. It had been a very pleasing day. He knew he'd gotten a good clean hit by the way the man had jerked and then slumped in the saddle, slowly tumbling to the ground, hitting the ground like a rag doll.

It was a good feeling knowing he had earned his pay. A day's work for a day's pay. Made a man feel needed. Yes, indeed.


At the Circle Double C, the men sat, mostly in small groups, and mostly in silence, cleaning weapons. The hands, not gunfighters, but just hard-working cowboys, were digging in warbags and taking out that extra holster and pistol, filling the loops of a spare bandoleer. They rode for the brand, and if a fight was what Dooley Hanks wanted, a fight would be what he would get.

The hands who had come over to Cord's side from the D-H did not have mixed feeling about it. They had been shoved aside in favor of gunhawks; they had seen Dooley and his ignorant sons go from bad to savage. There was not one ounce of loyalty left among them toward Dooley. They knew now that this was a fight to the finish. OK. Let's do it.

Just before dusk, Cord walked out to the bunkhouse, a grim expression on his face. "I sent Willie in for the doctor. Max is coughin' up blood. It don't look good. I can't stand to sit in

136

here and look at my wife tryin' to be brave about the whole damn thing when I know that what she really wants to do is bust out bawlin'. And the same goes for me."

Then he started cussing. He strung together some mighty hard words as he stomped around the big room, kicking at this and that; about every fourth and fifth word was Dooley Hanks. He traced the man's ancestry back to before Adam and Eve, directly linking Dooley to the snake in the Garden.

He finally sat down on a bunk and put his face in his hands. Smoke motioned the men outside and gently closed the door, leaving Cord with his grief and the right for a man to cry in private.

"It's gonna be Katy-bar-the-door if that boy dies," Hardrock said. "We just think we've seen a little shootin' up to now."

"I'm ready," Del said. "I'm ready to get this damn thing over with and get back to punchin' cows."

"It's gonna be a while 'fore any of us gets back to doin' that," Les said, one of the men who had come from the D-H.

"And some of us won't," Fitz spoke softly.

Someone had a bottle and that got passed around. Beans pulled out a sack of tobacco and that went the way of the bottle. The men drank and smoked in silence until the bottle was empty and the tobacco sack flat as a tortilla left out in the sun.

"Wonder how Dooley's ass is?" Gage asked, and the men chuckled softly.

"I hope it's healed," Del said. " 'Cause it's shore about to get kicked hard."

The men all agreed on that.

Cord came out of the bunkhouse and walked to the house, passing the knot of men without speaking. His face bore the brunt of his inner grief.

Holman got up from his squat and said, "I think I'm gonna go write my momma a letter. She's gettin' on in years and I ain't wrote none in near'bouts a year."

"That's a good idea," Bernie said. "If I tell you what to put on paper to my momma, would you write it down for me?"

"Shore. Come on. I print passable well."

They were happy-go-lucky young cowboys a few weeks ago, Smoke thought. Now they are writing their mothers with death on their minds.

That ghostly rider would be saddling up his fire-snorting stallion, Smoke mused. Ready for more lost souls.

"What are you thinking, amigo?" Lujan asked him.

Smoke told him.

"You are philosophical this evening. I had always heard that you were a man who possessed deep thoughts."

Smoke grunted. "My daddy used to say that we came from Wales—years back. Jensen wasn't our real name. I don't know what it was. But Daddy used to say that the Celts were mysterious people. I don't know."

"I know that there is the smell of death in the air," the Mexican said. "Listen. No birds singing. Nothing seems to be moving."

The primal call of a wolf cut the night air, its shivering howl touching them all.

"Folks cut them wolves down," Del spoke out of the darkness. "And I've shot my share of them when they was after beeves. But I ain't got nothing really agin them. They're just doing what God intended them to do. They ain't like we're supposed to be. They can't think like nothin' except what they is. And you can't fault them for that. Take a human person now, that's a different story. Dooley and them others, and I know that Dooley's done lost his mind, but I think his greed brung that on. His jealousy and so forth. But them gunning over yonder. They coulda been anything but what they is. They turned to the outlaw trail 'cause they wanted to. What am I tryin' to say anyways?"

Silver Jim stood up and stretched. "It means we can go in smokin' and not have no guilty conscience when we leave them bassards dead where we find them."

Lujan smiled. "Not as eloquently put as might have been, but it certainly summed it up well."

Cord stepped out on the porch just as Doc Adair's buggy pulled up. The men could hear his words plain. "Max just died."

138

# Twenty-One

Max McCorkle, the oldest son of Cord and Alice, and brother to Rock, Troy, and Sandi, was buried the next day. He was twenty-five years old. He was buried in the cemetery on the ridge overlooking the ranch house. Half a dozen crosses were in the cemetery, crosses of men who had worked for the Circle Double C and who had died while in the employment of the spread.

Sandi stood leaning against Beans, softly weeping. Del stood with Fae. Ring stood with Hilda and Hans and Olga. Gage with Liz. Cord stood stony-faced with his wife, a black veil over her face. Parnell stood with Smoke and the other hands and gunfighters. And Smoke had noticed something: the schoolteacher had strapped on a gun.

The final words were spoken over Max, and the family left while the hands shoveled the dirt over the young man's final resting place on this earth.

Parnell walked up to Smoke. "I would like for you to teach me the nomenclature of this weapon and the proper way to fire it."

A small smile touched Smoke's lips, so faint he doubted Parnell even noticed it. "You plannin' on ridin' with us, Cousin?"

The man shook his head. "Regretfully, no. I am not that good a horseman. I would only be in the way. But someone needs to be here at the ranch with the women. I can serve in that manner."

Smoke stuck out his hand and the schoolteacher, with a surprised look on his face, took it. "Glad to have you with us, Parnell."

139

"Pleased to be here, Cousin."

"We'll start later on this afternoon. Right now, let's wander on down to the house. Mrs. McCorkle and the others have been cookin' all morning. Big crowd here. I 'spect the neighbors will be visitin' and such all afternoon."

"Funerals are barbaric. Nothing more than a throwback to primitive and pagan rites."

"Is that right?"

"Yes. And dreadfully hard on the family."

Weddings and funerals were social events in the West, often drawing crowds from fifty to seventy-five miles away. It was a chance to catch up on the latest gossip, eat a lot of good food—everybody brought a covered dish—and see old friends.

"We got the same thing goin' on up on the Missouri," Smoke heard one man tell Cord. "Damn nesters are tryin' to grab our land. Some of the ranchers have brung in some gunfighters. I don't hold with that myself, but it may come to it. I writ the territorial governor, but he ain't seen fit to reply as yet. Probably never even got the letter."

Smoke moved around the lower part of the ranch house and listened. Few knew who he was, and that was just fine with him.

"Maybe we could get Dooley put in the crazy house," a man suggested. "He's sure enough nuts. All we got to do is find someone to sign the papers."

"No," another said. "There's one more thing: findin' someone stupid enough to serve the papers when Dooley's got hisself surrounded by fifty or sixty gunslicks."

"I wish I could help Cord out, but I'm shorthanded as it is. The damn Army ought to come in. That's what I think."

Smoke heard the words "vigilante" and "regulators" several times. But they were not spoken with very much enthusiasm.

Smoke ate, but with little appetite. Cord was holding up well, but his two remaining sons, Rock and Troy, were geared up for trouble, and unless he could head them off, they would be riding into disaster. He moved to the boys' side, where they stood backed up against a wall, keeping as far away from the crowd as possible.

"You boys best just snuff out your powder fuse," Smoke told them. "Dooley and his bunch will get their due, but for right now, think about your mother. She's got enough grief on her shoulders without you two adding to it. Just settle down."

The boys didn't like it, but Smoke could tell by the looks on their faces his words about their mother had hit home. He felt they would check-rein their emotions for a time. For how long was another matter.

Having never liked the feel of large crowds, Smoke stayed a reasonable time, paid his respects to Cord and Alice, and took his leave, walking back to the bunkhouse to join the other hands.

"When do we ride?" Fitz asked as soon as Smoke had walked in.

"Don't know. Just get that burr out from under your blanket and settle down. You can bet that Dooley is ready and waiting for us right this minute. Let's don't go riding into a trap. We'll wait a few days and let the pot cool its boil. Then we'll come up with something."

Fine words, but Smoke didn't have any plan at all.


They all worked cattle for a few days, riding loose but ready. In the afternoons, Smoke spent several hours each day with Parnell and his pistol. Parnell was very fast, but he couldn't hit anything but air. On the third day, Smoke concluded that the man never would be able to hit the side of a barn, even if he was standing inside the barn. Since they had plenty of rifles, Smoke decided to try the man with a Winchester. To his surprise, Parnell turned out to be a good shot with a carbine.

"You can tote that pistol around if you want to, Parnell," Smoke told him. "But you just remember this: out here, if a man straps on a gun, he best be ready and able to use it. Don't go off the ranch grounds packing a short gun, 'cause somebody's damn sure going to call your hand with it. Stick with the rifle. You're a pretty good shot with it. We got plenty of rifles, so keep half a dozen of them loaded up full at all times."

"I need to go in and get some books and papers from the school."

"I wouldn't advise it, Cousin. You'd just be askin' for trouble. Tell me what you need, and I'll fetch it for you."

"Perhaps," the schoolteacher said mysteriously, and walked away.

Smoke had a feeling that, despite his words, the man was

going into town anyway. He'd have to keep an eye on him. He knew Parnell was feeding on his newly found oats, so to speak, and felt he didn't need a baby-sitter. But Smoke had a hunch that Parnell really didn't know or understand the caliber of men who might jump him, prod him into doing something that would end up getting the schoolteacher hurt, or dead.

Smoke spread the word among the men to keep an eye on Parnell.

"Seems to me that Rita's been lookin' all wall-eyed at him the last couple of days," Pistol said. "Shore is a bunch of spoonin' goin' on around here. Makes a man plumb nervous."

"Wal, you can re-lax, Pistol," Hardrock told him. "No woman in her right mind would throw her loop for the likes of you. You too damn old and too damn ugly."

"Huh!" the old gunfighter grunted. "You a fine one to be talkin'. You could hire that face of yours out to scare little children."

Smoke left the two old friends insulting each other and walked to the house to speak with Cord sitting on the front porch, drinking coffee.

Cord waved him up and Smoke took a seat.

"I'm surprised Dooley hasn't made a move," the rancher said. "But the men say the range has been clear. Maybe he's counting on that Danny Rouge to pick us off one at a time."

"I doubt that Dooley even knows what's in his mind," Smoke replied. "I've been thinking, Cord. If we could get a judge to him, the judge would declare him insane and stick him in an institution."

"Umm. Might be worth a shot. I can send a rider up to Helena with a letter. I know Judge Ford. Damn! Why didn't I think of that?"

"Maybe he'd like to come down for a visit?" Smoke suggested. "Has he been here before?"

"Several times. Good idea. I'll spell it all out in a letter and get a man riding within the hour. I'll ask him if he can bring a deputy U.S. marshal down with him."

"We just might be able to end this mess," Smoke said, a hopeful note in his voice. "With Dooley out of the picture, Liz could take over the running of the ranch, with Gage to help her, and she could fire the gunslicks."

"It sounds so simple."

"All we can do is try. Have you seen Parnell and Rita?"

"Yeah. They went for a walk. Can't get used to the idea of that schoolteacher packin' iron. It looks funny."

"I warned him about totin' that gun in town."

"And I told Rita not to go into town. However, since I'm not her father, it probably went in one ear and out the other. Dooley and me told those girls fifteen years ago not to see one another. Did a hell of a lot of good, didn't it? Both those girls are stubborn as mules. Did Parnell get his back up when you warned him?"

"I . . . think perhaps he did. I tell you, Cord, he can get that six-shooter out of leather damn quick. He just can't hit anything with it."

The men chatted for a time, then Smoke left the rancher composing the letter he was sending to Judge Ford. The rider would leave that afternoon. Smoke saddled up and rode out to check on Fae's cattle. As soon as he pulled out, Parnell and Rita left in the buggy, heading for town.


"I shan't be a moment, Rita," Parnell said as they neared Gibson. "I only need to gather up a few articles from the school."

Rita put a hand on Parnell's leg and almost curled his toenails. "Take as long as you like. I'll be waiting for you . . . darling."

Parnell's collar suddenly became very tight.

He gathered up his articles from the school and hurried back to the buggy.

"Would you mind terribly taking me over to Mrs. Jefferson's house, Parnell? I have a dress over there I need to pick up."

"Not at all . . . darling."

Rita giggled and Parnell blushed. He clucked the horse into movement and they went chatting up the main street of Gibson. They did not go unnoticed by a group of D-H gunslicks loafing in front of the Hangout, the busted window now boarded up awaiting the next shipment of glass.

"Yonder goes Miss Sweety-Baby and Sissy-Pants," Golden said, sucking on a toothpick.

"Let's us have some fun when they come back through," Eddie Hart said with a wicked grin.

"What'd you have in mind?"

"We'll drag Sissy-Britches out of that there buggy and strip him nekkid right in the middle of the street; right in front of Pretty-Baby."

They all thought that would be loads of fun.

Golden looked at an old rummy sitting on the steps, mumbling to himself. "What the hell are you mumbling about, old man?"

"I knowed I seed that schoolteacher afore. Now it comes to me."

"What are you talkin' about, you old rum-dum?"

"'Bout fifteen year ago, I reckon it was. Back when Reno was just a sandy collection of saloons and hurdy-gurdy parlors. They was a humdinger of a shootin' one afternoon. This kid come riding in and some hombres decided they'd have some fun with him. In 'bout the time hit'd take you to blink your eyes four times, they was four men in the street, dead or dyin'. The kid was snake quick and on the mark. He disappeared shortly after that." The old man pointed toward the dust trail of the buggy. "That there, boys, is the Reno Kid!"

# Twenty-Two

"The *Reno Kid!*" Golden hissed, as his front chair legs hit the boardwalk.

"He's right!" Gandy, a member of Cat Jennings's gang almost shouted the words. "I was there! I seen it! That there is shore nuff the Reno Kid. He's all growed up and put on some weight, but that's him!"

"Damn right!" the wino said. "I said it was, din I. I was thar, too."

"That's why he don't never pack no gun," another said. "Who'd have thought it?"

"He's mine," Golden said.

"We'll both take him," Gandy insisted. "Man lak 'at you cain't take no chances with."

"But he ain't packin' no iron!" another said. "Hit'd be murder, pure and simple."

Golden said a cuss word and leaned back in his chair.

"Here they come!" Gandy looked up the street. "To hell with it. I'll force his hand and call him out. Make him git a six-gun."

"I'll keep you covered in case he's packin' a hideout gun," Golden told him.

Both men stood up, Gandy stepping out into the wide street, directly in the path of the buggy.

Parnell whoaed the horse and sat glaring at the gunslick.

Gandy glared back.

"Will you please remove your unwashed and odious presence from the middle of the street, you ignorant lout!" Parnell ordered.

"Whut the hale did you say to me, Reno?"

Parnell blinked and looked at Rita, who was looking at him.

"I'm afraid you have me confused with someone else," Parnell said. "Now kindly step out of the way so we may proceed on our journey."

"Git outta that thar buggy, Reno! I'm a gonna kill you."

"He thinks you're the Reno Kid." Rita gripped Parnell's arm.

"Who, or what, is the Reno Kid?"

"A legendary gunfighter from the Nevada Territory. He'd be about your age now. No one has seen him in fifteen years."

"What the hale-far is y'all whisperin' about?" Gandy hollered. "What'd the matter, Reno, you done turned yeller?"

"I beg your pardon !" Parnell returned the shout. "Begone with you before I give you a proper hiding with a buggy whip, you fool!"

No one seemed to notice the tall, lean, darkly tanned stranger standing in the shadows of the awning in front of the Pussycat. He was wearing a gun, but then, so did nearly every man. He stood watching the goings-on with a faint twinkle of amusement in his dark eyes.

If it got out of hand, he would interfere, but not before.

"Y'all heard it!" Gandy shouted. "He called me a fool! Them's fightin' words, Reno. Now get out of that there buggy."

"I most certainly will not, you . . . you . . . hooligan!"

"I think I'll just snatch your woman outta there and lift her petticoats. Maybe that'll narrow that yeller stripe a-runnin' down your back."

Before he even thought about the consequences, Parnell stepped from the buggy to the street. His coat was covering his pistol. "I demand you apologize to Miss Rita for that remark, you brute!"

"I ain't a-gonna do no sich of a thing, Reno."

"My name is not Reno and oh, yes, you will!"

"Your name shore as hell is Reno and I will not!"

Gandy could not see most of Parnell for the horse. Parnell brushed back his coat and put his hand on the butt of his gun, removing the leather thong from the hammer and stepping forward, drawing as he walked.

Gandy saw the arm movement and grabbed iron. Parnell stubbed his toe on a rock in the street and fell forward, pulling the trigger. The hammer dropped, the slug striking Gandy right between the eyes and knocking him down, dead before he hit the dirt.

Shocked at what he'd done, Parnell turned, the muzzle pointing toward Golden just as Golden jerked his gun out of leather.

Parnell instinctively cocked and fired, the bullet slamming into Golden's stomach and doubling him over. By this time, Rita had jerked a Winchester out of the boot and eared the hammer back.

"That's it, Reno!" Eddie Hart hollered. "We don't want no more trouble."

Parnell looked at the dead and dying men. He felt sick at his stomach; fought back the nausea as he climbed back into the buggy, first holstering his pistol. He picked up the reins and clucked the mare forward, moving smartly up the street.

"I feel quite ill," Parnell admitted.

"You're so brave!" Rita threw her arms around his neck and gave him a wet kiss in his ear.

Parnell almost lost the rig.

"I seen some fancy shootin' in my days, boys," Pooch Matthews said. "But I ain't never seen nothing like that. Damn, but that Reno is fast."

"Like lightnin'," another said. "Smoke's been holding an ace in the hole all this time."

The stranger walked back into the Pussycat and up to the bar. "You got rooms for rent upstairs?"

"Sure do. Bath's out back. That was some shootin', wasn't it?"

"Yes," the stranger chuckled. "I will admit I have never seen anything like it. I'll take a room; might be here several days."

"Fix you right up. Even give you a clean towel. Them sheets ain't been slept in but once or twice. Maybe three times. Clean sheets'll cost you a quarter."

The stranger laid a quarter down on the bar. "Clean ones, please."

"We ain't got no registry book. But I'm nosy. You ain't from around here, are you?"

"No."

"If you gonna hire on with Dooley, the room is gonna cost you fifty dollars a night."

"I never heard of anyone called Dooley. I'm just tired of

147

riding and would like to rest for a few days."

"Good. Fifty cents a night, then. The schoolteacher is really the Reno Kid. Dadgum! How about that? Where are you from, mister?"

"Oh, over Nevada way."


"Dammit, Parnell!" Smoke grabbed the reins behind the driving bit. "I told you not to go into town wearin' that gun."

"He's the Reno Kid!" Rita shouted, and everybody within hearing range turned and came running. "I just watched him beat two gunnies to the draw and kill them both. Right in front of the Hangout."

Smoke looked at Parnell, shock in his eyes. "You *hit* something? With a pistol?"

"I stubbed my toe. The gun went off. I am not the Reno Kid."

"He ain't the Reno Kid!" Charlie said. "I been knowin' Reno for twenty years."

Parnell turned to Rita. "You see. I told you repeatedly that I am not the Reno Kid."

"Oh, I know *that*, honey. But I sure got everybody's attention, didn't I?" She hopped from the buggy and raced over to Sandi to tell her story.

"Reno changed his name about fifteen years ago and went to ranchin' up near the Idaho border." Charlie cleared it up. "But he shore left a string of bodies while he was gunslingin'."

Smoke turned back to Parnell. "You really got them both?"

"One was hit between the eyes. I'm sure he's dead. The lout called Golden took a round in the stomach. If he isn't dead, he'll certainly be incapacitated for a very long time."

"What the hell is in-capassiated?" Hardrock muttered.

"Beats me," Pistol said. "Sounds plumb awful, though."

Parnell climbed down from the buggy and Corgill led the rig to the barn. Smoke faced the man. "All right, Parnell. You're tagged now. There'll be hundred guns looking for you . . ."

"That is perfectly ridiculous!" Parnell cut in. "I am not the Reno Kid!"

"That don't make no difference," Silver Jim told him. "This time tomorrow the story will be spread fifty miles that the Reno Kid has surfaced and is back on the prowl. By this time next week it'll be all over the territory and they'll be no tellin'

148

how many two-bit punks and would-be gunhawks comin' in to make their rep. By killin' you. Welcome to the club, Schoolteacher," he added bitterly.

Charlie patted Parnell on the back. "You go git out of them town duds, Parnell. The four of us is gonna take you under our wing and teach you how to handle that there Colt."

Parnell stood with his mouth open, unable to speak.

"But Parnell don't sound like no gunfighter's name to me," Silver Jim said. "Where was you born, Parnell?"

"In Iowa. On the Wolf River."

"That's it!" Charlie exclaimed. "You ain't the Reno Kid, so from now on, your handle is Wolf."

"*Wolf!*" Parnell stared at the man. "Have you taken leave of your senses?"

"Nope. Wolf, it is. The Wolf is on the prowl. I like it."

"This is madness!" Parnell yelled.

"Go on now, Wolf," Hardrock told him. "Git you some jeans and boots. Strap on and tie down that hogleg. We'll set up a target range."

"See you in a few minutes, Wolf." Pistol grinned at him.

"This is absurd!" Parnell muttered. He started up the steps, tripped, and fell facedown on the porch. He picked himself up with as much dignity as possible and entered the house.

Charlie shook his head. "We got our work cut out for us, boys."

Golden died that night, cursing the man he believed to be the Reno Kid as he slipped across that dark river. Twenty-four hours later, a dozen men were riding for Gibson, their burning ambition to be the one man who faced the Reno Kid and brought him down. Another twenty-four later, two dozen more punks and tinhorns would be on their way, until those looking to make a reputation by killing the Reno Kid would grow to a hundred. And the news had spread that Smoke Jensen was really in Gibson—nobody had believed it up to now; indeed, many people believed that Smoke Jensen really did not exist, he was such an elusive figure.

Telegraph wires began humming and a dozen big newspapers sent reporters into Montana to cover the story. Within a week, Gibson had a brand-spanking-new hotel and had been added to the stagecoach route.

The stranger from Nevada decided to stay, watching all the fuss with amusement in his eyes, spending most of his time sitting in a chair under the awning in front of the Pussycat.

Dooley had pulled in his men, cussing at all the notoriety and knowing this was no time to enlarge the range war. The hate within the man continued to fester, ready to erupt at any moment, spewing blood and violence all over the area.

Judge Ford was at some sort of conference, out of the state, and would be back in about a month.

"Another good idea shot down," Cord said, disgusted at the news.

Four more saloons had been thrown up in Gibson, along with several more stores, including a gunshop, a dress shop—for a lot of ladies of the evening were coming in—an apothecary shop, and another general store.

A lot had happened in a week.

Thanks to the Reno Kid aka Parnell.


"We found out what was wrong with Wolf not bein' able to shoot worth a damn," Charlie told Smoke.

Smoke closed his eyes for a few seconds and shook his head. "Wolf," he muttered. "What a name. What was wrong with him, Charlie?"

"He's scared of guns! Pistols 'specially."

"Good God! Charlie, there's about a hundred people in Gibson—new people—with one thought in mind: to kill the Reno Kid, real name Parnell, now called Wolf. He's a schoolteacher, Charlie. Not a gunfighter. The poor man is a walking target."

Hardrock grinned. "But we come up with something, Smoke. Lookee here." He held up the ugliest and most awesome-looking rig Smoke had ever seen.

"What in God's name . . . !"

The old gunfighters had taken two double-barreled shotguns and sawed the barrels down to about ten inches long. They had then fashioned a pistol-type butt for the terrible weapons.

"Those things would break a man's arm!" Smoke said, eyeballing the rigs.

"Not Wolf's arm. For a schoolteacher, he's powerful strong. And he's just as fast with these here things as he is with a pistol," Silver Jim said with a nearly toothless grin.

"That's all the booming I been hearing."

"Right! Man, Wolf is plumb awesome with these here things," Pistol said. "We got 'um loaded up with rusty nails and ball-bearin's and raggedly little rocks and the like. We done loaded up near'bouts a case of shells for him. He's ready to go huntin' him a rep."

"Pistol, Parn . . . Wolf doesn't want a rep," Smoke said.

Charlie grinned. "You ain't seen much of him for a week, Smoke. You gonna be ass-tonished at the change. Come on."

Smoke was more than astonished. He didn't even recognize the man. Parnell had grown a mustache, and that had completely changed his appearance. He was dressed all in black, from his hat down to his polished boots. He looked very capable and very tough.

"I gotta see him draw and cock and fire these hand cannons," Smoke said.

"With pleasure, Cousin." Parnell strapped on the weapons.

"You watch this," Charlie said, as Cord and several others gathered around.

Pistol and Silver Jim rolled several full water barrels out and backed away.

"They's a-facin' you, Wolf!" Charlie said, excitement in his voice. "Watch 'um now. Watch they eyes. That'll give 'em away ever time."

Parnell tensed, his hands hovering over the butts of the terrible weapons.

"They's about ready to make their play!" Hardrock called out. "You got to take out the man on your left first, he's the bad one."

"Now!" Silver Jim yelled.

Parnell's right hand dipped and his left hand came across to support the sawed-off shotgun. One barrel exploded in a roar of gunsmoke, the second barrel was shattered as Parnell let loose the second charge. As fast as anything Smoke had ever seen— considering the cumbersome weapons he was using—Parnell dropped the first sawed-off to the ground and drew the left hand shotgun. The third barrel was reduced to splinters.

"I'm impressed," Smoke said.

"I'm proud of you, Brother!" Fae said.

"I love you!" Rita yelled.

Hardrock looked close at Parnell and shook his head. "Furst time I ever seen a wolf blush!"

151

# Twenty-Three

"Feel like trying out the new general store?" Cord asked Smoke.

"I thought you'd never ask. I forgot to pick up some tobacco last time in."

"Ah . . . Parnell wants to go along. I refuse to call him Wolf. I just can't!"

Smoke laughed. "I can't either. Sure, if he wants to come along. I notice he's been in the saddle for the last week. He's turned out to be a pretty good rider."

"Man is full of surprises. And speaking of surprises, I'm told that we're all in for a surprise when we see what's happening, or has happened, to Gibson."

"Yeah. I hear there's even a paper."

"*The Gibson Express.* I want to pick up a copy."

"How about your boys?"

"I ordered them to stay close to their ma. They'll obey me."

"I'll put on a clean shirt and meet you out front."

Cord, Smoke, Parnell, Lujan, Beans, Del, Charlie, and Ring rode into Gibson. A wagon rattled along behind them to carry the supplies back, Cal at the reins. At the edge of town, they reined up and stared in disbelief. The once tiny and sleepy little town was now a full three blocks long and several blocks deep on either side. Many of the new stores were no more than knocked-together sideboards with canvas tops, but it was still a very impressive sight.

"This spells trouble, gentlemen," Lujan said.

"Yeah," Charlie agreed, standing up in his stirrups for a moment. "You bet your boots it does."

"I fail to see how the advancement of civilization, albeit at

152

first glance quite primitive in nature, could be called trouble," Parnell stated.

"That town ain't filled with nothin' but trash," Charlie told him. "Hurdy-gurdy girls, tin-horn hustlers and pimps, two-bit gunslingers, slick-fingered gamblers, and the like. It's dyin' while it seems to be growin'. As soon as this war is settled, one way or the other, ninety-nine percent of them down yonder will pull up stakes and haul their ashes. Town will be right back where it started from."

"How about the one percent that will stay?" Parnell questioned.

"Good point," Charlie agreed. "Wolf, you stay on top of things down yonder in that town. They's gonna be a bunch of people eyeballin' ever move you make. And you gonna get called out. Bet on it."

"I am aware of that," the schoolteacher turned gunfighter said. "I am ready to confront whatever comes my way."

"Me and you, Parnell," Beans said, "will have us a cool beer in one of them new saloons. Check things out."

Parnell glanced at him. "I detest the taste of beer. However, I might have a sarsaparilla."

The Moab Kid returned the glance. "You go sashayin' up in a saloon in the middle of a bunch of hardcases and order sodee pop, Parnell, you better be ready for trouble, 'cause it's shore gonna be comin' at you."

"I am aware of that, too."

"Let's go," Smoke said.

The men rode slowly toward the now-crowded street of the West's newest boom town. The news of their arrival spread as quickly as a prairie fire across dry grass. In less than a minute, the wide street had emptied. No one wanted to be caught in the middle of a gunfight, and that was something that everybody knew might be, probably was, only a careless word away.

As the men rode past the Pussycat, Charlie cut his flint-hard eyes to a stranger sitting on the boardwalk, his chair tilted back. Charlie smiled faintly.

Gonna get real interestin' around here, Charlie thought.

Ring reined up in front of Hans and dismounted. "I shall be visiting Hilda," he told them. "I will come immediately if there is trouble."

Cord, Del, and Cal pulled up in front of the new general store. "Which one of those new joints are you boys going to try?" Cord asked.

"How about Harriet's House?" Parnell asked. "That sounds quite congenial."

"Oh, I'm sure it will be," Beans said. "Harriet always runs a stable out back."

"Well, then, that will be a convenient place for our horses."

"A stable of wimmin, Parnell," Beans told him. "For hire."

"You mean . . . I . . . ladies who sell their . . . ?"

"Right, Parnell."

Smoke dismounted and almost bumped into a small man wearing a derby hat and a checkered vest. The man's head struck Smoke about chest-high.

"Horace Mulroony's the name, sir. Owner and editor of *The Gibson Express.* And you would be Smoke Jensen?"

"That's right."

Horace stuck out his hand and Smoke took it, quickly noticing that the hand was hard and calloused. He cut his eyes just for a flash and saw that the stocky man's hands were thick with calluses around the knuckles. A Cornish boxer sprang into Smoke's mind. Not very tall, but built like a boxcar. Something silently told him that Horace would be hard to handle.

"And your friends, Mister Jensen?"

Smoke introduced the man all around, pointing them out. "Charlie Starr, Lujan, The Moab Kid, Parnell Jensen."

"The man they're calling the Reno Kid."

"I am not the Reno Kid."

"Name's Wolf," Charlie said shortly. He didn't like newspaper people; never wanted any truck with them. They never got anything right and was always meddlin' in other folks' business.

"I see," Horace scribbled in his notebook. "That is quite an unusual affair strapped around your waist, Wolf."

"I would hardly call two sawed-off shotguns an affair, Mister Mulroony. But since this is no time to be discussing proper English usage, I will let your misunderstanding of grammer be excused—for now."

Mulroony laughed with high Irish humor. "You sound like a schoolteacher, Wolf."

"I am."

"Ummm. Are you gentlemen going to have a taste in Miss Harriet's saloon?"

154

"We was plannin' on it," Charlie said. "The sooner the better. All this palaverin' is makin' me thirsty."

"Do you mind if I join you?"

"Could we stop you?" Charlie asked.

"Of course not!" Horace grinned. "After you, Mister Starr." He waved at a man toting a bulky box camera and the man came at a trot. Horace grinned at the gunfighters. "One never knows when a picture might be available. I like to record events for posterity."

Charlie grunted and pushed past the smaller man, but not before he saw the stranger leave his chair in front of the Pussycat and walk across the street, toward the saloon they were entering.

Charlie had a hunch the stranger was thinking about joining the game. He knew from experience that the man was a sucker for the underdog.

The saloon was filled with hardcases, both real and imagined. Smoke's wise and knowing eyes immediately picked out the real gunslingers from the tinhorn punks looking for a reputation.

Smoke knew a few of the hardcases in the room. Several from Dad Estes's gang were sitting at a table. A few that had left Cord's spread were there. A couple of Cat Jennings's bunch were present. They didn't worry Smoke as much as the young tinhorns who were sitting around the saloon, their guns all pearl-handled and fancy-engraved and tied down low.

The known and experienced gunhandlers had stiffened when their eyes touched the awesome rig belted around Parnell's waist. Nobody in their right mind wanted to tangle with a sawed-off shotgun, since a buckshot load at close range would literally tear a man in two. Even if a man could get lead into the shotgun toter first, the odds were, unless the bullet struck him in the brain or the heart, that he could still pull a trigger.

"Beer," Smoke said.

"Tequila," Lujan ordered.

Beans and Charlie opted for whiskey.

Horace ordered beer.

Parnell, true to his word, looked the barkeep in the eyes and ordered sarsaparilla.

Several young punks seated at a nearby table started laughing and making fun of Parnell.

155

Parnell ignored them.

The barkeep served up the orders.

"What's the matter with you, slick?" a young man laughed the question. "Cain't you handle no real man's drink?"

Parnell took a sip of his sarsaparilla and smiled, setting the bottle down on the bar. He turned and looked the young man in the eyes. "Does your mother know where you are, junior?"

The punk's eyes narrowed and he opened his mouth to retort just as the batwings swung open and the stranger entered.

There is an aura about really bad men, and in the West a bad man was not necessarily an outlaw. He was just a bad man to fool with. The stranger walked between the punk and Parnell, his hands hanging loosely at his side. He wore one gun, a classic Peacemaker .45, seven-and-a-half-inch barrel. It was tied down. The man looked to be in his mid-to-late thirties, deeply tanned and very sure of himself. He glanced at Parnell's drink and a very slight smile creased his lips.

Walking to Charlie's side, he motioned to the barkeep. "A sarsaparilla, please."

Another loudmouth sitting with the punk started giggling. "Another sissy, Johnny. You reckon they gonna kiss each other."

"I wouldn't be surprised."

The barkeep served up the stranger's drink and backed away, to the far end of the bar. When they had entered, the bar had been full. Now only the seven of them remained at the long bar.

The stranger lifted his bottle. "A toast to your good health," he said to Charlie.

Charlie lifted his shot glass and clinked it against the bottle. "To your health," he replied. If the man wanted to reveal his real identity. That was up to him. Charlie would hold the secret.

"Hey, old man!" Johnny hollered. "You with them wore-out jeans on."

Charlie sipped his whiskey and then turned to face the mouthy punk. "You talkin' to me, boy?"

"I ain't no boy!"

"No," Charlie said slowly, drawling out the word. "I reckon you ain't. Strappin' on them guns makes you a man. A loudmouth who ain't dry behind the ears yet. And if you keep flappin' them lips at me, you ain't never gonna be dry behind

156

your dirty ears."

Johnny stood up, his face flushed red. "Just who the hell do you think you are, old man?"

"Charlie Starr."

The words were softly offered, but they had all the impact of a hard slap across Johnny's face.

Johnny's mouth dropped open. He closed it and swallowed hard a couple of times. Beads of sweat formed on his forehead.

Charlie spoke, his words cracking like tiny whips. "Sit down, shut your goddamned mouth, or make your play, punk!"

The experienced gunhandlers had noticed first off that the men at the bar had entered with the leather thongs off their hammers.

"You cain't talk to me lak 'at!" Johnny found his voice. But it was trembly and high-pitched.

"I just did, boy."

Johnny abruptly sat down. He tried to pick up his beer mug but his hand was shaking so badly he spilled some of it on the tabletop.

Charlie turned his back to the mouthy punk and picked up his shot glass in his left hand.

But there wasn't a man or woman in the bar who thought it was over. The punk would settle down, gulp a few more drinks to boost his nerve, and would have to try Charlie, or leave town with his tail tucked between his legs.

"Been a long time, Charlie," the stranger said.

"Near'bouts ten years, I reckon. You just passin' through?"

"I was. I decided to stay."

"What name you goin' by nowadays?"

"Same name that got hung on me seventeen-eighteen years ago."

Being a reporter—Charlie would call it being a snoop, among other things—Horace leaned around and asked, "And what name is that, sir?"

The stranger turned around, facing the crowd of punks and tinhorns, loudmouths and barflys, hurdy-gurdy girls, gamblers, and gunfighters, who were all straining to listen. He let his eyes drift around the room. "I never did like a lopsided fight, Charlie. You recall that, I suppose." It was not posed in question form.

"I allow as to how I do. I 'member the time me and you

157

stood up to a whole room filled to the rafters with trash and cleaned it out." He chuckled. "That there was a right good fight." Charlie held up his shot glass in salute and the stranger clinked his sarsaparilla bottle to the glass.

"I got my other gun in my kit over to the roomin' house. I reckon I best go on over and get it and strap it on. Looks like we got some house-cleanin' to do."

"I couldn't agree more."

Smoke was smiling, nursing his beer. He'd already figured out who the stranger was.

One of Cat Jennings's men lifted his leg and broke wind. "That's what I think about you, stranger."

"How rude!" Parnell said.

"Sissy-pants," the man who had made the coarse social comment stood up. "I think I'll just kill you. 'Cause I don't believe you're the Reno Kid."

"Of course, he isn't," the stranger said. "I am!"

# Twenty-Four

That news broke the spirit of a couple of men who had already been toying with the idea of rattling their hocks. They stood up and walked toward the door. Charlie Starr and them old gray-headed he-cougars with him was bad enough. Add the Moab Kid and Lujan to that mixture and you was stirrin' nitro too fast with a flat stick. Smoke Jensen was the fastest gun in the West. Now here comes the Reno Kid, and there goes anybody with a lick of sense.

The batwings squeaked and two gunnies were gone.

The gunhand facing Parnell didn't back down. Without taking his eyes from Parnell, he said, "Did anybody pull your chain, Reno?"

"Nope," Reno answered easily.

"You gonna fight Sissy-pants' battles for him?"

"Nope."

"You ready to die, Sissy-pants?"

"Oh, I think not." Parnell had turned, facing the man, his right hand hovering near the butt of the holstered sawed-off. "But I do have a question?"

"Ax it!"

"What is your name?"

"Readon. What's it to you?"

"I just wondered what to have carved on the marker over your grave."

"Draw, damn your eyes!" the man shouted, and grabbed for his six-gun.

Parnell was calm and quick. Up came the awesome weapon, the right side hammer eared back. Across went his left hand in a practiced move, gripping the short barrels. The range was no

159

more than twelve feet and the booming was enormous in the beery, smoky room. The ball-bearings and rusty nails and ragged rocks hit the gunhand in the belly and lifted him off his boots while the charge was tearing him apart. He landed on a table several feet away from where he had been standing, smearing the tabletop with crimson and collapsing the table. He had never even cleared leather.

The hurdy-gurdy girls began squalling like hogs caught in barbed wire and ran from the room, their short dresstails flapping as they ran.

Parnell, seeing that no one was going to immediately take up the fight, but sensing that was only seconds away, broke open the shotgun pistol and tossed aside the empty, loading it up full. He snapped it shut and eared back both hammers.

The gunhand Smoke had first seen at that little store down on the Boulder stood up. "Me and Readon had become pals, Jensen," Dunlap said. "You a friend of that shotgun-toter, so that makes you my enemy. I think I'll just kill you."

He grabbed for his guns.

Smoke shot Dunlap in the chest just as his hands gripped the butts of his guns. Dunlap looked puzzled for a moment, coughed up blood, and sat down in the chair he should never have gotten out of. He slowly put his head on the tabletop and sighed as that now-familiar ghost rider came galloping up, took a look around, and grinned in a macabre fashion. He decided to stick around. Things were quite lively in this little town.

The ghost rider put a bony hand on another's shoulder as half the men in the barroom grabbed for iron and Lujan shot one between the eyes.

Mulroony jumped behind the bar and landed on top of the barkeep who was already on the floor. He'd been a bartender in too many western towns not to know where the safest place was.

Parnell's sawed-off shotgun-pistol roared again, the charge knocking two gunnies to the floor. Johnny picked that time to make his move. Just as he was reaching for his guns, Parnell stepped the short distance as he was reversing the weapon. Using it like a club, he hit Johnny in the mouth. Teeth flew in several directions and Johnny was out cold. Parnell dropped to the floor and once more loaded up.

The Reno Kid was crouched by the bar, coolly and carefully picking his shots.

160

Charlie had dropped two before a bullet took him in the shoulder and slammed him against the bar. He did a fast border-roll with his six-gun and kept on banging. When his gun was empty, Lujan grabbed the older man and literally slung him over the bar, out of the line of fire.

The Moab Kid took a round in the leg and the leg buckled under him, dropping him to the floor, his face twisted in pain.

But it was Parnell who was dishing out the most death and destruction. Firing and loading as fast as he could, the schoolteacher did the most to clear out the room and end the fighting.

The gunnies and tinhorns gave it up, one by one dropping their still-smoking six-guns and raising their hands in the air. Cord, Del, Ring, and Cal stepped through the batwings, pistols drawn and cocked, Ring with his double-barrel express gun.

"Get Doc Adair," Smoke said, his voice husky from the thick gunsmoke in the saloon.

Cal was gone at a bow-legged trot to fetch the doctor.

Lujan helped Charlie to a chair. The front of the old gunslinger's shirt was soaked with blood.

"Did I get the old bassard?" a gunhawk moaned the question from the floor. He had taken half a dozen rounds in the chest and stomach and death was standing over him, ready to take him where the fires were hot and the company not the best.

"You got lead in me," Charlie admitted. "But I'm a long ways from accompanyin' you."

"If not today, then some other time. So I'll see you in hell, Starr," the gunny grinned the words, his mouth bloody. He started to add something but the words would not form on his tongue. His eyes rolled back in his head and he mounted up behind the ghost rider.

Smoke had reloaded. He stood by the bar, his hands full of Colts, his eyes watching the gunnies who had chosen to give up the fight.

Johnny moaned on the floor and rolled over on his stomach, one hand holding his busted mouth. The other hand went to his right hand gun. But it was gone.

"Are you looking for these?" Parnell asked, holding out the punk's guns in his left hand. His right hand was full of twelve gauge sawed-off blaster.

Johnny mumbled something.

"You're diction is atrocious," Parnell told him. He looked at Smoke and smiled. "My, Cousin, but for a few moments, it was quite exhilarating."

Smoke grinned and shook his head. "Yeah, it was, Parnell. I'll stand shoulder-to-shoulder with you anytime, Cousin."

Mulroony had crawled from behind the bar and waved his photographer in. The man set up his bulky equipment and sprinkled the powder in the flashpan. "Smile, everyone!" he hollered, then popped his shot, adding more smoke to the already eye-smarting air.

Beans had cut his jeans open to inspect the wound, and it was a bad one. "Leg's busted," he said tightly. "Looks like I'm out of it."

The flashpan popped again, the lenses taking in the bloody sprawl of bodies and the line of gunhawks standing against a wall, their hands in the air, their weapons piled on a table.

While Doc Adair tended to Charlie and Beans, Smoke faced the surrendered gunhandlers. His eyes were as cold as chips of ice and his words flint-hard.

"You're out of it. Get on your horses and ride. If I see any of you in this area again, I'll kill you! No questions asked. I'll just shoot you. And no, you don't pack your truck, you don't get your guns, you don't draw your pay—you ride! Now! Move!"

They needed no further instrucitons. They all knew there would be another time, another place, another showdown time. They rushed the batwings and rattled their hocks, leaving in a cloud of dust.

"You tore up my place!" a woman squalled, stepping out of a back room.

"Howdy, Harriet," Beans called. "Right nice to see you again."

"You!" she hollered. "I might have known it'd be you, Moab." Her eyes flicked to the Reno Kid. "You back gunhandlin', Reno?"

"I reckon."

She looked at Smoke. Took in his rugged good looks and heavy musculature. "Remember me, big boy?"

"I remember you, Harriet. You were one of the smart ones who left Fontana early."

"Did you kill Tilden Franklin?"

"I sure did."

"Man ever deserved killin', that one did. You gonna run me

162

out of Gibson?"

"I didn't run you out of Fontana, Harriet."

"For a fact. See you around, baby." She turned and pushed through a door.

"He can't sit a saddle," Adair said, standing up from working on Beans's leg. "And I'd rather he didn't for a few days." The doctor pointed to Charlie.

"I'll put some hay in the wagon," Cal said, and left the saloon.

The undertaker and his helper, both of them trying very hard to keep from smiling, entered the saloon and walked among the dead and dying, pausing at each body to go through the pockets.

"Does I get my guns back?" Johnny pushed the words through mashed lips and broken teeth.

Parnell looked at Smoke. Smoke nodded his head. "Give them to the punk. He'd just find some more. One of us is gonna have to kill him sooner or later."

The flashpan belched once again.

"What a story this will make!" Horace chortled, rocking back and forth on his feet. "I shall dispatch it immediately to New York City."

"Do try to be grammatically correct," Parnell reminded him.

Horace gave him a smile. A very thin smile.


Sandi hollered and bawled and carried on something fierce when she saw Beans in the back of the wagon but then brightened up considerably when she realized he'd be laid up for several weeks and she could nurse him.

Reno had checked out of his room and rode back to the Circle Double C with the men. He had strapped on his other Peacemaker and was in the fight to the finish.

Charlie bitched about having to be bedded down in the main house so the ladies could take proper care of his wound. Hardrock told him to shet his mouth and think about what a relief it would be to the others not to have to look at his ugly face for a spell.

"It works both ways," Charlie popped back, smiling as the ladies fussed over him.

Parnell had taken a slight bullet burn on his left arm. But the way Rita acted a person would have thought he'd been riddled. She insisted on spoon-feeding him some hot soup she fixed—just for him.

"What did we accomplish?" Cord asked Smoke.

"Damn little," he admitted. "Seems like every time we run off or kill a gunhawk, there's ten to step up, taking his place."

Cord added some more numbers in his tally book and shook his head at the growing number of dead and wounded. "Why did the Reno Kid toss in with us, Smoke? Charlie says he's married, with several children."

"So am I," Smoke reminded the man.

Something good did come out of the gunfight inside Harriet's saloon: many of the hangers-on decided to pull out; the fight was getting too hot for many of the tin-horn and would-be gunfighters. They'd go back to their daddy's farms and be content to milk the cows and gather the eggs, their guns hanging on a peg.

But it left the true hardcases, many of them on no one's payroll. Like buzzards, they were waiting to see the outcome and perhaps pick up a few crumbs of the pie.

Johnny and his punk sidekick, Bret, were still in town, swaggering around, hanging on the fringes of the known gunslingers, talking rough and tough and lapping up the strong beer and rotgut and snake-head whiskey served at most of the newer saloons.

Crime had increased in Gibson, with foot-padders and petty thieves plying their trade on the unsuspecting men and women who had to venture out after dark. And the hardcases were getting surly and hard to handle, craving action.

There were several minor run-ins among the gunhawks, provoked by recklessness and restlessness and booze and the urge to kill and destroy. The leaders of the gangs had to step in and calm the situation, reminding the outlaws that their fight was not with each other, but with the Double Circle C.

"Then gawddammit!" Lodi snarled. "Let's *make war* on them!"

The Hangout, jammed full of hired guns, shook with the roars of approval.

Dad Estes did his best to shout his boys down while Jason Bright and Cat Jennings and Lanny Ball tried to calm their people.

They were only half successful.

The leaders looked at each other and shrugged their shoulders. Dad jerked his head toward the boardwalk and the men stomped outside, to stand in the night.

"We got to use them or lose them," Dad summed it up. "My boys ain't gonna stand around here much longer twiddlin' their thumbs."

The others agreed with Dad.

"So you got some sort of a plan, Dad?"

"We hit them, tonight."

"What does Dooley have to say about that?" Jason asked.

"I ain't discussed it with him."

The others smiled, Dad continuing, "Look here, we could turn this into a right nice town, and if we was all big land owners, why, we'd also own the sheriff and deputies and the like."

"We got to kill Dooley and them first," he was reminded by Cat Jennings.

Dad shifted his chewing tobacco to the other side of his mouth. He took out an ornate pocket watch and clicked it open. "Well, boys, I got some people doin' that little thing in about an hour."

# Twenty-Five

Dooley came awake, keeping his eyes closed. The slight creaking of the hall door had brought him awake. He had drank himself to sleep, sitting in the big chair just inside the living room. The first time he'd ever done that. Now wide awake, he sat very still in the darkness and opened his eyes.

"I tole you to oil that door!" his oldest boy, Sonny, hissed the words.

"Shet your mouth," Bud whispered. "The old fool was prob'ly so drunked up when he went to bed a shotgun blast wouldn't wake him up."

Conrad giggled. "A shotgun blast is what we're goin'give him!"

Cold insane fury washed over the father as he froze still in his chair. If he'd had a gun in his hand, he'd have killed all three of them right this minute. But his gun belt was hanging on the peg in the hall.

Sonny shushed his brothers. "Stay here and keep watch, Conrad. Me and Bud will do the deed."

"I don't wanna keep no watch! I wanna see it when the buckshot hits him. And what the hell is I gonna be watchin' for anyways? There ain't nobody here but us. The others is all back in town."

"Do what I tell you to do."

Dooley carefully drew his feet up under the chair, hiding them from view should any of his traitorous offspring look into the living room. The sorry sons of bitches.

The dark humor and irony of that thought almost caused him to chuckle.

166

The stillness of the house was shattered by twin shotgun blasts.

Then he remembered he hadn't made up his bed from the past night; the pillows and covers must have fooled the boys into thinking their dad was lying in bed.

Boots ran up the hall. "Got the old nut-brain!" Sonny shouted. "The ranch is ourn. Let's go join the other boys and finish the deed."

The front door slammed shut.

What deed? Dooley thought.

The thunder of hooves hammered past the house. Dooley moved to the window and watched his bastard sons gallop out of sight.

That damn Cord put them up to this! Dooley's fevered brain quickly reached that conclusion. He jerked on his boots and ran into the hall, pausing to yank his gun belt from the peg and belt it around his waist. He ran to the kitchen and filled a gunnybag with cans of food, a side of bacon, some hardtack. He took a big canteen and filled that at the kitchen pump. Then he ran to the study and quickly opened his safe, stuffing a money belt full of cash money he'd just received from the army cattle buyer. He belted the money bag around his middle. In his bedroom, he rolled up some clothes in a blanket and slipped out the back of the house, stopping only once, to fill his pockets with .44 rounds and pick up a small coffeepot and skillet.

Dooley saddled a horse and stuffed the saddlebags full of supplies. He hung the canteen and bag on the saddle horn and took off into the timber of the Little Belt Mountains. When his boys come back, they'd find that what they'd shot was only a bed, and they'd come lookin' to kill their pa.

"Come on, you miserable whelps," Dooley muttered, talking to his horse. His best horse. His favorite horse. Dooley could sleep in the saddle and his horse would never falter. The horse also knew where Dooley was going as soon as Dooley guided the way toward the old Indian trail that wound in a circuitous route to the base of Old Baldy, the highest peak in the Little Belts, which ran for some forty miles from southeast of Great Falls to the Musselshell. Dooley and his horse had come here often, just to think—to let the hate fester over the past few years.

"Goddamn you, Cord," Dooley muttered. "You heped take

167

my woman from me and now you done turned my sons agin me. I'm a-gonna kill ever' one of you. Ever' stinkin' one of you!"

"Here they come!" the shout from Smoke was only seconds before the mass of riders entered the Circle Double C ranch complex. But it was enough to roust everybody out of bed.

Smoke's shout was followed by a war whoop from Hardrock that echoed across the draws and hollows and grazing land of the ranch.

"Hep me clost to that winder." Charlie told Parnell. "I'll take it from there. I can shoot jist as good with my left hand as I can with my right."

Across the hall, Beans told Sandi, "Get some help and shove my bed to that window and hand me my rifle. Then you and Rita get on the floor."

The girls positioned the bed and reached for their own rifles.

"Cain't you wimmin take orders?" Beans asked over the thunder of hooves.

"We stand by our men," Sandi told him. "Now shut up and shoot!"

"Yes, dear," Beans said, just as a bullet from an outlaw's gun knocked a pane of glass out of the window.

Before Beans could sight the rider in, Parnell's sawed-off blaster roared, the charge lifting the man out of the saddle and hurling him to the ground, his chest and throat a bloody mess.

"Give 'em hell, baby!" Rita shouted her approval.

"You curb that vulgar tongue, woman!" Parnell glared at her.

"Yes, dear," Rita muttered.

From the bunkhouse, Ring was deadly with a rifle, knocking two out of the saddle before a round misfired and jammed the action. Ring turned just as a man was crawling in through a rear window. Reversing the Winchester, Ring used the rifle like a club and smashed the outlaw on the forehead with the butt. The sound of a skull cracking was evident even over the hard lash of gunfire. Ring grabbed up the man's Colts and moved to a window. He wasn't very good with a pistol, but he succeeded in filling the night with a lot of hot lead and made the evening very uncomfortable for a number of outlaws.

Smoke and the Reno Kid had grabbed up rifles and

bandoleers of ammunition and raced to the barn and corral, knowing that if the outlaws succeeded in stampeding their horses they were doomed. Reno climbed into the loft, with Jake and Corgill. Fitz, Willie, and Ol' Cook stayed below, while Smoke and Gage remained outside, behind watering troughs by the corral.

The outlaw, Hartley, who was wanted for murder down in the Oklahoma Nations, tried to rope the corral gates and bring them down. Smoke leveled his pistol and the hammer fell on an empty chamber. Running to the man, Smoke jerked him off his horse and smashed the man in the face with a balled right fist, then a left to the man's jaw. He jerked Hartley's pistol from leather and rapped the outlaw on the head-bone with it. Hartley lay still in the dirt.

Smoke stuck both of Hartley's pistols behind his belt, reloaded his own .44's, and climbed onto Hartley's horse, a big dun. He would see how the outlaws liked the fight taken to them.

Smoke charged right into the middle of the confusing dust-filled fray. He saw the young punk gunslick Twain and shot him out of the saddle, one of Twain's boots caught in the stirrup. Twain's horse bolted, dragging the wounded and screaming young punk across the yard. His screaming stopped when his head impacted against a tree stump.

Smoke stayed low in the saddle, offering as little target as possible for the outlaws' guns. He slammed the horse's shoulder into an outlaw's leg. The gunny screamed in pain from his bruised leg and then began screaming in earnest as the horse lost its balance and fell on him, breaking the outlaw's other leg. The horse scrambled to its feet, the steel-shod hooves ripping and tearing flesh and breaking the outlaw's bones.

Cat Jennings rammed his big gelding into Smoke's horse and knocked Smoke to the ground. Rolling away from the hooves of the panicked horse, Smoke jumped behind a startled outlaw, stuck a pistol into the man's side, and pulled the trigger. Shoving the wounded man out of the saddle, Smoke slipped into the saddle, grabbed up the reins, and put his spurs to the animal's sides, turning the horse, trying to get a shot at Cat.

But the man was as elusive and quick as his name implied, fading into the milling confusion and churning dust. Smoke leveled his pistol at Ben Sabler and missed him clean as the man wheeled his horse. The bullet slammed into another out-law. The outlaw was hard-hit, but managed to stay in the saddle and gallop out of the fight.

"Back! Back!" Lanny Ball screamed, his voice faint in the booming and spark-filled night. "Fall back and surround the place."

Smoke tried to angle for a shot at Lanny and failed. Jumping off his horse, Smoke rolled behind a tree in the front yard of the main house, and with a .44 in each hand, emptied the guns into the backs of the fast-retreating outlaws. He saw several jerk in their saddles as hot lead tore into flesh and one man fell, the back of his head bloody.

Smoke ran to the house. Jumping on the front porch, he saw the body of Willie, draped over the porch railing. On the other side of the porch, Holman was sprawled, a bloody hole in his forehead.

"Damn!" Smoke cursed, just as Cord pushed open the screen door and stepped out.

Cord's face was grim as he looked at the body of Willie. "Been with me a long time," the rancher said. "He was a good hand. Loyal to the end."

"Man can't ask for a better epitaph," Smoke said. "Cord, you take the barn and I'll run to the bunkhouse. Tell the men to fortify their positions and fill up every canteen and bucket they can find." He cut his eyes as Liz and Alice came onto the porch. "You ladies start cooking. The men are going to need food and lots of it. We might be pinned down here for days."

Cord said, "I'll have some boys gather up all the guns and ammo from the dead. Pass them around." He stepped off the porch and trotted into the night.

"Larry!" Smoke called, and the hand turned. "Get the horses out of the corral and into the barn. Find as much scrap lumber as you can and fortify their stalls against stray lead."

The cowboy nodded and ran toward the corral, hollering for Dan to join him.

Smoke and Parnell carried the bodies of Holman and Willie away from the house, placing them under a tree; the shade would help as the sun came up. The men covered them with blankets and secured the edges with rocks.

Snipers from out in the darkness began sending random rounds into the house and the outbuildings, forcing everyone to seek shelter and stay low.

"This is going to be very unpleasant," Parnell said, lying on

170

the ground until the sniping let up and he could get back to the house.

"Wait until the sun comes up and the temperature starts rising," Smoke told him. "Our only hope is that cloud buildup." He looked upward. "If it starts raining, I plan on heading into the timber and doing some head-hunting. The rain will cover any sound."

"Do you think prayer would help?" Parnell said, only half joking.

"It sure wouldn't hurt."


There were seven dead outlaws, and all knew at least that many more had been wounded; some of them were hard-hit and would not live.

But among their own, Corgill and Pat had been wounded. Their wounds were painful, but not serious. They could still use a gun, but with difficulty.

Smoke and Cord got together just after first light and talked it out, tallying it up. They were badly outnumbered, facing perhaps a hundred or more experienced gunhandlers, and the defenders' position was not the best.

They had plenty of food and water and ammunition, but all knew if the outlaws decided to lie back and snipe, eventually the bullets would seek them out one by one. The house was the safest place, the lower floor being built mostly of stone. The bunkhouse was also built of stone. The wounded had been moved from the upstairs to the lower floor. Beans, with his leg in a cast, could cover one window. Charlie Starr, the old warhoss, had scoffed off his wound and dressed, his right arm in a sling, but with both guns strapped around his lean waist.

"I've hurt myself worser than this by fallin' out of bed," he groused.

Parnell had gathered up a half dozen shotguns and loaded them up full, placing them near his position. The women had loaded up rifles and belted pistols around their waists.

Silver Jim almost had an apoplectic seizure when he ran from the bunkhouse to the main house and put his eyes on the women, all of them dressed in men's britches, stompin' around in boots, six-guns strapped around their waists. He opened his mouth and closed it a half dozen times before he could manage to speak. Shielding his eyes from the sight of women all dressed up like men, with their charms all poked out ever'

171

whichaway, he turned his beet-red face to Cord and found his voice.

"Cain't you do something about that! It's plumb indecent!"

"I tried. My wife told me that if we had to make a run for it, it would be easier sittin' a saddle dressed like this."

"Astride!" Silver Jim was mortified.

"I reckon," Cord said glumly.

"Lord have mercy! Things keep on goin' like this, wimmin'll be gettin' the vote 'for it's over."

"Probably," Parnell said, one good eye on Rita. There was something to be said about jeans, but he kept that thought to himself.

"Wimmin a-voting'?" Silver Jim breathed.

"Certainly. Why shouldn't they? They've been voting down in Wyoming for years."

The old gunfighter walked away, muttering. He met Charlie in the hall. "What's the matter, that bed get too much for you?"

"'Bout to worry me to death. Layin' in there under the covers with nothing on but a nightgown and wimmin comin' and goin' without no warning. More than a body can stand."

"Where are you fixin on shootin' from?"

"I best stay here with these folks. Come the night they'll be creepin' in on us."

"Gonna rain in about an hour. My bones is talkin' to me."

"Then Smoke is gonna be goin' headhuntin'. Preacher taught him well. He'll take out a bunch."

"You reckon some of us ought to go with him?"

"Nope. You know Smoke, he likes to lone-wolf it."

"He's been diggin' in his war bag and he's all dressed up in buckskin, right down to his moccasins. He was sittin' on a bunk, sharpenin' his knife when I left."

Charlie's grin was hard. "Them gunhandlers is gonna pay in blood this afternoon. Bet on that, old hoss."

"Who's gonna pay in blood?" Cord asked, walking up to the men.

"Them mavericks out yonder. Smoke's fixin' to go lookin' for scalps come the rain."

"Sounds dangerous to me," the rancher shook his head.

Silver Jim laughed. "Oh, it will be." He jerked his thumb toward the hills. "For them out there."

172

# Twenty-Six

The sky darkened and lightning began dancing around the high mountains of the Little Belt, thunder rolling ominously. Then the sky opened and began dumping torrents of rain. With his rifle slung over his shoulder with a strap, hanging barrel down, and his buckskin shirt covering his six-guns and a long-bladed Bowie knife sheathed, Smoke slipped out into the rain on moccasin-clad feet. He kept low to the ground, utilizing every bit of natural cover he came to. He moved swiftly but carefully and made the timber and brush without drawing a shot.

Once in the brush, he paused, studying every area in his field of vision before moving out. He had shifted his long-bladed knife to just behind his right hand .44.

He froze still as a mighty oak at the sound of voices. Clad in buckskins, with the timber dark and gloomy as twilight, Smoke would be hard to spot unless he was right on top of a man.

And he was just about was!

"I shore wants me a crack at that Sandi McCorkle," the voice came to him very clear, despite the driving rain and gusts of wind.

"We'll use all them pretty gals 'fore we kill them," a second voice was added. "You see anything movin' down yonder?"

"Naw. They all shet up in the buildings."

"I be back, Tabor. I got to . . ." His words were drowned out by a clap of thunder. ". . . Must have been somethang I et."

Slowly Smoke sank down behind a bush as a red-and-white checkered shirt stood and began moving toward him. The pair must be Tabor and Park. Two thoroughly tough men. When Park passed the bush, Smoke rose up like a brown fog. His

173

Bowie in his right hand. He separated Park's head from his shoulders with one hard slash, catching the headless body before it could come crashing to the ground and alert Tabor.

Easing the body to the wet earth, Smoke picked up the head and placed it in a gunnybag he'd tucked behind his belt.

Then he went looking for Tabor.

Circling around to come in behind the Oklahoma outlaw, Smoke laid his bloody-bottomed sack down on a rock and Injuned up to Tabor, coming in slowly and making no sound.

Tabor never knew what happened. The big-bladed and heavy knife flashed in the stormy light and another head plopped to the earth. That went in the sack with Park's head.

Smoke moved on through the rain and spots of fog that clung low to the ground, swirling around his moccasined feet, as silent as his footsteps.

Someone very close to him began firing—not at Smoke, for at the sound of the hammer being eared back, Smoke had bellied on the gound—but at the house. More guns were added to the barrage and Smoke added his .44 to the manmade thunder, his bullet striking a gunman in the head.

"Hey!" a man shouted, his voice just audible over the roar of rifles. "Pete's hit!" He stood up, an angry look on his face, sure that someone on his side was getting careless.

Smoke shot him between the eyes and the man fell back with a thud that only Smoke could feel as he lay on the ground.

Smoke worked his way back into the timber, climbing up the hill as he moved. Behind a thick stand of timber, he paused for a break and squatted down, the bloody sack beside him. He hadn't made up his mind what to do with the heads, but an idea was formed.

He ate a biscuit and cupped his hands for a drink of rainwater. He did not have one ounce of remorse or regret for what he was doing. He knew only too well that to fight the lawless, one must get down and wallow in the muck and the crud and the filth with them, using the same tactics, or worse, that they would use against an innocent. To win a battle, one must understand the enemy.

Rested, Smoke moved out, staying above the positions of the outlaws. He circled wide, wanting to hit them at widely separated spots, wanting them to know they had not been alone and had been attacked by someone who had walked among them with the stealth of a ghost.

A hard burst of gunfire came from the house, the bullets hitting the rocks and the rain-soaked earth several hundred feet below Smoke's position. As the outlaws returned the fire, Smoke leveled his Winchester and counted more coup, his fire covered by the outlaw's own noise. The lone outlaw—Smoke did not know his name and did not recall ever seeing him before—slumped forward, his rifle sliding from lifeless hands, a bloody hole in the man's back.

Smoke slipped down to the man's position and left the bloody bag of heads by the dead man's side. He added his ammunition to that he'd gathered from the others and moved on.

He had planned on sticking the heads up on poles but decided this way would be just as effective.

He continued his circling, which would eventually bring him out on the north end of the ranch complex. He caught just a glimpse of the Hanks boys. Bellying down, he started working his way to their position, freezing log-still as two gunslicks, wearing canvas ponchos, stepped out of the timber and headed in his direction. They were so sure of themselves they were not expecting any trouble and were not checking their surroundings. Smoke could catch only a few of the words that passed between them.

". . . Never thought them boys would do it . . ."

". . . Didn't like my old man, but I don't think I'd have had the . . . kill him with a shotgun."

". . . Be gettin' ripe layin' up in that bed . . . Sonny pulled the trigger, I reckon."

". . . All three of um's crazy as a bessy-bug."

The outlaws moved out of earshot and Smoke lay for a moment, putting some sense into what he'd heard. The Hanks boys had killed their father with a shotgun, probably as he lay sleeping in bed.

Smoke broke off his head-hunting and began making his way back to the ranch. If the news was true, and he had no reason to doubt it, for the Hanks boys were as goofy as their father, that meant that part of the outlaws' plans had been accomplished. And everyone at the Circle Double C had to die for the outlaws' planned takeover to succeed.

Smoke moved quickly, always staying in the brush and timber. As he was approaching the ranch complex, he heard a horrified shout from the hills and knew that the bag of heads

175

had been found . . . either that or the headless bodies of the outlaws.

Smoke began moving cautiously, for at this point he was open to fire from either side. Closer to the house, he began a meadowlark's call. Charlie waited for a moment and then returned the call. When a human gives a birdcall, a practiced ear can pick up the subtle difference, no matter how good the caller is.

Smoke ran the last few hundred feet, zigging and zagging to offer a hard target. But if the outlaws saw him, they did not fire; probably they were too busy searching the ridges for the unknown headhunter. On the back porch, Liz and Alice had towels for him, a change of clothes—Cord's long underwear and jeans and shirt—and a mug of coffee, for Smoke was soaked and cold.

Smoke broke the news to a horrified audience.

Liz shook her head but shed no tears for her husband or sons. And neither did Rita.

"Killed their own father!" Cord was visibly shaken by the news. "Good God!"

Parnell was the first to put the upcoming horror into words. "Then we—all of us—have to die if their plans are to succeed."

The women looked at each other. They knew that for them, it would not be a quick bullet. They would be used, and used badly, until the outlaws tired of them. Only then would death bring relief.

"Reno comin' at a run," Charlie said, looking out the window. "He's been out eyeballin' the situation close to home."

The gunfighter was as soaked as Smoke had been. The women shooed him into a room and handed him towels and dry clothing. When he emerged, they had coffee waiting for him.

He took a gulp of the strong hot coffee. "They blocked off the road leading south and have men waiting in the passes. They have so many men it was no problem to seal us off. Any bust-out is gonna be difficult, if not downright impossible."

"And walking out will be tough with the wounded," Smoke added. "But if we stay here, they'll eventually overrun us by their number. Or they'll burn the buildings down around us. Beans is gonna have to be carried out of here. Pat and Corgill can walk out with him. I'm going to suggest that the women leave with them." He looked at Parnell. "Parnell, you and Gage, Del and Bernie will spell each other with the litter. Me and Reno will make the litter right now. You people pack some food and blankets; make a light backpack and get ready to move out at dark. Let's do it."

All knew that Smoke had casually but deliberately chosen the men to accompany the women. Then he irritated the hell out of Charlie Starr by suggesting that he accompany the foot party.

"I'll be damned if I will!" the old gunfighter flared up.

"Charlie . . .," Smoke put a hand on his friend's shoulder. "They need you. They need your experience in guiding them and they need your gun."

"Well . . ." Charlie calmed down. "If you put it that way. All right. But I hate like hell to miss out on this here fight."

"Damned ol' rooster with a busted wing." Hardrock told him. "You look after them folks, now, you hear me, you old coot?"

"I've told them to head for the old Fletcher gold mine in the Big Belt," Cord said. "It's been abandoned for years and we cache supplies there. From there, they can angle back East and make it into Gibson. But it's gonna be a long hard haul for them all."

"You just get me in a saddle!" Beans groused. "I ain't never seen the day I couldn't sit on a hurricane deck."

"Oh, hush up!" Lujan told him. "Just lay back and enjoy the trip. Amigo, you injure that leg again, and you'll be a cripple for the rest of your life. It's better this way and you know it."

Beans did some fancy cussing, but finally agreed to shut up about it and accept his fate.

Smoke pulled Cord to one side. "How do you feel about leaving your ranch to those jackals out there on the ridges?"

"I don't like it. But I think it's gonna happen. See if my plan agrees with yours: We give them walkin' out a full twenty-four hours. Then we saddle up, put sacks on the horses' hooves, and lead them out a'ways. Then we all hit one spot just as hard as we can."

"That's it. We'll get the foot party moving just after dark and pray that this rain doesn't let up. They're going to be wet

177

and cold and miserable, but I think they've got more of a chance out there than staying here."

Cord nodded his big head. "I'll pass the word to the hands. You sure you don't want a diversion?"

"No. That would be a sure tipoff that we're up to something. Anyway, I think they'll hit us at full dark. That'll be enough."

The afternoon wore on with only a few shots being exchanged from each side. Those in the house knew that the outlaws would be cold, soaking wet, miserable, and their patience would be growing thin with each sodden hour that passed.

And those in the ranch compound also knew, some more than others, that after finding the sack of bloody heads and several more of their kind shot to death, most of the outlaws would be wanting revenge in the worst sort of way, for they would know it had been Smoke stalking them silently on the ridges.

Smoke looked out onto the gray dripping afternoon. Twenty-four hours. They had to hold out for twenty-four hours.

Reno seemed to read his thoughts. "We'll hold, Smoke. Some of them might breech the house, but it'll be a death trap for them. One thing in our favor, they damn sure can't burn the place down . . . at least not this night."

"From the outside," Smoke stuck an amendment to that. "A couple of torches tossed inside, though . . ."

Cord heard it. "I've got some lumber out in the shed. Rock, Troy, you boys fetch the lumber while we get some nails and hammers. We'll board up windows we're not shooting from. On both levels of the house." He began ripping down curtains and drapes to lessen the fire hazard.

As the sounds of the muffled hammering began drifting to the outlaws on the ridges, the gunfire picked up, forcing the men to work more carefully, without exposing themselves. Those inside the house didn't have to worry about breaking a window with all the hammering; all the windows were already shot out.

Those windows not being used as shooters' positions boarded up, Smoke went to find Fae.

He put his arm around her shoulders and kissed her cheek. "I'm headin' back outside, Fae. I like to be outside when the action goes down." He looked at the other women. "You ladies watch your step this night. We'll see you all in a couple of days."

He shook hands with the men who were leaving that night. "You boys enjoy your stroll. As soon as it gets full dark, take off. And good luck."

He walked back into the living room, leaving Cord to say his goodbyes to wife and daughter.

"I'm going to pull Ring and Hardrock, Silver Jim, and Pistol in the house with you and Cord and the boys," he told Reno. "The rest of us will be in the bunkhouse and the barn." He looked outside. "Be dark shortly. I'm heading out yonder. The others will be showing up one at a time about five minutes apart. Good luck tonight."

"Luck to you, Smoke."

There was nothing left to say. The two famed gunhandlers looked at each other, nodded their heads, and Smoke slipped out onto the stone and wood porch. He knew the chances of his being seen from several hundred yards away were practically nonexistent, but he stayed low from force of habit.

Smoke darted off the porch and to a tree in the yard, then over the fence and a foot race to the corral. Then, as he got set for the run to the bunkhouse, a cold voice spoke from behind him.

"I'll be known as the man who kilt Smoke Jensen. Die, you meddlin' bastard!"

# Twenty-Seven

Smoke threw himself to one side just as the pistol roared. He could feel the heat of the bullet as it passed his arm. He twisted his body in the air and hit the muddy ground with a .44 in his hand, the muzzle spitting fire and smoke and lead.

Hartley took the first slug in his chest and Smoke fired again, the force of his landing lifting his gun hand, the second slug striking the gunhawk in the throat. Hartley, with a knot plainly visible on his rain-slicked head, the hair matted down, leaned up against a corral rail and lifted his six-gun, savage all the way to the grave.

A .44-.40 roared from the bunkhouse and Spring's aim was true. Hartley's head ballooned from the impact of the slug and he pitched forward, into a horse trough.

Riflemen from the ridges and the hills opened up, not really sure what they were shooting at, but filling the air with lead. Smoke lay where he was, as safe there as anywhere in the open expanse between house and bunkhouse. When the fire from the outlaws slacked up, Smoke scrambled to the bunkhouse and dove headfirst into the building, rolling to his feet.

"Thanks, Spring," he told the old hand. "Hartley must have laid out there in the corral all covered up with hay since I conked him on the noggin last night."

"Hell, he was dead on his feet when I shot him," the old hand said. "I just like some in'shorence in cases like that."

He poured Smoke a cup of coffee and returned to his post by a window.

Smoke drank the strong hot brew and laid out the plans. One by one, the old gunfighters began leaving the bunkhouse, heading for the house. Ring was the last to stand in the door.

He smiled at Smoke.

"You always bring this much action with you when you journey, Smoke?"

"It sure seems like it, Ring," Smoke said with a laugh.

The big man returned the laugh and then slipped out into the rapidly darkening day, the rain still coming down in silver sheets.

"I got to thinkin' a while back," Spring said. "After Ring asked me how it was nobody come to our aid. Smoke, they's sometimes two, three weeks go by don't none of us go to town. Ain't nobody comin' out here."

"And even if they did come out, what could they do? Nothing," he ansered his own question. "Except get themselves killed. It'd take a full company of Army troops to rout those outlaws."

There had been no fire from the ridges, so the men had safely made the house. Darkness had pushed aside the day. Those walking out would be leaving shortly, and they had a good chance of making it, for the move would not be one those on the ridges would be expecting. To try to bust out on horseback, yes. But not by walking out. Not in this weather.

When the wet darkness had covered the land for almost an hour, Smoke turned to Spring. He could just see him in the gloom of the bunkhouse.

"I don't think they'll try us on horseback this night, Spring. They'll be coming in on foot."

"You right," Donny whispered from the far end of the bunkhouse. "And here they come. You want me to drop him now or let them come closer?"

"Let them come on. This rain makes for deceptive shooting."

A torch was lighted, its flash a jumping flame in the windswept darkness. The torch bobbed as the carrier ran toward the house. From the house, a rifle crashed. The torch stopped and fell to the soaked earth, slowly going out as its carrier died.

All around the compound, muzzle flashes pocked the gloom, and the dampness kept the gunsmoke low to the ground as an arid fog.

A kerosene bomb slammed against the side of the bunkhouse, the whiskey bottle containing the liquid smashing. The flames were slow to spread and those that did were quickly put out by the driving rain. Spring's pistol roared and spat sparks. Outside, a man screamed as the slug ripped through flesh and shattered bone. He lay on the wet ground and moaned for a moment, then fell silent.

Smoke saw a moving shadow out of the corner of his eyes and lifted his pistol. The shadow blended in with the night and Smoke lost it. But it was definitely moving toward the bunkhouse. It was difficult, if not impossible, to hear any small sounds due to the hard-falling rain and the crash of gunfire. Smoke left the window and moved to the door of the bunkhouse, standing some six feet away from the door. Spring and Donny and two other hands kept their eyes to the front, occasionally firing at a dark running shape within their perimeter.

The bunkhouse door had no inner bar; most people didn't even lock their doors when they left for town or went on a trip. If somebody used the house to get out of the weather or to fix something to eat, they were expected to leave it as they found it.

The door smashed open and the doorway filled with men. Smoke's .44's roared and bucked in his hands. Screaming was added to the already confusing cacophony of battle. More men rushed into the bunkhouse, leaping over the bodies sprawled in the doorway. Smoke was rushed and knocked to the floor. He lost his left hand gun but jammed the muzzle of his right hand gun into the belly of a man and pulled the trigger. A boot caught him on the side of the head, momentarily addling him.

Smoke heaved the badly wounded man away and rolled to the far wall. Men were all over him swinging fists and gun barrels. Using his own now-empty pistol as a club, he smashed a face, the side of a head, Jerking the pistol from a man's holster, Smoke began firing into the mass of wet attackers. A bullet burned his side; another slammed into the wooden leg of a bunk, driving splinters into Smoke's face.

Jerking his Bowie from its sheath, Smoke began slashing out, feeling the warm flow of blood splatter his arm and face as the big blade drew howls of pain from his attackers.

He slipped to one side and listened to the cursing of the outlaws still able to function. Lifting the outlaw's pistol, Smoke emptied it into the dark shapes. The bunkhouse became silent after the battle.

"You hit, Smoke?" Spring called.

"Just a scratch. Donny?"

The young cowboy did not reply.

"I'll check," Fitz spoke softly. He walked to the cowboy's position and knelt down. "He rolled twelve," Fitz's voice came out of the darkness.

"Damn!" Smoke said.


Another attack from the outlaws had been beaten back, but Donny was dead and Cal had been wounded. Smoke's wounds were minor but painful. No one in the house had been hurt.

They had bought those walking out some time and distance. By this time, if they had not been discovered, they were clear. Clear, but facing a long, cold, wet, and slow march into the Big Belts. The house, the barn, and the bunkhouse were riddled with bullet holes. They had lost two horses, having to destroy them after they'd been hit by stray bullets. And no cowboy likes to shoot a horse.

The rain slacked and the clouds drifted away, exposing the moon and its light. With that, the outlaws slipped away into the shadows and made their way back to the ridges overlooking the ranch.

The moonlight cast its light upon the bodies of outlaws sprawled in death on the grounds. Some of those with wounds not serious tried to crawl away. Cord and Smoke and the others showed them no mercy, shooting them if they could get them in gunsights.

After the intitial attack had been beaten back, the outlaws fired from the ridges for several hours, finally giving it up and settling down for some rest.

The moonlight was both a blessing and a curse, for it would make their busting out a lot more difficult.

Smoke ran to the house to confer with Cord.

"I figure just after sunset," the rancher said. "After the moon comes up, it'll be impossible."

"All right. We'll head in the opposite direction of those walking out. We'll start out like we're trying to bust through the roadblock, then cut east toward the timber. That sound all right to you?"

"Suits me."

\*    \*    \*

183

Dooley had changed his mind about heading farther into the mountains, turning around when he was about halfway to Old Baldy. He rode slowly back toward Gibson.

At dawn of the second day of the attack on the Circle Double C, he was standing in front of the newly opened stage offices, waiting for the station agent. He plopped down his money belt.

"Stash that in your big safe and gimme a receipt for it," he told the agent.

That taken care of, Dooley walked over to the new hotel and checked in. He slept for several hours, then carefully bathed in the tub behind the barber shop, shaved, and dressed in clean clothes. He was completely free of the effects of alcohol and intended to remain that way. Nuts, but sober.

He walked over to Hans and enjoyed a huge breakfast, the first good meal he'd eaten in days. Hans and Olga and Hilda eyeballed the man suspiciously.

"Vere is everybody?" Hans broke the silence.

"I ain't got no idea," Dooley told him, slurping on a mug of coffee. "I ain't been to the ranch in two-three days." Really, he had no idea how long he'd been gone. Two days or a week. Time meant nothing to him anymore. He had only a few thoughts burning in his brain: to kill Cord McCorkle and then turn his guns on his traitor sons and watch them die in the muddy street. And if he didn't soak up too much lead doing that, and he could find her, he wanted to shoot his wife.

That was the sum total of all that was in Dooley Hanks's brain. He paid for his meal and took a mug of coffee with him, sitting in a chair on the boardwalk in front of the cafe. He would wait.

He sat in his chair, watching the town wake up and the people start moving around. He drank coffee and rolled cigarettes, smoking them slowly, his eyes missing nothing.

He watched as two very muddy and tired-looking riders rode slowly up the street, coming in from the north. Dooley set his coffee mug on the boards and stood up, staying in the morning shadows, only a dark blur to those still in the sunlight. He slipped the thongs from the hammers of his guns. The two riders reined up and dismounted, looping the reins around the hitchrail and starting up the steps to Hans. They stopped and stared in disbelief at the man.

Hector and Rod, two punk gunslicks Dooley had hired, stood with their mouths open.

"You 'pposed to be *dead!*" Hector finally managed to gasp.

"Well, I ain't," Dooley told them. "And I want some answers from you."

"We ain't got no quarrel with you," Rod told him. "All we want is some hot coffee and food."

"You'll get hot lead, boy," Dooley warned him. "Where the hell is my no'count sons?"

"I . . ." Hector opened his mouth. A warning glance from Rod closed it.

"You'd better talk to me, pup!" Dooley barked. "'Fore I box your ears with lead."

Hector laughed at the man. "You ain't seen the day you could match my draw, old man." Hector was all of nineteen. He would not live to see another day.

Dooley drew and fired. He was no fast gunslinger, but he was quick and very, very accurate. The slug struck Hector in the heart and the young man died standing up. He fell on his face in the mud.

Dooley turned his gun toward Rod, the hammer jacked back. "My boys, punk. Where is they?"

"They teamed up with Jason and Lanny and Cat Jennings," he admitted. "I don't know where they is," he lied.

Dooley bought it. He sat down in the chair, his gun still in his hand. He would wait. They would show up. Then he'd kill them. He'd kill them all.

Rod backed up and led his horse across the street, to a little tent-covered cafe. Horace Mulroony had stood on the boardwalk across the street and witnessed the shooting. He motioned for his cameraman to bring the equipment. They had another body to record for posterity.

"Mister Hanks," he said, strolling up. "I would like to talk to you."

"Git away from me!" Dooley snarled, spittle leaking out of one corner of his mouth.

Horace got.

# Twenty-Eight

In the middle of the afternoon, in order to keep suspicion down, Smoke risked a run to the barn and began saddling all the horses himself. He laid four gunnybags or pieces of ripped-up blankets in front of each stall, to be used to muffle the horses' hooves when they first pulled out. Smoke went over each saddle, either taping down or removing anything that might jingle or rattle.

That done, he climbed up into the warm loft to speak to the men. Lujan was reclining on some hay. He opened his eyes and smiled at Smoke.

"At full dark, amigo?"

"At full dark. If you know any prayers, you best be saying them."

The gunfighter grinned. "Oh, I have!"

The other men in the loft laughed softly, but in their eyes, Smoke could see that they, too, had been calling—in their own way—for some heavenly guidance.

He climbed back down and decided to stay in the barn until nightfall. No point in drawing unnecessary gunfire from the ridges. He lay down on a pile of hay and closed his eyes. Might as well rest, too. It was going to be a long night.


Gage and Del had led the party safely past the gunmen on the ridges. An hour later they were deep in the timber and feeling better. It was tough going, carrying Beans on the stretcher, but by switching up bearers every fifteen minutes, they made good time.

Dawn found them miles from the Circle Double C. But instead of following Cord's orders, Del had changed directions and was heading toward Gibson. He had not done it autocratically, but had called for a vote during a rest period. The vote had been unanimous: head for town.

By midafternoon they were only a few miles from town, a very tired and foot-sore group.

Late in the afternoon, they came staggering up the main street of Gibson. People rushed out of stores and saloons and houses to stand and stare at the muddy group.

"Them wimmin's wearin' men's britches!" a man called from a saloon. "Lord have mercy. Would you look at that."

Gage quickly explained what had taken place and why they were here, Dooley listening carefully.

Rod stood on the boardwalk and stared at the group, his eyes bugged out. Parnell felt the eyes on him and turned, his hot gaze locking with Rod's disbelieving eyes. Parnell slipped the thongs from his blasters and walked toward the young man.

"I ain't skirred of you!" Rod shouted.

"Good," Parnell said, still walking. "A man should face death with no fear."

"Huh! It ain't me that's gonna die."

"Then make your play," Parnell said, and with that he became a western man.

Rod's hands grabbed for iron.

Parnell's blaster roared, and Rod was very nearly cut in two by the heavy charge. It turned him around and tossed him through the window and into the cafe, landing him on a table, completely ruining the appetite of those having an early supper.

Beans had been keeping a good eye on Dooley; a good eye and his gun. Crazy as Dooley might be, he wasn't about to do anything with Beans holding a bead on him.

Dooley stood up slowly and held out his hand as he walked up to Gage. With a look of amazement on his face, Gage took the offered hand.

"You got a good woman, Gage. I hope you treat her better than I did." He turned to Liz and handed her the receipt from the stage agent. "Money from the sale of the cattle is over yonder in the safe. I'm thinkin' straight now, Liz. But I don't know how long it's gonna last. So I'll keep this short. Them boys of ourn took after me. They're crazy. And they got to be stopped. I sired them, so it's on my shoulders to stop them." Then, unexpectedly, and totally out of character for him, he took off his hat and kissed Liz on the cheek.

"Thank you for some good years, Liz." He turned around,

walked to his horse, and swung into the saddle, pointing the nose of the horse toward the Circle Double C.

"Well, I'll just be damned!" Gage said. "I'd have bet ever' dollar I owned—which ain't that many—that he was gonna start shootin.'"

Liz handed him the receipt. "Here, darling. You'll be handling the money matters from now on. You might as well become accustomed to it."

"Yes, dear," the grizzled foreman said meekly. Then he squared his shoulders. "All right, boys, we got unfinished business to take care of. Let's find some cayuses and get to it."

Their aches and pains and sore feet forgotten, the men checked their guns and turned toward the hitchrails, lined with horses. "We're takin' these," Del said. "Anybody got any objections, state 'em now."

No one had any objections.

Hans rode up on a huge horse at least twenty hands high. He had belted on a pistol and carried a rifle in one big paw. "I ride vit you," he rumbled. "Friends of mine dey are, too."

Horace came rattling up in a buggy, a rifle in the boot and a holstered pistol on the seat beside him. "I'm with you, boys."

More than a dozen other townspeople came riding up and driving up in buggies and buckboards, all of them heavily armed.

"We're with you!" one called. "We're tired of this. So let's ride and clean it out."

"Let's go, boys!" Parnell yelled.

"Oohhh!" Rita cooed. "He's so manly!"

"Don't swoon, child," her mother warned. "The street's too muddy."

Del leaned out of the saddle and kissed Fae right on the mouth, right in front of God and everybody.

Parnell thought that was a good idea and did the same with Rita.

The hurdy-gurdy girls, hanging out of windows and lining the boardwalks, all applauded.

Olga and Hilda giggled.

Gage leaned over and gave Liz a good long smack while the onlookers cheered.

Then they were gone in a pounding of hooves, slinging mud all over anyone standing close.

*       *       *

Dooley rode slowly back to his ranch. He looked at the buckshot-blasted bed and shook his head. Then he fixed a pot of coffee and poured a cup, taking it out to sit on the front porch. He had a hunch his boys would be returning to the ranch for the money they thought was still in the safe.

He would be waiting for them.


"I don't like it," Jason told Lanny, with Cat standing close. "Something's wrong down there. I feel it."

"I got the same feeling," Cat spoke. "But I got it last night while we was hittin' them. It just seemed like to me they was holdin' back."

Lanny snapped his fingers. "That's it! Them women and probably a few of the men walked out durin' the rain. Damn them! This ain't good, boys."

Cat looked uneasily toward the road.

Jason caught the glance. "Relax, Cat. There ain't that many people in town who gives a damn what happens out here." Then he smiled. "The town," he said simply.

Lanny stood up from his squat. "We've throwed a short loop out here, boys. Our plans is busted. But the town is standin' wide open for the takin'."

But Cat, older and more experienced in the outlaw trade, was dubious. "There ain't nobody ever treed no western town, Lanny. We done lost twenty-five or so men by the gun. Them crazy Hanks boys left nearabouts an hour ago."

"Nobody ever tried it with seventy-five-eighty men afore, neither. Not that I know of. 'Sides, all we've lost is the punks and tin-horns and hangers-on."

"He's got a point," Jason said.

"Let's ride!"


Dooley Hanks sat on his front porch, drinking coffee. When he saw his sons ride up, he stood up and slipped the thongs from the hammers of his guns. The madness had once more taken possession of his sick mind, leaving him with but one thought: to kill these traitor sons of his.

He drained his coffee mug and set the mug on the porch railing. He was ready.

The boys rode up to the hitchrail and dismounted. They were muddy and unshaven and stank like bears after rolling in rotten meat.

"If you boys come for the money, you're out of luck," Dooley called. "I give it to your momma. Seen her in town hour or so back."

The boys had recovered from their initial shock at seeing their father alive. They pushed through the fence gate and stood in the yard, facing their father on the porch. The boys spread out, about five feet apart.

"You a damn lie, you crazy old coot!" Sonny called. "She's over to Cord's place. Trapped with the rest of them."

"Sorry, boys." Dooley's voice was calm. "But some of 'em busted out and walked into town, carrying the Moab Kid on a stretcher. Now they's got some townspeople behind 'em and is headin' back to Cord's place. Your little game is all shot to hell."

Sonny, Bud, and Conrad exchanged glances. Seems like everything that had happened the last several days had turned sour.

"Aw, hell, Daddy!" Bud said, forcing a grin. "We knowed you wasn't in that there bed. We was just a-funnin' with you, that's all. It was just a joke that we made up between us."

"Yeah, Daddy," Sonny said. "What's the matter, cain't you take a joke no more?"

"Lyin' scum!" Dooley's words were hard, verbally tossed at his sons. "And you knowed who raped your sister, too, didn't you?"

The boys stood in the yard, sullen looks on their dirty and unshaved faces.

*"Didn't you?"* the father screamed the question at them. "Damn you, answer me!"

"So what if we did?" Sonny asked. "It don't make no difference now, do it?"

A deadly calm had taken Dooley. "No, it doesn't, Sonny. It's all over."

"Whut you mean, Daddy?" Conrad asked. "Whut you fixin' to do?"

"Something that I'm not very proud of," the father said. "But it's something that I have to do."

Bud was the first to put it together. "You can't take us, Daddy. You pretty good with a gun, but you slow. So don't do nothing stupid."

"The most stupid thing I ever done was not takin' a

horsewhip to you boys' butts about five times a day, commencin' when you was just pups. It's all my fault, but it's done got out of hand. It's too late. Better this than a hangman's noose."

"I think you done slipped your cinches agin, Pa," his oldest told him. "You best go lay down; git you a bottle of hooch and ponder on this some. 'Cause if you drag iron with us, you shore gonna die this day."

Dooley shot him. He gave no warning. He had faced men before, and knew what had to be done, so he did it. His slug struck Sonny in the stomach, doubling him over and dropping him to the muddy yard.

Bud grabbed iron and shot his father, the bullet twisting Dooley, almost knocking him off his boots. Dooley dragged his left hand gun and got off a shot, hitting his middle son in the leg and slamming the young man back against the picket fence, tearing down a section of it. The horses at the hitchrail panicked, breaking loose and running from the ugly scene of battle.

Conrad got lead in his father before the man turned his guns loose on his youngest boy. Conrad felt a double hammer-blow slam into his belly, the lead twisting and ripping. He began screaming and cursing the man who had fathered him. Raising his gun, the boy shot his father in the belly.

But still Dooley would not go down.

Blood streaming from his chest and face, the crazed man took another round from his second son. Dooley raised his pistol and shot the young man between the eyes.

As the light began to dim in Dooley's eyes, he stumbled from the porch and fell to the muddy earth. He picked up one of Sonny's guns just as the gut-shot boy eared back the hammer on his Colt and shot his father in the belly. Dooley jammed the pistol into the young man's chest and emptied it.

Dooley fell back, the sounds of the pale rider's horse coming closer.

"Daddy!" Conrad called, his words very dim. "Help me, Daddy. It hurts so bad!"

The ghost rider galloped up just in time to see Dooley stretch his arm out and close his fingers around Conrad's hand. "We'll ride out together, boy."

The pale rider tossed his shroud.

# Twenty-Nine

"They're pullin' out!" Lujan yelled from the loft.

Smoke was up and running for his horse as the men streamed out of the bunkhouse, all heading for the barn.

"Why?" Reno asked.

"That damn crazy Del led 'em into town!" Cord said, grinning. "We got help on the way. Bet on it."

In the saddle, Smoke said, "That means the town is gonna get hit. That's the only thing I can figure out of this move."

"Let's go, boys!" Cord yelled the orders. "They'll hit that town like an army."

The men waited for a few minutes, to be sure the outlaws had really pulled out, then mounted up and headed for town. They met the rescue party halfway between the ranch and Gibson.

Smoke quickly explained and the men tore out for Gibson.


"There she is, boys," Lanny pointed toward the fast-growing town. "We hit them hard, fast, grab the money, and get gone."

"I gotta have me a woman," one of Cat Jennings's men said. "I can't stand it no more."

"Mills," Cat said disgustedly. "You best start thinkin' with your brain instead of that other part. You can always find you a woman."

"A woman," Mills said, his eyes bright with his inner cruelty.

"Let's go." Jason spurred his horse.

Some seventy strong, the outlaws hit the town at a full gallop, firing at anything that came into sight. They rampaged through on the first pass, leaving several dead in the muddy main street and that many more wounded, crawling for cover.

At the end of the street, the men broke up into gangs and began looting the stores and terrorizing the citizens. Mills blundered into Hans's cafe and eyeballed Hilda.

"You a fat pig, but you'll do," he told the woman, walking toward her.

Hilda threw a full pot of boiling coffee into the man's face.

Screaming his pain and almost blind, Mills stumbled around the cafe, crashing into tables and chairs, both hands covering his scalded face.

Olga ran from the upstairs, carrying two shotguns. She tossed one to Hilda and eared back the hammers of her own, leveling the double-barrel twelve gauge at Mills. She gave him both barrels of buckshot. The outlaw was slung out the window and died on the boardwalk.

Mills's buddy and cohort in evil, Barton, ran into the cafe, both pistols drawn. He ran right into an almost solid wall of buckshot. The charges blew him out of one boot and sent him sailing out of the cafe, off the boardwalk, and into a hitchrail. Barton did a backflip and landed dead in the mud.

Hilda and Olga picked up his dropped pistols and reloaded their shotguns, waiting for another turkey to come gobbling in.

Harriet and her hurdy-gurdy girls had armed themselves and already had accounted for half a dozen outlaws, the bodies littering the floor of the saloon and the boardwalk out front a clear warning to others not to mess with these short-skirted and painted ladies.

The smithy, a veteran of The War Between The States and several Indian campaigns, stood in his shop with a Spencer .52 and emptied several saddles before the outlaws decided there was nothing of value in a blacksmith shop anyway.

Some of Dad Estes's men had charged the general store and laid a pistol up side Walt Hillery's head, knocking the man unconscious. They then grabbed his sour-faced wife, Leah, dragging her to the storeroom and having their way with her.

Leah's screaming brought Liz and Alice and Fae on the run, the women armed with pistols and rifles. Sandi and Rita were at the doctor's office with the wounded men.

Fae leveled her .45 at a man with his britches down around his boots and shot him in the head just as Alice and Liz began pulling the trigger and levering the action, clearing the storeroom of nasties.

Liz tossed a blanket over the still-squalling and kicking and pig-snorting Leah and gave her a look of disgust. "They must have been hard up," she told the shopkeeper.

Leah stopped hollering long enough to spit at the woman. She stopped spitting when Liz balled her right hand into a fist and started toward her.

"You wouldn't dare!" Leah hissed.

"Maybe you'd like to bet a broken jaw on it?" Liz challenged.

Leah pulled the blanket over her head, leaving her bony feet sticking out the other end.

The agent at the stagecoach line had worked his way up the ladder: starting first as a hostler, then a driver, then as a guard on big money shipments from the gold fields. He didn't think this stop would be in operation long, but damned if a bunch of outlaws were going to strip his safe.

When some of No-Count George Victor's bunch shot the lock off the door, the agent was waiting behind the counter, with several loaded rifles and shotguns and pistols. With him was his hostler and two passengers waiting for the stage, all heavily armed.

The first two outlaws to step through the door were shot dead, dying on their feet, riddled with bullet holes. Another tried to ride his horse through the big window. The animal, already frightened by all the wild shooting, resisted and bolted, running up the boardwalk. The outlaw, just able to hang on, caught his head on the side of an awning and left the saddle, missing most of his jaw.

Beans was sitting next to an open window of the doctor's office, a rifle in his very capable hands. He emptied half a dozen saddles.

And Charlie Starr was calmly walking up the boardwalk, a long-barreled Colt in his hand. He was looking for Cat Jennings. One of Cat's men, a disgustingly evil fellow who went by the name of Wheeler, saw Charlie and leveled his pistol at him.

Charlie drilled him between the eyes with one well-placed shot and kept on walking.

A bullet slammed into Charlie's side and turned him around. He grinned through the pain. Doc Adair had seen the lump pushing out of Charlie's side and their eyes had met in the office.

"Cancer," Charlie had told him.

Charlie lifted his Peacemaker and another outlaw went on that one-way journey toward the day he would make his peace with his Maker.

"Cat!" Charlie called, and the outlaw wheeled his horse around.

Charlie shot him out of the saddle.

Cat came up with his hands full of Colts, the hate shining in his eyes.

Charlie took two more rounds, both of them in the belly, but the old gunfighter stayed on his feet and took his time, carefully placing his shots. Cat soaked up the lead and kept on shooting.

Charlie border-rolled his second gun just as he was going to his knees in the muddy street. He could hear the thunder of hooves and something else, too: singing. It sounded like a mighty choir was singing him Home.

Charlie lifted his Peacemaker and shot Cat Jennings twice in the head. Propped up on one elbow, the old gunfighter had enough strength to make sure Cat was dead, then slumped to the floor.

Hardrock and Silver Jim and Pistol LeRoux had seen Charlie go down, and they screamed their rage as they jumped off their horse, their hands full of guns.

Silver Jim stalked up the boardwalk, holding his matched set of Remington .44's, looking for No-Count George Victor. Hardrock was by his side, his hands gripping the butts of his guns, his eyes searching for Three-Fingers Kerman and his buddy, Fulton. Pistol had gone looking for Peck and Nappy.

The Sabler Brothers, Ben, Carl, and Delmar were waiting at the edge of town, waiting for Lujan.

Diego, Pablo, and a gunfighter called Hazzard were waiting to try Smoke.

Twenty or more gunslicks had already hauled their ashes out of town. They had realized what the townspeople already knew: nobody hogties and trees a western town.

The Larado Kid had teamed up with several more punks, including Johnny and his buddy, Bret, and the backshooter, Danny Rouge. They had turned tail and galloped out of town. There would be another day. There always was. Besides, Johnny had him a plan. He wanted to kill Smoke Jensen. And he knew this fight was just about over. Smoke would be heading home. And a lot could happen between Montana and Colorado.

"No-Count!" Silver Jim yelled, his voice carrying over the din of battle, the screaming of the wounded, and the sounds of panicked horses.

No-Count whirled around, his hands full of pistols. Silver Jim drew and fired as smoothly as he had forty years back, when he had cut the flap off a soldier's holster and tied it down.

Both the old gunfighter's slugs struck true and No-Count squatted down in the muddy alley, dropped his pistols, and fell over facefirst in the mud.

Hardrock felt a numbing blow striking him in the shoulder, staggering him. He turned, falling back up against a building front, his right hand gun coming up, his thumb and trigger finger working as partners, rolling thunder from the muzzle.

Three-Finger Kerman went down, the front of his shirt stained with blood. Fulton fired at Hardrock and missed. Hardrock grinned at the outlaw and didn't miss.

Pistol Le Roux rounded a corner and came face-to-face with Peck and Nappy. Pistol's guns spat fire and death before the two so-called badmen could react. Pistol looked down at the dead and damned.

"Pikers!" he snorted, then turned and walked into one of the new saloons, called the Pink Puma, and drew himself a cool one from the deserted bar. He could sense the fight was over. He had already seen Dad Estes and his gang hightail it out of town.

Damn! but he hated that about Charlie. Him and Charlie had been buddies for nigh on . . . Hell, he couldn't remember how many years.

He drew himself another beer, sat down, and propped his boots up. It could be, he mused, he was getting just too old for this type of nonsense.

Naw! he concluded. He looked up as Hardrock came staggering in, trailed by Silver Jim.

"What the hell happened to you, you old buzzard?" he asked Hardrock.

"Caught one, you jackass!" Hardrock snapped. "What's it look like—I been pickin' petunias?"

"Wal, sit down." He shoved out a chair. "I'll fetch you a beer and then try to find the doctor. If I don't, you'll probably whine and moan the rest of the day." He took his knife and cut away Hardrock's shirt. "Bullet went clear through." He got

Hardrock a beer and picked up a bottle of whiskey. "This is gonna hurt you a lot more than it is me," he warned.

Hardrock glared at him.

Pistol poured some whiskey on the wounds, entrance and exit, and took a reasonably clean bar towel that Silver Jim handed him and made a bandage.

"You'll keep. Drink your beer."

"Make your play, gentlemen," Lujan told the Sabler Brothers.

Parnell stood by Lujan's side, smiling faintly.

The sounds of battle had all but ceased.

The Sablers grabbed for iron.

Lujan's guns roared just a split second before Parnell's blasters boomed, sending out their lethal charges. In the distance, a bugle sounded. Someone shouted, "The Army's here!"

Ben, Carl, and Delmar Sabler lay on the muddy bloody ground. Ben and Carl had taken slugs from Lujan. Delmar had taken a double dose from Parnell's blasters. He was almost torn in half.

Lojan holstered his guns and held out his hand. "My friend, you can stand shoulder-to-shoulder with me anytime you like. You are truly a man!"

Parnell blushed.

"Thank you, Lujan." He shook the hand.

"Come on, amigo. Let's go have us a . . . sarsaparilla."

# Thirty

The commander of the Army contingent, a Captain Morrison, met with Cord, Smoke, and a few others in what was left of the Hangout, while the undertaker and his helper roamed among the carnage.

"A lot of bad ones got away," Smoke told the young captain. Smoke's shirt was stiff from sweat and dirt and blood. "I expect I'll meet up with some of them on the trail home."

"Are you really Smoke Jensen?" The captain was clearly in awe.

"Yes."

Horace's photographer popped another shot.

The captain sighed. "Well, gentlemen. This is not an Army matter. I will take a report, certainly, and have it sent to the sheriff. But I imagine it will end there. I'm new to the West; just finished an assignment in Washington. But during my short time here, I have found that western justice is usually very short and very final."

"I don't understand part of what you just said," Cord leaned forward. "You mean you weren't sent in here?"

"No. We were traveling up to Fort Benton and heard the gunfire. We just rode over to see what was going on."

Smoke and Cord both started laughing. They were still laughing as they walked out of the saloon.

"The strain of battle," Captain Morrison spoke the words in all seriousness. "It certainly does strange things to men."

A grizzled old top sergeant who had been in the Army since before Morrison was born shifted his chew of tobacco to the other side of his mouth and said, "Right, sir."

\*　　　\*　　　\*

Smoke went to the tubs behind the barber shop and took a long hot bath. He was exhausted. He dressed in clean clothes purchased at the new general store and walked over to Hans for some hot food. The bodies of the outlaws were still being dragged off the street.

Hans placed a huge platter of food before the man and poured him a cup of coffee. Smoke dug in. Cord entered the cafe and sat down at the table with Smoke. He waved away the offer of food and ordered coffee.

"We have a problem about what to do with the wounded, Smoke."

"I don't have any problem at all with it. Treat their wounds and when they're well, try them."

"We don't have a jail to hold them."

"Build one to hold them or hang them or turn them loose."

"Captain Morrison is leaving a squad here to see that we don't hang them."

"Sounds like a real nice fellow to me. Very much law and order."

"You're being sarcastic, Smoke."

"I'm being tired, is what I am. Sorry to be so short with you. Is it OK to have Charlie buried out at the ranch?"

"You know it is," the rancher replied, his words softly spoken. "I wouldn't have it any other way."

"Any reward money goes to Hardrock and Silver Jim and Pistol."

"I've already set that in motion." He smiled. "You really think they're going to open a home for retired gun-fighters?"

"It wouldn't surprise me at all."

"I tell you what: I'd hate to have them for enemies."

The men sat and watched as wagons pulled up to the four new saloons and began loading up equipment from Big Louie's, the Pink Puma, The JimJam, and Harriet's House.

"I'll be glad to see things get back to normal," Cord said.

"It won't be long. I been seeing that fellow who opened up the new general store makin' trips to Walt and Leah's place. Looks like he's tryin' to buy them out."

Cord's smile was not of the pleasant type. "Liz and Alice paid Walt and Leah a visit. They convinced Walt that it would be the best thing if they'd sell out and get gone. Parnell is buyin' their house. Him and Rita will live there after they're married."

"Beans?"

"I told him he was my new foreman. He's gonna file on some sections that border my spread."

Smoke finally smiled. "Looks like it's going to be a happy ending after all."

"A whole lot of weddin's comin' up next week. You are goin' to stay for them, aren't you?"

"Oh, yeah. I couldn't miss those." He looked up at Hans, smiling at them from behind the counter. "Hilda and Ring gonna get hitched up, Hans?"

The man bobbed his big head. "*Ja.* Ever'boody vill be married at vonce."

Smoke looked out at the muddy, churned-up street. All the bodies had been toted off.

"I reserved all the rooms above the saloon," Cord said. "The hands are back at the ranch, cleaning it up and repairing the damage. Bartender has your room key."

Smoke stood up, dropped some money on the table, and put on his hat. "I think I'll go sleep for about fifteen hours."


Bob and Spring and Pat and some hands from the D-H and the Circle Double C began rebuilding Fae's burned-down house and barn. Smoke, Hardrock, Silver Jim, and Pistol began driving the cattle back onto Box-T Range.

The legendary gunfighter, Charlie Starr, was buried in a quiet ceremony in the plot on the ridge above the ranch house at the Circle Double C. His guns were buried with him. He had always said he wanted to be buried with his boots on. And he was; a brand-new pair of boots.

Dooley Hanks and his sons were buried in the family plot on the D-H.

Horace Mulroony said he would stay around long enough to photograph the multiple weddings and then was going to open a paper up in Great Falls. Things were just too quiet around Gibson.

"How about you, Lujan?" Smoke asked the gunfighter.

"Oh, I think that when you pull out I might ride down south with you. I have talked it over with Silver Jim and the others. They're coming along as well." He lit a long slender cigar and looked at Smoke. "You know, amigo, that this little war is far from over."

"I think they'll wait until we're out of Montana Territory to hit us."

"Those are my thoughts as well."

"We'll hang around until Hardrock's shoulder heals up. Then we'll ride."

Lujan smiled. "The first of the reward money has arrived. The old men said I would take a thousand dollars of it or we'd drag iron. I took the money. It will last a long time. I am a simple man and my needs are few."

"I'd hate to have to drag iron against those old boys," Smoke conceded. "They damn sure don't come any saltier."

Lujan laughed. "They have all bought new black suits and boots and white dusters. They present quite a sight."

Parnell packed away his double-barreled blasters. But his reputation would never quite leave him. He would teach school for another forty years. And he would never have any problems with unruly students.

Walt and Leah Hillery pulled out early one morning in a buckboard. They offered no goodbyes to anyone, and no one lifted a hand in farewell. It was said they were going back East. They just weren't cut out to make it in the West.

Several of the wounded outlaws died; the rest were chained and shackled and loaded into wagons. They were taken to the nearest jail—about a hundred miles away—escorted by the squad of Army troops.

The brief boomtown of Gibson settled back into a quiet routine.

Young Bob drew his time and drifted, as Smoke had predicted he would. The hard-eyed young man would earn quite a name for himself in the coming years.

Then came the wedding day, and the day could not have been any more perfect. Mild temperatures and not a cloud in the sky.

Del and Fae, Parnell and Rita, Liz and Gage, Ring and Hilda, and Beans and Sandi got all hitched up proper, with lots of fumbling around for rings and embarrassed kisses and a big hoo-rah right after the weddings.

Beans took time out after the cake-cuttin' to speak to Smoke.

"When you pullin' out, partner?"

"In the morning. I'm missin my wife and kids. I want to get back to the Sugarloaf and the High Lonesome. Reno is pullin' out today; headin' back to Nevada."

"Them ol' boys is gonna be comin' at you, you know that, don't you?"

"Oh, yes. Might as well get it over with, 'way I look at it. No point in steppin' around the issue."

"You watch your backtrail, partner."

Smoke stuck out his hand and Beans took it. "We'll meet again," Smoke told him.

"I'm countin' on it."

As was the western way, there were no elaborate or prolonged goodbyes. The men simply packed up and mounted up before dawn and pointed the noses of their horses south, quietly riding down the main street of Gibson, Montana Territory, without looking back.

"Feels good to be movin'," Pistol said. "I git the feelin' of being all cooped up if I stay too long in one place."

"Not to mention the fact that your face was beginnin' to frighten little children," Hardrock needled him. "All the greenbacks you got now you ought to git you a bag special-made and wear it over your head."

Smoke laughed and put Dagger into a trot. It did feel good to be on the trail again.

They followed the Smith down to the Sixteenmile and then followed an old Indian trail down to the Shields—the trail would eventually become a major highway.

The men rode easily, but always keeping a good eye out for trouble. None of them expected it until they were out of the territory, but it never hurt to be ready.

They began angling more east than south, crossing the Sweetgrass, taking their time, enjoying some of the most beautiful scenery to be found. They would stop early to make camp, living off the land, hunting or fishing for their meals, for the most part avoiding any towns. They ran out of coffee and sugar and bacon just north of the Wyoming line and stopped in a little town to resupply.

The man behind the counter of the general store gave Smoke and the others a good eyeballing as they walked into the store. The men noticed the clerk seemed awfully nervous.

"Feller's got the twitchies," Hardrock whispered to Silver Jim.

"I noticed. I'll take me a stroll down to the livery; check out the horses there."

"I'll go with you," Hardrock said. "Might be walkin' into something interestin'."

"You Smoke Jensen, ain't you?" the clerk asked.

"Yes."

"You know some hard-lookin gents name of Eddie Hart and Pooch Matthews? They travelin' with several other gents just as hard-lookin'."

"I know them."

"They here. Crost the street in the saloon. My boy—who earns some pennies down to the stable—heared them talkin'. They gonna kill you."

"They're going to try." Smoke gave the man his order and then took a handkerchief and wiped the dust from his guns. Hardrock stepped back into the store.

"Half a dozen of them ol' boys in town, Smoke."

"I know. They're over at the saloon."

As the words were leaving his mouth, the town marshal stepped in.

"Jackson Bodine!" Hardrock grinned at the man. "I ain't seen you in a coon's age."

"Hello, Hardrock." The marshal stuck out his hand and Hardrock gripped it.

"When'd you take up lawin'?"

"When I got too old to do much of anything else." He looked at Smoke. "I don't want trouble in my town, Mister-whoever-you-are."

"This here's Smoke Jensen, Jackson," Hardrock said.

The marshal exhaled slowly. "I guess a man don't always get his wishes," he said reluctantly.

"I don't want trouble in your town or anybody else's town, marshal. But I'm afraid this is something those men over in the saloon won't let me sidestep." Briefly, he explained what had taken place over the past weeks.

The marshal nodded his head. "Give me ten minutes before you call them out, Smoke. That'll give me time to clear the street and have the kids back at home."

"You can have as much time as you need, Marshal."

The marshal smiled. "I never really knew for sure whether you were real or just a made-up person. They's a play about you, you know that?"

"No, I didn't. Is it a good one?"

The marshall laughed. "I ain't seen it. Folks that have gone to the big city tell me they got you somewheres between Robin Hood and Bloody Bill Anderson."

Smoke chuckled. "You know Marshal, they just may be right."

Jackson Bodine left the store to warn the townspeople to stay off the streets.

"He's a good man," Hardrock said. "Come out here 'bout, oh, '42 or '43, I reckon. Preacher knows him. 'Course, Preacher knows just about ever'body out here, I reckon."

Silver Jim stepped inside. "I could have sworn we dropped Royce back yonder at the ranch," he said. "But he's over yonder, 'live and well and just as ugly as ever."

"Anybody else?" Lujan asked.

"Lodi, Hazzard, Nolan . . ." His eyes touched Lujan's unblinking stare. "And Diego and Gomez. Three or four more I know but can't put no names to."

The Chihuahua gunfighter grunted. "Well, gentlemen, shall we cross the street and order us a drink?"

"I am a mite thirsty," Hardrock said. "Boredom does that to me," he added with a smile.

# Thirty-One

The men walked across the dusty street, all of them knowing the gunfighters in the saloon were waiting for them, watching them as they crossed the street.

Smoke was the first to push open the batwings and step inside, moving to one side so the others could follow quickly and let their eyes adjust to the dimmer light.

The first thing Smoke noticed was that Diego and Gomez were widely separated, one standing clear across the room from the other. It was a trick they used often, catching a man in a crossfire.

Smoke moved to the bar, his spurs jingling softly with each step. He walked to the far end of the bar while Lujan stopped at the end of the bar closest to the batwings. The move did not escape the eyes of Diego and Gomez. Both men smiled knowingly.

Only Smoke, Lujan, and Hardrock were at the bar. Pistol and Silver Jim positioned themselves around the room, and that move made several of the outlaws very nervous.

Smoke decided to take a chance and make a try for peace. "The war is over, boys. This doesn't have to be. You're professionals. Dooley is dead. You're off his payroll. There is no profit in dying for pride."

A very tough gunfighter that Pistol knew only as Bent sighed and pushed his chair back. "Makes sense to me. I don't fight for the fun of it." He walked out the batwings and across the boardwalk, heading for the livery.

"One never knows about a man," Diego spoke softly. "I was certain he had more courage than that."

"I always knowed he was yeller," Hazzard snorted.

"Maybe he's just smart," Smoke said.

Diego ignored that and stared at Lujan. "The noble Lujan," he said scornfully. "Protector of women and little children." He spat on the floor.

"At least, Diego," Lujan said, "I have that much of a reputation for decency. Can you say as much?"

"Who would want to?" the gunfighter countered. "Decency does not line my pockets with gold coins."

There was no point in talking about conscience to the man—he didn't have one.

Lujan flicked his dark eyes to Smoke. No point in delaying upcoming events, the quick glance seemed to say.

Smoke shot the Mexican gunfighter. He gave no warning; just drew, cocked, and fired, all in a heartbeat. Lujan was a split second behind him, his slug taking Gomez in the belly.

Hardrock took out Pooch Matthews just as Smoke was pouring lead into Eddie Hart and Silver Jim and Pistol had turned their guns on the others.

Royce was down, hanging onto a table. Dave and Hazzard were backed up against a wall, the front of their shirts turning crimson. Blaine and Nolan were out of it, their hands empty and over their heads, total shock etched on their tanned faces.

Diego raised his pistol, the sound of the cocking loud in the room.

"Don't do it, Diego," Smoke warned him.

The gunfighter cursed Smoke, in English and in Spanish, telling him where he could go and in what part of his anatomy he could shove the suggestion.

Smoke shot him between the eyes just as Lujan was putting the finishing touches to Gomez.

The batwings pushed open and Jackson Bodine walked in, carrying a sawed-off double barrel express gun.

"There might be re-ward money for them two," Hardrock said, pointing to Blaine and Nolan. "You might send a telly-graph to Fort Benton."

Hazzard finally lost the strength to hang onto the table and he fell to the floor. Dave hung on, looking at Smoke through eyes that were beginning to lose their light.

"We was snake-bit all through this here job," he said, coughing up blood. "Didn't nothin' turn out right." The table tipped over under his weight and he fell to the floor. He lay amid the cigar and cigarette butts, cursing Smoke as life left him. Profanity was the last words out of his mouth.

"Anyone else gunnin' for you boys?" the marshall asked.

"Several more," Smoke told him.

"I sure would appreciate it if y'all would take it on down the road. This is the first shootin' we've had here in three years."

Hardrock laughed at the expression on the marshal's face. "I swear, Jackson. I do believe you're gettin' crotchety in your old age."

"And would like to get older," the marshal replied.

Hardrock slapped his friend on the back. "Come on, Jackson, I'll buy you a drink."


The men rode on south, crossing the Tongue, and rode into the little town of Sheridan, Wyoming. There, they took their first hot soapy bath since leaving Gibson, got a shave and a trim, and enjoyed a cafe-cooked meal and several pots of strong coffee.

The sight of five of the most famous gunslingers in all the West made the marshal a tad nervous. He and some of the locals, armed with shotguns, entered the cafe where Smoke and his friends were eating, positioning themselves around the room.

"I swanny," Silver Jim said. "I do believe the town folks is a mite edgy today." He eyeballed the marshal. "Ain't it a bit early for duck-huntin'?"

"Very funny," a man said. "We heard about the shootin' up North. There ain't gonna be no repeat of that around here."

"I shore hope not," Hardrock told him. "Violence offends me turrible. Messes up my di-gestive workin's. Cain't sleep for days. I'm just an old man a-spendin' his twilight years a-roamin' the countryside, takin' in all the beauty of nature. Stoppin' to smell the flowers and gander at the birds."

"Folks call me Peaceful," Silver Jim said, forking in a mouthful of potatoes and gravy. "I sometimes think I missed my callin'. I should have been a poet, like that there Longbritches."

"Longfellow," Smoke corrected.

"Yeah, him, too."

"I think you're all full of horse hocky," the marshal told them. "No trouble in this town, boys. Eat your meal and kindly leave."

"Makes a man feel plumb unwanted," Pistol said.

They made camp for the night a few miles south of town. Staying east of the Bighorns, they pulled out at dawn. They rode for two days without seeing another person.

Over a supper of beans and bacon, Smoke asked, "Where do you boys pick up the rest of your reward money?"

"Cheyenne," Silver Jim replied.

"You best start anglin' off east down here at the Platte."

"That's what we was thinkin'," Pistol told him. "But I just don't think it's over, Smoke."

"You can't spend the rest of your life watching my backtrail." He looked across the fire at Lujan. "How about you, Lujan?

"I'll head southwest at the Platte." He smiled grimly. "My services are needed down on the Utah line."

Smoke nodded. "Are you boys really going to start up a place for old gunfighters and mountain men?"

"Yep," Hardrock said. "But we gonna keep quiet about it. Let the old fellers live out they days in peace and quiet. Soon as we get it set up, we'll let you know. We gonna try to get Preacher to come and live thar. You think he would?"

"Maybe, You never know about that old coot. He's nearabouts the last mountain man."

"No," Silver Jim drawled the word. "The last mountain man will be ridin' the High Lonesome long after Preacher is gone."

"What do you mean?"

"You, boy. You be the last mountain man."


The men parted ways at the Platte. They resupplied at the trading post, had a last drink together, and rode away; Lujan to ply his deadly trade down on the Utah line; Silver Jim and Pistol Le Roux and Hardrock to get the bulk of their reward money and find a spot to build a home for old gunfighters. Smoke headed due south.

"We're goin' home, boy," he spoke to Dagger, and the horse's ears came up. "It'll be good to see Sally and the babies."

Smoke left the trail and took off into the wild, a habit he had picked up from Ol' Preacher. He felt in his guts that he was riding into trouble, so he would make himself as hard to find as possible for those wanting to kill him.

He followed the Platte down, keeping east of the Rattlesnake Hills, then crossing the Platte and making his way south, with Bear Mountain to his east. He stayed on the west side of the Shirley Mountains and rode into a small town on the Medicine Bow River late one afternoon.

He was clean-shaven now, having shaved off his mustache before leaving Gibson, although he did have a stubble of beard on his face, something he planned to rectify as soon as he could get a hot bath and find a barber.

He was trail-worn and dusty, and Dagger was just as tired as he was. "Get you rubbed down and find you a big bucket of corn, boy," Smoke promised the horse. "And me and you will get us a good night's sleep."

Dagger whinnied softly and bobbed his head up and down, as if to say, "I damn well hope so!"

Smoke stabled Dagger, telling the boy to rub him down good and give him all the corn he could eat. "And watch my gear," he said, handing the boy a silver dollar.

"Yes, *sir!*"

Slapping the dust from his clothes, Smoke stopped in the town's only saloon for a drink to cut the dry from his throat.

He was an imposing figure even in faded jeans and worn shirt. Wide-shouldered and lean-hipped, with his arms bulging with muscle, and cold, emotionless eyes. The men in the saloon gave him a careful onceover, their eyes lingering on the guns around his waist, the left gun butt-forward. Don't see many men carrying guns thataway, and it marked him immediately.

Gunfighter.

"Beer," Smoke told the barkeep and began peeling a hardboiled egg.

Beer in front of him, Smoke drank half of the mug and wiped his mouth with the back of his hand and then ate the egg.

"Passin' through?" the barkeep asked.

"Yeah. Lookin' for a hot bath and a shave and a bed."

"Got a few rooms upstairs. Cost you . . ."

"He won't be needin' no bath," the cold voice came from the batwings. "Just a pine box."

Smoke cut his eyes. Jason Bright stepped into the room, which had grown as silent as the grave.

Smoke was tired of killing. Tired of it all. He wanted no

trouble with Jason Bright. But damned if he could see a way out of it.

"Jason, I'll tell you the same thing I told Diego, just before I killed him."

Chairs were pushed back and men got out of the line of fire. Diego dead? Lord have mercy! Who was this big stranger anyways?

"Speak your piece, Jensen," Jason said.

*Smoke Jensen!* Lordy, Lordy!

"The war is over," Smoke spoke softly but firmly. "Nobody's paying you now. There are warrants all over the place for you. Ride out, man."

"You queered the deal for me, Smoke. Me and a lot of others. They scattered all around, from here to Colorado, just waitin' for a shot at you. But I think I'll just save them the trouble."

"Don't do it, Jason. Ride on out."

The batwings were suddenly pushed inward, striking Jason in the back and throwing him off balance. Smoke lunged forward and for the second time in about a month, Jason Bright was about to get the stuffing kicked out of him.

Smoke hit the gunfighter in the mouth and floored him, as the man who had pushed open the batwings took one look inside and hauled his freight back to the house. He didn't need a drink noways.

Smoke jerked Jason's guns from leather and tossed them into a man's lap, almost scaring the citizen to death.

"I'm tired of it, Jason," Smoke told the man, standing over him like an oak tree. "Tired of the killing, tired of it all."

Jason came up with the same knife he once tried to use on Cord. Smoke kicked it out of his hand and decked the man with a hard right fist. He jerked Jason up and slammed him against the bar. Then Smoke proceeded to hammer at the man's midsection with a battering ram combination of left's and right's. Smoke both felt and heard ribs break under the hammering. Jason's eyes rolled back in his head and Smoke let him fall to the floor.

"You ought to go on and kill him, Smoke," a man called from the crowd. "He ain't never gonna forget this. Someday he'll come after you."

"I know," Smoke panted the words. "But I'm tired of the

killing. I don't want to kill anybody else. Ever!"

"We'll haul him over to the doc's office for you, Smoke," a man volunteered. "He ain't gonna be ridin' for a long time to come. Not with all them busted ribs. And I heard 'em pop and crack."

"I'm obliged to you." He looked at the bartender. "The tub around back."

"Yes, sir. I'll get a boy busy with the hot water right away."

"Keep anybody else off me, will you?"

Several men stood up. "Let us get our rifles, Mister Jensen. You can bathe in peace."

"I appreciate it." He looked down at Jason. "You should have kept ridin', Jason. You can't say I didn't give you a chance."

# Thirty-Two

Dagger was ready to go when Smoke saddled up the next morning. Not yet light in the east. He wanted to get gone, get on the trail home. He would stop down the road a ways and fix him some bacon to go with the bread he'd bought the night before. But he would have liked some coffee. He looked toward the town's only cafe. Still dark. Smoke shrugged and pointed Dagger's nose south. He had his small coffeepot and plenty of coffee. No trouble to fix coffee when he fixed the bacon.

About an hour after dawn, he stopped by a creek and made his fire. He fixed his bacon and coffee and sopped out the pan with the bread, then poured a cup of coffee and rolled a cigarette.

The creek made happy little sounds as it bubbled on, and the shade was cool. Smoke was reluctant to leave, but knew he'd better put some miles behind Dagger's tail.

Jason's words returned to him: "They scattered all around, from here to Colorado, just waitin' for a shot at you."

He thought back: Had there been a telegraph wire at that little town? He didn't think so. And where would the nearest wire office be? One over at Laramie, for sure. But by the time he could ride over there and wire Sally to be on the lookout, he could be almost home.

He really wasn't that worried. The Sugarloaf was very isolated, and unless a man knew the trails well, they'd never come in from the back range. If any strangers tried the road, the neighbors would be instantly alerted.

Smoke made sure his fire was out, packed up his kit, and climbed into the saddle. He'd make the northermost edge of the Medicine Bow Range by nightfall. And he'd stay in the timber into Colorado, doing his best to avoid contact with any of the outlaws. Ol' Preacher had burned those trails into his head as a boy. He could travel them in his sleep.

Nightfall found him on the ridges of the Medicine Bow Range. It had been slow going, for he followed no well-traveled trails, staying with the trails in his mind.

He made his camp, ate his supper, and put out his fire, not wanting the fire's glow to attract any unwanted gunslicks during the night. Smoke rolled up in his blankets, a ground sheet under him and his saddle for a pillow.

He was up before dawn and built a hat-size fire for his bacon and coffee. For some reason that he could not fathom, he had a case of the jumps this morning. Looking over at Dagger, he could see that the big horse was also uneasy, occasionally walling his eyes and laying his ears back.

Smoke ate his breakfast and drank his coffee, dousing the fire. He filled his canteens from a nearby crick and let Dagger drink. Smoke checked his guns, wiping them free of dust and then loaded up the chamber under the hammer, usually kept empty. He checked his Winchester. Full.

Then, on impulse, he dug out a bandoleer from the saddlebags and filled all the loops, then added a handful of cartridges to his jacket pocket.

He would be riding into wild and beautiful country this day and the next, with some of the mountains shooting up past twelve thousand feet. It was also no country to be caught up high in a thunderstorm, with lightning dancing all around you. That made a fellow feel very small and vulnerable.

And it could also cook you like a fried egg.

The farther he rode into the dark timber, the more edgy he became. Twice he stopped and dismounted, checking all around him on foot. He could find nothing to get alarmed about, but all his senses were working hard.

Had he made a mistake by taking to the timber? The outlaws knew—indeed, half the reading population of the States knew—that Smoke had been raised in the mountains by Preacher, and he felt more at home in the mountains.

He pressed on, slowly.

He came to a blow-down, a savage-appearing area of about thirty or forty acres—maybe more than that—that had suffered a ravaging storm, probably a twister touch-down. It was a dark and ominous-looking place, with the trees torn and ripped from the earth, piled on top of each other and standing on end and lying every which-a-way possible.

He had dismounted upon sighting the area, and the thought came to him that maybe he'd better picket Dagger and just wait here for a day, maybe two or three if it came to that. He did not understand the thought, but his hunches had saved his life before.

He found a natural corral, maybe fifty by fifty feet, with three sides protected by piled-up trees, the front easily blocked by brush.

He led Dagger into the area and stripped the saddle from him.

There was plenty of grass inside the nature-provided corral, so he covered the entrance with brush and limbs and left Dagger rolling; soon he would be grazing. There were pools where rainwater had collected, and that would be enough for several days.

Taking a canteen and his rifle, Smoke walked several hundred yards from where he left his gear, reconnoitering the area.

Then he heard a horse snort, another one doing the same. Faint voices come to him.

"Lost his damn trail back yonder."

Smoke knew the voice: Lanny Ball.

"We'll find it," Lodi said. "Then we'll torture him 'fore we kill him. I done had some of that money spent back yonder till he come along and queered it for us."

Smoke edged closer, until he could see the men as they passed close by. Cat Jennings's gang were in the group.

"Hell, I'm tarred," a man complained. "And our horses are all done in. We gonna kill them if we keep on. And we got a lot of rough country ahead of us."

"Let's take a rest," Lodi said. "We can loaf the rest of the day and pick up the trail tomorrow."

"Damn good idee," an outlaw named Sutton said. "I could do with me some food and coffee."

"All right," Lanny agreed. "I'm beat myself."

Smoke kept his position, thinking about this new pickle he'd gotten himself into.

It was only a matter of time—maybe minutes or even seconds—before Dagger caught the scent of other horses and let his presence be known. Then whatever element of surprise

Smoke had working for him would be gone.

There were few options left for him. He could backtrack and saddle up, hoping Dagger didn't give his position away, and try to ride out. But he knew in his heart that was grabbing at straws.

His other option was to fight.

But he was body and soul sick of fighting. If he could ride out peacefully and go home and hang up his guns and never strap them on again he would be content. God, but that would be wonderful.

The next statement from the mouth of a outlaw drifted to him, and Smoke knew this fight had to be ended right here and now.

"They tell me that Jensen's wife is a real looker. When we kill him, let's ride on down to Colorado. I'd like to have me a taste of Sally Jensen. I like it when they fight." Then he said some other things he'd like to do to Sally. The filth rolled in a steady stream from his mouth, burning deep into Smoke's brain. Finally he stood up , the verbal disgust fouling the pure clean mountain air.

Smoke lifted his Winchester and shot the man in the belly.

Smoke shifted position immediately, darting swiftly away. He was dressed in earth colors, and had left his hat back at the corral. He knew he would be nearly impossible to spot. And after hearing the agreeing and ugly laughter of the outlaws at the gut-shot man's filthy, disgustingly perverted suggestions, Smoke was white-hot angry and on the warpath.

He knelt behind a thick fallen log, all grown around with brush, and waited, his Winchester at the ready, hammer eared back.

Movement to his right caught his eyes. He fired and a wild shriek of pain cut the air. "My elbow's ruint!" a man wailed.

Smoke fired again into the same spot. The man with the ruined elbow stood up in shock and pain as the second bullet slammed into him. He fell forward onto his face.

As the lead started flying around him, thudding into the fallen logs and still-standing trees, Smoke crawled away, working his way around the outlaw's position, steadily climbing uphill.

He swung wide around them, moving through the wilderness just as Ol' Preacher had taught him, silently flitting from cover to cover, seething mad clear through; but his brain was clear and cold and thinking dark primal thoughts that would have made a grizzly back up and give him room.

In the West, a man just didn't bother a good woman—or even a bad woman for that matter. Or even say aloud the things the now-dead outlaw had mouthed. Molest a woman, and most western men would track that man for days and either shoot him or hang him on the spot.

Smoke caught a glimpse of color that did not fit into this terrain. He paused, oak-tree still, and waited. The man's impatience got the better of whatever judgment he possessed, and he started to shift positions.

Smoke lifted his rifle and drilled the outlaw, the bullet entering his right side and blowing out the left side.

Smoke thought the man's name was Sweeney; one of Cat Jennings's crud.

Lead splattered bark from a tree and Smoke felt the sting of it. He dropped to one knee and fired just under the puff of gunsmoke drifting up from the outlaw's position, working the lever just as fast as he could, filling the cool air with lead.

A crashing body followed the spray of bullets.

"He ain't but one man!" a harsh voice shouted. "Come on, let's rush him."

"You rush him, Woody" was the reply. "If you so all-fired anxious to get kilt."

"I'm gonna kill you, Jensen!" Woody hollered. "Then drag your stinkin' carcass till they ain't nothing left for even the varmits to eat."

Smoke remained still, listeneing to the braggard make his claims.

"I'll take him," a high thin voice was added to the brags. Danny Rouge.

The only thing that moved was Smoke's eyes. He knew he couldn't let Danny live, couldn't let Danny get him in gunsights, for the punk's aim was deadly true.

There, Smoke's eyes settled on a spot. That's where the voice came from. But was the back-shooter still there? Smoke doubted it. Danny was too good to speak and then remain in the same spot. But which direction did he take?

There was only one direction that was logical, at least to Smoke's mind. Up the rise.

Smoke sank to the cool moist earth that lay under the pile of storm-torn and tossed logs. As silent as a stalking snake he inched his way under a huge pile of logs and paused, waiting.

"Well, dammit, boy!" Woody's voice cut the stillness, broken only by someone's hard moaning, probably the gut-shot outlaw. "What are you waitin' on, Christmas?"

But Danny was too good at his sneaky work to give away his location with a reply.

Smoke lay still, waiting.

Someone stepped on a dry branch and it popped. Smoke's eyes found the source and he could have easily killed the man. He chose to wait. He had the patience of an Indian and knew that his cat-and-mouse game was working on the nerves of the outlaws.

"To hell with you people!" a man spoke. "I'm gone. Jensen ain't no human person."

"You git back here, Carlson!" Lanny shouted.

Carlson told Lanny, in very blunt and profane language, where to go and how to get there.

That would be very painful, Smoke thought, allowing himself a thin smile.

He heard the sound of horses' hooves. The sound gradually faded.

Rifle fire slammed the air. A man cursed painfully. "Dammit, Dalton, you done me in."

A rifle clattered onto wood and fell to the earth with a dull thud. The outlaw mistakenly shot by one of his own men fell heavily to the earth. He died cursing Dalton.

Still Smoke did not move.

"Smoke? Smoke Jensen? It's me, Jonas. I'm gone, man. Pullin' out. Just let me get to my hoss and you'll never see me agin."

"Jonas, you yeller rabbit!" Lanny yelled. "Git back here."

But the fight had gone out of Jonas. He found his tired horse and mounted up. He was gone, thinking that Smoke Jensen was a devil, worser than any damn Apache that ever lived.

Smoke sensed more than heard movement behind him. But he knew that he could not be spotted under the pile of tangled logs, and he had carefully entered, not disturbing the brush that grew around and over the narrow entrance.

For a long minute the man, Danny, Smoke felt sure, did not move. Then to Smoke's surprise, boots appeared just inches from his eyes. Danny had moved, and done so with the stealth of a ghost.

He was good, Smoke conceded. Very good. Maybe too good for his own good.

Very carefully, Smoke lifted the muzzle of his rifle, lining it up about three feet above the boots. The muzzle followed the boots as they moved silently around the pile of logs, then stopped.

Smoke caught a glimpse of a belt buckle, lifted the muzzle an inch above it, and pulled the trigger.

Danny Rouge screamed as the bullet tore into his innards. Smoke fired again, for insurance, and Danny was down, kicking and squalling and crying.

"I'm the bes'," he hollered in his high, thin voice. "I'm the bes' they is."

Wild shooting drowned out whatever else Danny was saying. But none of the bullets came anywhere near to Smoke's location. None of the outlaws even dreamed that Smoke had shot the back-shooter from almost point-blank range.

Danny turned his head and his eyes met those of Smoke, just a couple of yards away, under the pile of logs.

"Damn you!" Danny whispered, his lips wet with blood. "Damn you to hell!" He closed his eyes and shivered as death took him.

Smoke waited until the back-shooter had died, then took a thick pole and shoved the body downhill. It must have landed near, or perhaps on, an outlaw, for the man yelped in fright.

"Lanny, let's get out of here," a man called. "He ain't gonna get Jensen. The man's a devil."

"He's one man, dammit!" Lanny yelled. "Just one man, that's all."

"Then you take him, Lanny." The outlaw's voice had a note of finality in it. "'Cause I'm gone."

Lanny cursed the man.

"Jensen, I'm hauling my freight," Hayes called. "I hope I don't never seen you no more. Not that I've seen you this day," he added wearily.

Another horse's hooves were added to those already riding down the trail, away from this devil some called the last mountain man.

Smoke remained in his position as Lanny, Woody, and a few more wasted a lot of ammunition, knocking holes in trees and burning the air.

Smoke calmly chewed on a piece of jerky and waited.

# Thirty-Three

Smoke had carefully noted the positions of those left. Five of them. He had heard their names called out. Woody, Dalton, Lodi, Sutton, and Lanny Ball.

The outlaws had tried to bait Smoke, cursing him, voicing what they were going to do to his wife and kids. Filthy things, inhuman things. Smoke lay under the jumble of logs and kept his thoughts to himself. If he had even whispered them, the white-hot fury might have set the logs blazing.

After more than two hours, Sutton called, "I think he's gone, Lanny. I think he suckered us and pulled out and set up a new position."

"I think he's right, Lanny," Woody yelled. "You know his temper; all them things we been sayin' about his wife would have brought him out like a bear."

Sutton abruptly stood up for a few seconds, then dropped to the ground. Lodi did the same, followed by the rest of them, and cautiously, tentatively, the outlaws stood up and began walking toward each other. Lanny was the last one to stand up.

He began cursing the rotten luck, the country, the gods of fate, and most of all, he cussed Smoke Hensen.

Smoke emptied his rifle into Lodi, Sutton, Dalton, and Woody, knocking them spinning and screaming to the littered earth.

Lanny hit the ground.

Smoke had dragged Danny's fancy rifle to him with a stick. Dropping his empty Winchester, Smoke ended any life that might have been left in the quartet of scum, then backed out of his hiding place and stretched his cramped muscles, protected by the huge pile of logs.

Smoke carefully checked his Colts, wiping them free of dirt with a bandana. "All right, Lanny!" he called. "You made your brags back in Gibson. Let's end this madness right here and now. Let's see if you've got the guts to face a man. You sure have been real brave telling me what you planned to do with my wife."

"You know I wouldn't do that to no good woman, Jensen. That was just to make you mad."

"You succeeded, Lanny."

"Let's call it off, Smoke. I'll ride away and you won't see me no more."

"All right, Lanny. You just do that little thing."

"You mean it?"

"I'm tired of this killing, Lanny. Mount up and get gone."

"You'll back-shoot me, Jensen!" There was real fear in the outlaw's voice.

"No, Lanny. I'll leave that to punks like you."

Lanny cursed him.

"I'm steppin' out, Lanny." This was to be no fast draw encounter. Smoke knew Lanny was going to try to kill him any way he could. Smoke's hands were full of Colts, the hammers eared back.

At the edge of the piled-up logs, Smoke started running. Lanny fired, missed, and fired again, the bullet burning Smoke's side. He turned and began pulling and cocking, a thunderous roar in the savage blow-down.

Lanny took half a dozen rounds in his upper torso, the force of the striking slugs driving him back against a huge old stump. He tried to lift his guns. He could not. His strength was gone. Smoke walked over to him, reloading as he walked.

"You ain't human," Lanny coughed up the words. "You a devil."

"You got any kin you want me to write?"

"You go to hell!"

Smoke turned his back to the man and walked away.

"You ain't gonna leave me to die alone, is you?" Lanny called feebly.

Smoke stopped. With a sigh, he turned around and walked back to the outlaw's side. Lanny looked up as the light in his eyes began to dim. Smoke rolled a cigarette, lit it, and stuck it between Lanny's lips.

"Thanks."

Smoke waited. The cigarette fell out of Lanny's lips. Smoke

picked it up and ground it out under the heel of his boot.

"Least I can go out knowin' it wasn't no two-bit tinhorn who done me in," were Lanny's last words.


Smoke returned to the natural corral and saddled up. He wanted no more of this blown-down place of death. And from Dagger's actions, the big horse didn't either. Smoke rode out of the Medicine Bow Range and took the easy way south. He crossed the Laramie River and made camp on the shores of Lake Hattie.

He crossed over into Colorado the next morning and felt he was in home territory, even though he had many, many hard miles yet to go.

He followed the Laramie down into the Medicine Bow Mountains, riding easy, but still with the smell of sudden and violent death seeming to cling to him. He wanted no more of it. As he rode he toyed with the idea of selling out and pulling out.

He rejected that almost as quickly as the thought sprang into his brain.

The Sugarloaf belonged to Smoke and Sally Jensen. Fast gun he might be, but he wasn't going to let his unwanted reputation drive him away. If there were punks and crud in the world who felt they just had to try him . . . well, that was their problem. He had never sought the name of Gunfighter; but damned if he was going to back down, either.

The West was changing rapidly. Oh, there would be a few more wild and woolly years, but probably no more than a decade before law and order settled in. Law and order was changing everything and everybody west of the Mississippi. Jesse James was dead, killed in 1882. Clell Miller had been dead for years. Clay Allison had died a very ignoble death back in '77. Sam Bass was gone. Curley Bill Brocius had been killed by Wyatt Earp in Tombstone in '82. John Wesley Hardin was in a Texas prison. Rowdy Joe Lowe had met his end in Denver, killed in a gunfight over his wife. Mysterious Dave Mather had vanished about a year back and no one knew where he was.

Smoke doubted Dave would ever resurface. Probably changed his name and was living respectable.

Smoke rode the old trails, alive with the ghosts of mountain men who had come and gone years back, blazing the very trails he now rode. He thought of all the gunfighters and outlaws that were gone.

Charlie Storms was dead—and not too many folks mourned his passing. Charlie had been sitting at the table in Deadwood back in '76 when Cross-Eyed Jack McCall walked up behind Wild Bill and blew his brains out. Charlie tried to brace Luke Short in Tombstone back in '81. He rolled twelve.

I've known them all, Smoke mused. The good and the bad and that curious combination of both.

Dallas Stoudenmire finally saw the elephant back in '82.

Ben Thompson had been killed just the year back, Smoke recalled, down in San Antonio. Killed while watching a play.

The list was a long one, and getting longer.

And me? Smoke reflected. How many men have gone down under my guns?

He really didn't know. But he knew the count was awesomely high. He knew that he was rated as the number-one gunfighter in all the West; knew that he had killed a hundred men—or more. Probably more.

He shook those thoughts out of his head. There was no point in dwelling on them, and no point in trying to even think that he could live without his guns. There was no telling how many tin-horn punks and would-be gunslicks would be coming after him after the news of Gibson hit the campfires and the saloons of the West.

He stopped at a small four-store town and bought himself a couple of sacks of tobacco and rolling papers. He cut himself a wedge of cheese and got him a pickle from the barrel and a sackful of crackers. He went outside to sit on the porch of the store to have his late-afternoon snack.

"That there's Smoke Hensen." The words came to him from inside the store.

"No!"

"Yeah. He's killed a thousand men. Young, ain't he?"

"A thousand men?"

"Yeah. 'Course, that ain't countin' Indians."

Small children came to stand by the edge of the store to stare at him through wide eyes. Smoke knew how a freak in a carnival must feel. But he couldn't blame the kids. He'd been written about so much in the penny dreadfuls and other books of the time that the kids didn't know what to think of him.

Or the adults, either, for that matter.

Damn! but he was tired. Tired both physically and mentally.

Once he got back to Sally and the Sugarloaf, he didn't think he'd ever leave her side until she got a broom and ran him off.

He offered a cracker to a shy little girl and she slowly took it.

"Jeanne!" her mother squalled from a house across the dusty street. "You get away from him!"

Jeanne smiled at Smoke, grabbed the cracker and took off.

Smoke looked up at the sounds of horses walking toward him. He sighed heavily. The two-bit punk who called himself Larado and that pair of no-goods, Johnny and Brett, were heading his way.

He slipped the thongs off his hammers and called over his shoulder, "Shopkeep! Get these kids out of here—right now!"

Within half a minute, the street was deserted.

Smoke stood up as the trio dismounted and began walking toward him.

"Back off, boys!" Smoke called. "This doesn't have to be."

Larado snorted. "What's the matter, Jensen? You done turned yeller on us?"

"Don't be a fool!" Smoke's words were hard. "I'm tryin' to make you see that there is no point to this."

"The point is, Mister Big-Shot," Johnny said, and Smoke could smell the whiskey from all them even at this distance, "we gonna kill you."

Smoke shook his head. "No, you're not, boys. If you drag iron, you're dead. All of you." He started walking toward them.

Bret's eyes widened in fear. Johnny and Larado wore looks of indecision on their young faces.

"Well!" Smoke snapped, closing the distance. "At this range we're all going to die, you know that don't you boys?"

They knew it, and it literally scared the pee out of Bret.

Smoke slapped Larado with a hard open palm, knocking the young man's hat off and bloodying his mouth. He backhanded Johnny with the same hand and drove his left fist into Bret's stomach.

Reaching out, he tore the gunbelt from Larado and hit the young man in the face with it, breaking his nose and knocking him to the ground.

Smoke tossed the gunbelt and pistols into a watering trough. He looked down at the young men, lying on the ground.

"It's not as easy as the books make it out to be, is it, boys?" Smoke asked them. He expected no reply and got none.

Smoke reached down and jerked guns from leather, tossing them into the same trough.

"You can keep your rifles. Keep them and ride out. Go on

back home and learn you a trade. Go to school; make something out of yourselves. But don't ever brace me again. For if you do, I'll kill you without hesitation. I'm giving you a chance. Take it."

The young men slowly picked themselves up off the ground and mounted up. They rode out without looking back.

"Mighty fine thing you done there, Mister Smoke," a man said. "Mighty fine. You could have killed them all."

Smoke looked at the citizen. "I'm tired of killing. I know that I'll have to kill again, but I'm not looking forward to it."

"The wife is fixin' a pot roast for supper. We'd be proud to have you sit at our table. She's a good cook, my old woman is. And the kids would just be beside themselves if you was to come on over. Don't a home-cooked meal sound good to you?"

A smile slowly creased Smoke's lips. "It sure does."


Smoke did not leave the Sugarloaf for a week. He got reacquainted with Sally every time she bumped into him . . . and she bumped into him a lot.

He rolled on the floor with the babies and acted a fool with them, making faces at them, letting them ride his back like a horse, and in general, settling back into the routine of being a husband, father, and rancher.

On the morning that he decided to ride into town, Sally's voice stopped him in the door.

"Aren't you forgetting something, Smoke."

He turned. She was holding his guns in her hands.

He stared at her.

"I know, honey," she said. "I've known for a long time that you're tired of the killing."

"It just seems like a man ought to be able to ride into town without strapping on a gun."

"I don't know whether that day will ever come, honey. As long as you are Smoke Jensen, the last mountain man, there will be people riding to try you. And you know that." She came to him and pressed against him. "And speaking very selfishly, I kind of like to have you around."

Smoke smiled and took the gunbelt, hooking it on a peg.

She looked up at him, questions in her eyes.

He whispered in her ear.

She laughed and bumped into him again.